CA$HIN' OUT

A NOVEL BY JAI NICOLE

Life Changing Books in conjunction with Power Play Media
Published by Life Changing Books
P.O. Box 423 Brandywine, MD 20613

Library of Congress Cataloging-in-Publication Data;

www.lifechangingbooks.net
13 Digit: 978-1934230435
10 Digit: 1-93423043X

www.facebook.com/lifechangingbooks
www.twitter.com/lcbooks

ACKNOWLEDGMENTS

Well, of course, first and foremost, I have to thank the Lord because without Him giving me this talent, the ability to make my thoughts speak on pen and paper, you wouldn't be reading this novel. No matter how hard things got, I just kept praying and look at me now. *smiles*

My Ma & Daddy-sama, I love y'all, but y'all better not **EVER** read my book. Gotta thank you, Ma, for always reading to me when I was little. You gave me that hunger for reading and encouraged me to write. I still remember the 3rd grade when I won 2nd place in the writing contest and you stayed up with me all that night to type up my story on the Word Processor, long before we had a computer. And for letting me read your secret stash of V.C. Andrews novels. And Daddy-sama, you're the best truck driver and father a girl could have! A lot of this wouldn't be possible without you! I love y'all and thanks for bein' the best parents a girl could have.

Gotta thank my kid sis, Jyun, for staying up and listening to me rant and rave about this book and offering your ideas. Meant a lot to me, kiddo. And thanks for sneaking and buying 'Flyy Girl' and 'The Coldest Winter Ever' back when we were kids. If it hadn't been for that, I would have never starting writing or reading, street lit for that matter. So, a lot of this is possible because of things you did inadvertently.

My son, DJ, I do this for us and to ensure that you have everything you deserve! I love you! You are definitely the love of my life!

I have to shout out my family, both in NC and in GA. The Lynch's (Aunt Annette, Uncle Joe), the Gowdy's (Grandma Lizzie, Grandpa Walter, Uncle Darryl, Uncle Tony, Aunt Gena, my cousins Amanda & Charles Ray, Aunt Chele, etc.), the Pender's, the Cook's (Darnell & Mick), the Teasley's (Kim, Keith, Killer, etc), the Thurmond's (Aunt Bev, Kayla, Quin, Tesh, Jordan, Aunt Chele, Aunt Fab, etc)... Too many of y'all to name and I don't wanna leave out anybody, but I love y'all. Y'all know who you are!!!

Treasure E. Blue & Queen, I'm super thankful for y'all teaching me a lot about this business and helping me to believe in myself. I think if I'd never met y'all, I wouldn't be writing professionally, (or probably would have made a lot of major mistakes if I did) LOL, so I owe a lot of this to you guys! David Weaver, thanks for your encouragement. You put a lot of things into perspective for me!

My best friends and my son's Godparents: Katrina Kent-Saunders and AJ Saunders! I love y'all and my lil' Maliyah! Thanks for bein' there for me and I'm so happy y'all are finally back in the Peach State!

The bestie, Chelly-Mae!!! Thanks for always bein' there for me! I love our daily convos on Voxer too! I'll be in the 'A' before you know it and things will go back to how they used to be!!! Hey, Che-baby!!!

The best writer friend a girl could have, Jade! I'm so so glad that I met you and that we're friends!!! We've both shaped each other's writing style and I'm grateful to have a friend in this industry! Oh and Team FLGM. {insider}

My cuzzo, Jonique, for your entertaining stories and some of which you will see in future novels. Know it was your mastermind. LOL. My cousin, Monique, for your encouragement and for keepin' all my secrets. Love you, cuz.

My cuz, Denisha, I miss you! Kiss Tamia-mia for me and tell her that her 'Godmomma Auntie Cuz misses her'. Tell

Aunt Deb and Uncle Allen hello!

My Jenni-oneesama. I appreciate all the guidance throughout the years and you allowin' me into your world in West Monroe, LA. J I still remember (and have a few) of the chapters we used to write. I can't WAIT until you debut your novel to the world! You're going places!!!

My friends Titia-Ann (Thanks for listenin' to me through all the countless, STUPID stuff I've gone through with dudes. You've always had a good head on your shoulders and I appreciate all of your advice!), Chanelle (thanks for letting me use your name), 'Ronica, 'Mone, 'Leze, Lynn, Brina-ann, Quon (for your words of reason and helping me see things from a man's POV), Yulander Covington, Stepmomma (Lakyndra), Nicole-cole, Sept, Sheneka-ann, Momma Vette, Tabby-Mae (my wonderful stylist!), Cee, Kesha-Lou, Tora, Cole, Janine, T, Ray, Ben Blaze…Everybody from all of my fifty million jobs that I was cool with, LOL. Also, RIP Petrina Davis, you will be missed. 1978-2011. You were a great, kind-hearted person. I hate that you left so soon.

I even have to thank Young A.C. LOL My favorite rapper! Lawd, I swear by his music! It's played while I write, while I'm in my car… helped me to come up with ideas sometimes, too. Forever live young, Ferrari Young!

Now a **BIG** word of thanks to my LCB family!!!

Miss Leslie, I appreciate the hours we spent making sure that my book made sense. Being able to bounce ideas off you and work collaboratively was a great experience! You were hard on me, but it paid off.

Miss Azarel, thank you for giving me a chance and letting me be a part of the team. You extended your help to me and I'm eternally grateful! Thank you for being so uplifting when I was feeling down. Your pep talk helped me tremendously! It's nothing like being part of a crew that truly cares about your success and getting things right.

To the the rest of the LCB crew, including the editors,

and test readers, I thank you for your input on this project. Shout out to the LCB authors, I can't wait to meet each one of you.

And I can't forget, you, the readers! Thank you so much for purchasing this novel. You truly don't understand how much you mean to me. I love all of you. Haters included. MUAH!

To my city, Augusta, GA…Richmond County to be exact. Oh, and we're still the 2nd largest in the state, LOL. Never forget it. Always gonna have love for where I'm from!

Now, I'm sure somebody is probably mad that their name wasn't in here, but trust me, it wasn't done purposefully. Even if you're not in here, you're still in my heart. There is a lot of stress in doing acknowledgments because I don't wanna offend anybody.

R.I.P. to my Grandma Beulah Mae (1927-2012). You raised nine kids on your own and *always* put the needs of your children before your own. You are a true example of how strong a mother's love is: pure, unselfish, and forgiving. I love you so much; words cannot express it and I'm glad that you're no longer hurting but to not have you here with us is really eating me up inside. I will never forget and will always remember you saying, "Family s'posed to help family." Don't worry, Grandma Chick, I got us. I just wish you could've been here for my book release…Crying as I type this, so I'll end it here. I hope I've made you proud.

Love,
Jai Nicole

$ONE

Chanelle watched her boyfriend, JaQuez, intently as he placed the last stack of dead presidents into the money counter. They'd been going at it for hours, counting and recounting, making sure that their eyes weren't playing tricks on them.

A wide grin spread across JaQuez's face as he looked over at his girl. "You see this shit, baby? And this is only the muthafuckin' beginnin'!"

Chanelle was speechless. It was the most money that she'd seen in her entire life. She couldn't believe that he'd actually made $400k in less than a month. While JaQuez had been a dope boy ever since Chanelle had known him, he wasn't moving weight on the scale that he was now. Back then, he was clocking no more than a couple thousand a week working for an older cat named Chaos. Now, he was running shit in a major way as the head of his own drug operation.

Chanelle never imagined that JaQuez would make it to this level, but was glad that she'd stuck with him. Standing behind her man and dealing with his bullshit for years had finally paid off. Chanelle vowed that she would never go back to living a hard knock life…especially not as long as she had JaQuez by her side.

"I can't wait to blow a couple stacks," she said after placing a rubber band around the last bills.

JaQuez let out a slight chuckle as he exhaled the smoke from his blunt. "You know most of this is for me to re-up, Cha, so you won't be blowin' shit." As Chanelle looked at him skeptically, he nodded his head to reassure her. "I promise you we'll go shoppin' next time."

Chanelle rolled her eyes. "Whatever, nigga."

"Quit trippin', girl," JaQuez responded as he placed his blunt in the ashtray and sat next to her on the bed.

He nudged her with a smile, but she only rolled her honey colored eyes at him once again. To JaQuez, she was a prime example of how a female could look sexy while she was mad. Mixed with Puerto Rican and Black, Chanelle was a dead ringer for the R&B singer Cassie. This gave her a pretty, cinnamon-colored complexion and long, jet black hair without the help of extensions. Standing at 5'3, her petite body was like that of video vixen, Melyssa Ford. Chanelle was a certified dime and without a doubt, one of the baddest bitches in Raleigh. JaQuez was proud to have her on his arm.

Seeing the pout on her face, he relented. "You know I gotchu, Cha. Don't I always?" He lifted her chin and attempted to kiss her lips, but she only turned away. JaQuez let out a sigh before reaching into the pocket of his Crown Holder jeans. Handing over a wad of money, he kissed her on the cheek and said, "You lucky I love yo' spoiled ass."

Chanelle let out a squeal of delight as she thumbed through twenty, one-hundred dollar bills. "Thank you, baby. Now, I can get those Isabel Murant sneakers I want, along with some other goodies." She cupped his face with her petite hands and kissed him passionately. As the kiss deepened, she could feel herself becoming moist and reached for his belt buckle.

"Stop, Cha, you gonna make my dick hard," JaQuez warned while pushing her away. He had business to handle and couldn't let sex cloud his brain. He stood up from the bed and began placing the money into an over-sized duffle bag. "I gotta meet Rob at the stash house so he can make the drop and…"

Chanelle sucked her teeth. "Damn, you can't chill with me for a minute? You always on the go."

"Cha, why you trippin'? You knew I had some shit to do before I came home."

"Well, how long are you gonna be gone?"

JaQuez shrugged nonchalantly. "However long it takes. If you want them damn red bottoms and all that other designer shit, then you need to let me do what I gotta do."

"Maybe sometimes all I want is my nigga here at home with me instead of out in the streets all the time," Chanelle replied quietly, although she already knew where the conversation was going.

JaQuez let out a loud sigh as he slung the duffle bag over his shoulder and stood up. Too often they bickered about the lack of time he had to spend with her. JaQuez had to admit that Chanelle was right, but she never complained while she was out spending his money.

"You need to stop fakin'. All yo' money-hungry ass really cares about is how much I'm gonna give you to blow at the mall," JaQuez said in an agitated tone.

Chanelle bit her lip as she tried to calm herself down. She already knew what was about to happen next and thought frantically of a way to diffuse the situation. She definitely had to choose her words carefully or he would walk out on her like he always did.

"JaQuez," she spoke calmly, "if you feel that way, why are you with me then?"

He shrugged nonchalantly with his back still turned to her. "I ask myself that same shit every fuckin' day."

JaQuez didn't mean to be that harsh, but he needed to hurry up and leave. Not only did he have to get the money to Rob, but unbeknownst to Chanelle, JaQuez had promised his mistress that he'd swing by and spend some quality time with her and their son. He didn't have time to talk about the same old shit. He would worry about Chanelle's hurt feelings later. He knew that she would come around easily after he threw a couple stacks at her.

While he didn't doubt Chanelle's love for him, he also knew that her love of money and her insistence to never return to the projects ensured that she didn't leave him. There was also the fact that no other nigga in the Raleigh-Durham area would fuck with her. Everybody understood that she was JaQuez's wifey and no one wanted to deal with the possible repercussions. To put it simply, she wasn't going anywhere and he took full advantage of that fact by doing whatever the hell he wanted.

"Fuck you, JaQuez!" Chanelle screeched as she lost her composure. She threw the wad of bills he'd given her at his retreating figure. "Fuck your money, too!" He'd never gone that far before and it really got under her skin. The conversation wasn't going anything like she'd intended.

"Fuck you, too, then." He waved her off dismissively, not even bothering to look in her direction as he continued towards the door.

Chanelle couldn't let him leave despite his cruel words and rushed behind him, pulling him into an embrace. "Baby," she whimpered as her lip trembled, "I don't wanna fight. I just want you."

Chanelle's tears caused her words to come out broken as her voice cracked. JaQuez was shocked by her show of emotion because what had just transpired was nothing new for them. The outcome was usually very different though. They would get into a shouting match and Chanelle would be practically pushing him out of the door. For her to break down let him know that she was fed up because she *rarely* cried.

JaQuez shook his head as he sat the duffle bag on the floor and took her into his arms. "C'mon, baby, stop all that crying and shit. You know I hate to see you cry."

"Then stop treating me like this!" she yelled, her voice muffled due to burying her head in his chest. "Do you still love me?"

"What? Why would you say that?" His brow wrinkled in confusion. "Of course I do."

It was true. He did love her, but JaQuez knew that he didn't always show it by the way he treated her. Since he was rarely ever home and always in the streets, money was the only way he knew how to show her. His newfound fame in the streets had his full attention and getting to the money and hoes was all that he knew how to do lately.

Chanelle lifted her head as he wiped away her tears. "I really can't tell anymore. You know sometimes I think its best that we just leave each other alone. Maybe I should get my own place."

"Man, stop talkin' crazy. You know I love you, Cha. And as soon as I make a few more business moves, I promise you that a nigga gonna make you his wife."

JaQuez spoke sincerely as he stared into her eyes. His hand caressed the side of her face, lightly tracing over the faded scar he'd given her from a prior altercation.

Chanelle had heard it all before. He'd been telling her that since she was nineteen. It was five years later and nothing had changed despite his shift in the drug game. That promise just seemed to be something that he dangled in front of her to convince her to stay. Up until about a month ago, it had been working.

At first, marrying him had been something that Chanelle looked forward to. She loved her status in the hood. While bitches envied her, niggas wanted to fuck her and wished she was the chick lying in their bed every night. Even though they never tried to holla, it was obvious from the lustful gazes she received whenever JaQuez wasn't looking that she was highly sought after.

Chanelle's shoe game was sick and she pushed a foreign whip. It was part of the lifestyle as a hustler's wifey. However, while there were advantages, there were a handful of disadvantages. The nights of not knowing where he was, who he was fucking, and the STD's he brought home to her twice, once while she was pregnant, was too much for her. Being his wife was now the last thing she would ever want to be in life.

JaQuez could see the uncertainty and skepticism in her eyes so he kissed her, hoping to erase any doubts. "Trust me, you the only one I want, baby," he whispered before pushing her down on the bed. "You the only one I want," he repeated. JaQuez stared into her eyes hoping to convince her of his sincerity.

As he led Chanelle to the bed and removed her La Perla boyshorts, she didn't say one word. She wanted to protest, seeing as sex was his misguided solution to all of their problems, but he was hard to resist. His smooth, brown sugar complexion, chiseled build, and baby face ensured that she would never say 'no' to his advances. That and his impeccable tongue game.

Wasting no time, JaQuez buried his head between her thick thighs hoping to appease her "You still wanna leave me?" he asked, continuing to French kiss her southern lips.

"No, baby," Chanelle moaned with delight. She placed her hands on top of his head to ensure that he didn't stop hitting her spot. "Right there, baby… Please don't stop."

No sooner than the words came out of her mouth, she was requesting him to do just the opposite. "J-JaQuez!" Her voice was filled with urgency and her eyes widened. "No… stop JaQuez. Get up!"

"Hell no," he said, wiping his mouth free of her juices. "I'm not about to stop now. I'm just gettin' started."

"Behind you…" Chanelle was so scared that she wasn't sure how she'd managed to even get the words out.

JaQuez looked at her puzzled, not realizing how serious the situation was until the sound of a gun being cocked back echoed across the room.

$TWO

"Put yo' hands up, muthafucka!" the intruder barked as he kept his Glock pointed directly at JaQuez. Immediately, he hoisted the duffle bag over his shoulder like he knew exactly what was inside. He was a big man, resembling Rick Ross in body mass, with a ski mask pulled over his face to conceal his identity. "Don't try any slick shit because I don't mind puttin' one in ya dome."

Although it was obvious that JaQuez wasn't in control of the situation, he still couldn't allow the man to feel like he had the upper hand. He figured that if the masked man wanted him dead, he would have already done it. His failure to do so told JaQuez that he wasn't a killer.

"Muthafucka, do you realize who the fuck I am? You walk out with my muthafuckin' money and you a dead man. I promise you that shit!"

"You talk a lot of shit to be the nigga held up at gunpoint with his bitch!" the goon commented with a small smirk. "You got a lot of heart, lil' nigga."

"Fuck you," JaQuez shot back. He couldn't believe that he'd been caught slipping.

He'd always taken extra precautions to ensure that shit like this didn't happen, but evidently somehow he'd been careless. Immediately, JaQuez wished that he'd counted the money at the stash house like he wanted to in the beginning. It was at Chanelle's insistence that he come home in the first place. Still, he only expected to be in and out. If JaQuez had left when he'd intended, this wouldn't be happening.

"I know you got some more bread in here, nigga," the goon spoke.

"Even if I did, I wouldn't tell yo' fat ass," JaQuez retorted.

He was stalling for time as he tried to think of a plan. He refused to let some nigga walk out with all the money that he'd earned.

I worked too hard for that shit, JaQuez thought.

Still, JaQuez knew that he couldn't afford to act recklessly since Chanelle was with him. If he could just get to the Beretta he kept under his bed without the goon noticing, their problems would be solved.

"Where is it?" This time the goon's voice was more boisterous.

"He keeps it under the floorboard in the living room. It's a spot near the chaise that creaks," Chanelle blurted out without hesitation.

"Chanelle!" JaQuez yelled angrily. "What the fuck are you doin'?"

"Do you wanna live?" she asked, glaring at him. "I'm not dying over no muthafucking money!"

"Show me!" the man barked. He pointed his gun towards Chanelle, motioning for her to get up.

"At least let her put on some clothes first. Don't be gawkin' at my girl, nigga," JaQuez snapped.

"Go ahead." The man nodded his approval as Chanelle quickly slipped her clothes on. "And tie this pussy ass nigga up, too." The man tossed Chanelle the rope that he'd stored in the pocket of his hoodie. He then looked back at JaQuez with a smirk, "You try some slick shit and I'll rock yo' bitch to sleep."

Chanelle eyed JaQuez the entire time, pleading with him

silently not to screw things up. Quickly, she tied him to the bed post as she'd been instructed and mean mugged the intruder. "Follow me," she told him before guiding the man out of the bedroom.

When they were in the living room and out of earshot, Chanelle finally spoke up. "You were just supposed to get the money from the duffle bag and get ghost! You getting carried away."

The goon chuckled, as he removed his ski mask. "Go big or go home, baby. Why shouldn't we wipe this nigga out for all the shit you said he did to you? You need to go ahead and let me murk his ass since he seems to think he's untouchable."

"Desmond, stick to the fucking plan. You just got out of prison for murder. You tryna go back?" Chanelle chastised in a harsh whisper.

She just wanted to make a smooth getaway, not create a crime scene. So far things were going good and she couldn't allow him to fuck it up. Chanelle and Desmond had been planning this set-up for about three weeks since JaQuez had made the mistake of telling her when he would be collecting the money. Half of it was supposed to go to the connect to re-up and pay back his consignment, but now *all* of it would be going to them. This lick was sure to have them set for a good minute.

So far, she'd delivered a performance worthy of an Academy Award, an Emmy or at least a standing ovation. Chanelle couldn't believe how convincing she'd been. For the past month, she'd been playing the role of the doting wifey and was surprised at the way she'd kept in character. Chanelle just had to keep it up since they weren't home free until Desmond secured the money and they got the fuck out of the house.

A small part of her was nervous despite her calm composure. If JaQuez ever figured out that she had something to do with setting him up, he would surely put a bounty on her head. He'd done it before with other niggas who'd crossed him, so she figured that her fate would be no different.

Fuck that. The difference is that he'll never find me and he'll never know, Chanelle reasoned, dismissing her grim thoughts. She would be getting away with more than enough money to ensure her safety and she was going to be over three hundred miles away from Raleigh. Still, it was important that Desmond stuck with the script because even the slightest deviation had the possibility to fuck up everything and jeopardize her livelihood.

Making her way over to the creaky floorboard, Chanelle perched down and gently lifted the rug. As she removed the large square tile, the safe was revealed. It had been placed there a year ago as soon as they moved in. JaQuez had been stacking the money for lawyer fees and retainers just in case he ever got locked up.

"How much is it?" Desmond asked as he watched Chanelle punch in the code, then quickly pull out bundles of money stuffed into freezer bags.

"At least three hundred thousand."

"That's it?" Desmond snorted loudly. "The nigga should have more than that. How long he been in the game?"

"Can you keep your voice down?" Chanelle hissed again. "You want him to hear us before we get all this shit out?"

"I don't give a fuck. If you had agreed to let me murk the nigga, then it wouldn't matter," Desmond said as he took the money Chanelle handed him and continued to cram it into the already stuffed duffle bag. "Now, let's get the fuck up out of here."

Chanelle nodded in agreement before changing her mind. "Wait! I have to do something first."

"What the fuck are you doin'?" Desmond asked. "Let's go."

Chanelle's heart pounded out of her chest as she ran up the stairs, despite Desmond's protests. She'd made up her mind. There was no way that she could leave yet…not without doing one last thing.

"What the fuck is going on? Is he gone? Quick…grab the phone and call Rob," JaQuez continued to rant as she rushed past him. After entering the adjoining bathroom and rummaging through the cabinets, Chanelle emerged with a bottle of prescription pills in her hand and began untwisting the cap.

"So, what do you have *this* time? Chlamydia or Gonorrhea?" Flinging the medicine in his face violently, she shook her head. "You nasty bastard."

"What the fuck, Chanelle? Chill out!" he yelled, attempting to dodge the shower of pills.

"So, I guess you weren't gonna tell me, huh?"

"Ay yo', chill. You doin' this shit right now? A muthafucka just robbed us and you wanna talk about that right now?" JaQuez asked with a frown. Thinking about the fact that he'd just been robbed for his hard-earned cash had him beyond pissed as he struggled to free himself. "Yo' untie me!"

"I don't think so."

JaQuez displayed a confused expression. "What the fuck do you mean, you don't think so."

"Do your other women know that you're probably fucking every girl in Raleigh? Do they know that you keep a damn STD?"

"Stop playin' fuckin' games, Cha. I need to get that nigga before he gets too far away!"

"Chanelle! Hurry up! Let's go!" Desmond shouted from downstairs.

JaQuez's eyes enlarged. "What the fuck?" he mumbled, trying to piece the puzzle together. "So, you in it with this nigga?"

She smirked. "How does it feel to have some shit go down and not suspect a thing? It doesn't feel good, does it?" Chanelle didn't wait for a response before continuing. "That's exactly how I felt when I found out you got that bitch, Tiffanie, pregnant!"

"Look…"

"Shut up!" Chanelle roared. He's almost one year's old, and he's named after you! Did you think I wasn't gonna find out? I even know his birthday." Chanelle paused as tears welled up in her eyes. "It's funny how you could beat our baby out of me, but you let that bitch keep hers!"

"Chanelle, you know that was a fuckin' accident!" JaQuez protested. "I didn't know you were pregnant!"

"Liar!" she spat, slapping him forcefully. "I told you, but you *still* didn't stop beating me! I've taken so much shit from you. I don't even know why I stayed this long," her voice trailed off. "I shoulda *been* working on getting away from your ass a long time ago, but it's all good though. I got the last muthafucking laugh now. This money will be a small payback for all the bullshit you put me through."

Chanelle shook her head in disgust as she turned to exit the room. "Oh, by the way, thanks for making the code to the safe your son's birth date. That made shit so much easier. You know…I got more than enough justifiable reasons to kill your ass, but luckily, I'm gonna let you live to see another day."

JaQuez instantly started yelling obscenities to her re-treating figure, but she didn't care. Chanelle knew that it was risky to leave him alive, but she just didn't have it in her to kill him.

"Damn. You ready now?" Desmond asked impatiently as she sauntered down the stairs.

A huge grin graced her face. "Yup. Now that I got every-thing off my chest, I can leave."

"I still don't know why you won't let me off his ass." Desmond shook his head as he led the way to the front door. "Let me find out you still got feelings for that nigga."

"Desmond, please. Don't get it twisted! I don't give a damn about his ass," Chanelle defended. "Fuck him. Let's just go."

"You shoulda let him kill me, bitch, because I'll be

damned if I spare your life!" JaQuez roared from the top of the stairs.

He'd managed to free himself and quickly retrieve the Beretta. His aim was directly at the back of her head and he wasted no time pulling the trigger. Chanelle didn't even have time to react.

Click…Click…

JaQuez looked at the gun in horror as no bullets exited the chamber.

That shiesty ass bitch, he thought, realizing that Chanelle had removed the bullets from his clip. He wasn't sure how long they'd been plotting on him, but it was obvious that they'd covered all their bases.

"I'ma kill y'all muthafuckas!" JaQuez belted angrily, rushing down the stairs towards them. However, he didn't make it within two feet before Desmond ripped a bullet through his abdomen.

JaQuez's pupils widened as he clutched his stomach and stumbled to the foot of the staircase. Blood drenched the front of his shirt, turning his white tee into a scarlet color. His eyes were still filled with hatred and locked on Chanelle, giving her an eerie feeling.

As much as she wanted to, she never broke her gaze, instead watching as his eyes slowly rolled to the back of his head and his breaths appeared faint. It was only a matter of seconds before he was gone.

"Chanelle, let's go!" Desmond yelled as he started for the door. He was sure someone had overheard the gunshot and wasn't trying to stick around until the police came. After several years in the peniteniary, he didn't want to go back anytime soon.

Chanelle stood there in a daze, as he yelled once again. "Ay, go get that nigga's jewelry, too!"

She raised an eyebrow, reluctantly breaking her gaze on JaQuez, "What are you gonna do, sell it? Everybody knows that's JaQuez's chain."

"Just get the shit," Desmond commanded, "And hurry up." With that said, he walked out of the door.

Wasting no time, Chanelle rushed up the stairs to their bedroom. She was familiar with the chain Desmond was referencing. It was a custom made necklace that had a diamond encrusted pendant hanging from it, resembling a crack vial with crushed diamonds inside serving as the crack. It was a hefty size and she knew that he'd paid over fifteen thousand for it. It was one of the first things he'd purchased when he started blowing up in the drug game.

After grabbing it from where it hung in his valet box, she rushed back down the stairs. She walked briskly to the front door and slipped on her sandals. They never wore shoes in the house for fear of ruining the carpet. For once Chanelle was thankful for the rule she'd initially deemed as silly.

"Good riddance, muthafucka," Chanelle said as she opened the coat closet and pulled out the suitcases that she'd packed two nights before. She'd packed lightly, anticipating that she would buy plenty more thanks to JaQuez's money.

"Cha… Chanelle…"

The voice was low, but Chanelle was sure that she'd heard her name being called. *Can't be,* she thought shaking her head. *I must be losing it. Ain't no way he survived that shit.*

She stared at JaQuez's body for a few seconds to see if he was breathing. Even though she hadn't seen his chest move, Chanelle walked over and kicked him just for extra confirmation. After realizing her ex was indeed dead, she shrugged off the voice as her imagination. Chanelle figured that Desmond was probably calling her from outside.

Stop being so paranoid, she chastised herself. She blamed her guilt as the cause for her imagining things. No matter how hard she tried to convince herself or play it off, she did feel bad about what happened. Chanelle didn't want JaQuez to die, but there was no other option. It was either him or her, and she was determined not to let him shit on her again.

But…just to be sure, she drew in a deep breath before stooping down and quickly reaching into his pocket to retrieve his phone. *I gotta make sure his ass can't call for help… if he is alive. Thank God we don't have any house phones either.* Chanelle smiled as she looked at at his phone and headed back towards the door. *Fuck that nigga. I'm moving on to bigger and better things,* Chanelle thought as she twisted the doorknob, preparing to leave.

$THREE

"Got damn! We really hit a fuckin' lick!" Desmond exclaimed as he glided JaQuez's new Jaguar XJL Supersport down I-40. It was a hundred thousand dollar car and he felt like the man as he sat behind the wheel. "I can't wait to blow this money!"

"Me either. Now, I can finally get my boutique!" Chanelle smiled at the thought.

Taking orders from the next man had never been her forte, so she thought it was only natural that she'd start her own business. Besides, she knew that JaQuez's money wouldn't last forever with the way she blew cash.

Desmond chuckled. "All that money and that nigga couldn't even get you a store?"

"Yeah." Chanelle sighed. "He didn't want me to work. I think he just liked being in control. At first I was cool with not having to work, but having to depend on him for cash all the time got old real fast."

Desmond nodded his head in agreement. "I feel you. But you don't have to worry about that shit anymore. Now, it's me and you against the world like it used to be." He took her hand and kissed it gently.

"2012 Bonnie and Clyde…" Chanelle murmured with a wide grin. "Don't ever leave me again, Desmond Parker."

"Nah. I got your back and I ain't never leavin' you

again, Ma. Believe that."

She smiled at him before placing a kiss on his cheek. Desmond was Chanelle's first love. They'd met back when she was sixteen and although he was six years her senior, she only found that aspect of him more alluring. Originally from Queens, New York, the slick-talking Desmond blew her young mind and showed her a world that she didn't even know existed.

After only a few months he'd moved her out of the hell-hole that was her mother's house. They'd been inseparable for nearly three years until Desmond got locked up for second degree murder. Even though he professed his innocence to Chanelle, he refused to snitch on his homeboy taking the fall for him instead. Due to the amount of time that he was facing, he urged her to move on without him. She was reluctant at first, but didn't really have a choice after he started to avoid her calls.

"I hear you talking," she teased.

"For real. I came back for you, didn't I?"

"Boy, it was a coincidence that we ran into each other at Triangle Town Center that day."

"Nah. That was fate, Ma. We are meant to be together." Desmond grinned. "I thought you was playin' when you first talked about settin' that nigga up, but after seein' all that cash, I'm glad you weren't. That nigga definitely didn't see that shit comin'."

"Nope," Chanelle agreed.

The smile on her face seemed to be tatted on. She was in a great mood. She had her man, she had her money, and they were moving to Atlanta to start a brand new life. Things couldn't get any better. It was true what they said about after the rain there would be a brighter day. Chanelle was living proof.

"If Mario had never come clean, I don't know how my life would be right now," Chanelle confessed. Mario was the man that Desmond had taken the rap for. Although it had taken him five years, he finally came forward and professed his involvement, allowing Desmond to be freed. "I'd probably still be putting up with that nigga's shit."

Desmond nodded his head. "It don't matter now, baby. Leave that bullshit in the past. Let this be the last time you ever mention that nigga's name, a'ight?"

He was in disbelief hearing all of the things that she'd told him about JaQuez. They'd had plenty of late night conversations about it while JaQuez was out parlaying around town. It was enough to make Desmond want to go over and beat his ass, but at Chanelle's insistence he refrained.

"That nigga deserved what happened to him after all the shit he put you through. One bullet wasn't enough. Puttin' his hands on you and killin' y'all seed was foul."

"Leave it in the past, remember?" Chanelle said, wanting to change the subject. Just thinking about it would cause her to relive the moment and become angry all over again. "I don't wanna talk about it anymore."

Desmond shook his head in understanding. "Ay, Chanelle?"

"What's up?"

"I love you, girl."

A wide smile spread across her face. "I love you, too."

$$\$$$

"Desmond?" Chanelle called from inside the shower of the ritzy hotel room they'd rented at The St. Regis, Atlanta the night before. "Desmond?"

Chanelle frowned when she still hadn't received a response from him. After waiting for a few more seconds, she immediately jumped out of the shower and threw a towel around her body. She nearly slipped on the marble tile, but quickly regained her balance, holding on to the wall for support.

"Desmond!" she yelled again, then pushed the bathroom door open furiously. When Chanelle looked around the room and he was nowhere to be found, her heart immediately sank. "No! This shit can't be happening!"

Making her way over to the bed, Chanelle dropped on her hands and knees. She'd stashed the duffle bag of money underneath despite Desmond's protests. He felt the money would be safer in the trunk of the car, but Chanelle insisted they bring it with them. She'd worked too damn hard to let the smallest mishap fuck up her future.

"It's still here," Chanelle whispered in surprise when she saw the bag in its same location.

"What's still here?" Desmond asked, startling her.

"You scared the shit out of me!" she jumped, placing a hand over her heart. "I called out your name. Where the hell were you?"

"Stepped out for a minute to smoke a cigarette." He held up a pack of Newports. "Why you trippin'?"

"No reason," she lied.

He narrowed his eyes. "You real paranoid, Ma. Ever since we got here all you been doin' is checkin' on the money. It's not goin' anywhere. Damn. What you think I'ma do…take the money and run off?" Realizing that was exactly what she'd thought, he sighed. "Damn, Ma. I thought you knew me better than that. After knowin' the shit that you went through with JaQuez, do you really think I would fuck you over like that?"

"I mean, honestly…" Chanelle's voice spoke. "I wanna say 'no', but at the same time I don't wanna be fooled like I was before. I trusted JaQuez and he fucked me over. I was like a prisoner in my own damn home."

"That's because you put your trust in the wrong nigga. When have I ever done anything shiesty to you?"

"Never," she admitted, suddenly feeling foolish for thinking that he would try to dip on her.

Desmond had never given her reason to think that he would do something so foul, but despite knowing him forever, they'd also been separated for five years. She didn't know if anything had changed. While he felt so familiar, at the same time he was also like a stranger to her. They would definitely have to get to know each other all over again.

Desmond shook his head. "You gonna have to work on that. For real. I can't be with somebody that's always thinkin' some crazy shit about me. You feel me?" Chanelle nodded as he continued. "Either you trust me or you don't. Don't let the last nigga's actions dictate how you treat the next nigga, a'ight? We got history, so it shouldn't even be like that."

"You right. My bad, baby. I'm sorry."

"Yeah?" Desmond asked, licking his lips. "How sorry?"

From the look in his eyes, Chanelle already knew what he wanted and removed her towel seductively. "I can show you better than I can tell you," she flirted.

Desmond wasted no time coming out of his pants and tossing his boxers on the floor. He left on the chain they'd swiped from JaQuez. He had put it on the moment Chanelle had gotten into the car and hadn't taken it off since. Knowing how much it was worth, she wished that he would pawn it, but he wasn't trying to hear it. He viewed it as some sort of trophy from killing JaQuez. Apparently rocking a dead man's chain was something to be proud of.

"That's what I like to hear," Desmond grinned. His dick stood at attention, but his huge gut nearly concealed it. Desmond's size was a little less than average, but let him tell it, he was King Ding-a-Ling.

"Put it on me, big daddy," Chanelle cooed as she spread eagle on the bed.

"Girl, you don't know how bad I missed my pussy." Desmond kissed her lips sloppily as he guided himself inside of her. "Did you miss me, too?"

Chanelle nodded, stroking his ego. It was time to put her acting skills back to work, just as she'd done the night before when they'd made love for the first time in years. After all the shit that he'd talked about what he was going to do to her,

Chanelle had definitely been expecting more. Something more passionate, more animalistic.

Something more than just five minutes.

"Got damn, girl. You still got that good shit," Desmond praised as he pumped in and out of her quickly, resembling a stray dog in heat.

Sweat dripped from his body and Chanelle had to resist the urge to frown. She gazed at the clock on the nightstand that read 10:40 a.m. Only two minutes had passed since they started and she could see it was going to be a disappointing repeat of the night before.

Guess this is the price I have to pay for a good man. Sex ain't better than love, Chanelle tried to remind herself.

Chanelle remembered Desmond as being an excellent lover in bed, but at sixteen she was far less experienced than she was now. After sleeping with JaQuez, who was blessed with a ten inch Mandingo dick and the stamina of a horse, Desmond paled in comparison with a stubby five inches. She'd never had this problem with JaQuez. He'd always succeeded in making her cum at least twice, but Desmond couldn't even give her one. All he'd accomplished so far was turning her off.

"Did you hear me, girl? I said take this dick!"

Take what? Boy please, Chanelle thought as she laughed inwardly. She was trying hard not to compare JaQuez and Desmond, but it was difficult not to. Ironically, as much as she despised JaQuez, she had to think of him to even get wet.

Chanelle stared into Desmond's dark, beady eyes and really took in his facial features. His beard was rough and rugged, and his hair was a mini afro. It was apparent that he was obviously trying to grow his hair out, but the look wasn't attractive on him. Little patches of hair were sprouting from his chest and the sight was turning her off. It was a big contrast to what she was used to. His skin was as dark as charcoal and at the moment, beads of sweat rolled furiously down his forehead.

"You taking this dick, girl?" Desmond prompted again.

"I'm taking that big dick, baby," she lied.

Despite the fact that Desmond was trying his damndest to get her off, Chanelle couldn't focus. She could barely feel him moving inside of her and honestly she just wanted it to be over. She'd always thought that bigger men would be better in bed since they had something to prove, but Desmond obviously didn't get that memo. His weight gain over the years had taken a toll on his sex game. True enough, she still loved him though. She'd just have to find a different way to cope.

"Aw shit," Desmond cursed, snapping her back to reality as he came all over her stomach. "Damn, that was good."

"Uhm hmm," she agreed softly. Chanelle wasted no time wiping herself off with the towel, slightly disgusted and annoyed.

Desmond let out several exhausted breaths. "Listen, Ma I been thinkin'." He said as she sat back down on the bed. "This is somethin' I wanted to ask you about last night. ATL is nice and all, but what about Miami? It's a real different look from this and I think we'd be better off there. What is Atlanta anyway except an overrated and overcrowded city? Miami has palm trees and shit. It never gets cold. We could rent one of them condos on the beach….Think about it. Just me and you, baby girl."

Momentarily Chanelle forgot all about her sour thoughts about Desmond and their sex session. He loved her, he was down for her, and he wanted to be with her. With all that she'd been through in her life, she needed someone loyal in her life. He'd done more than enough to prove himself to her.

"Okay, let's do it," Chanelle agreed.

$FOUR

"Tell 'em we on pump five," Desmond told Chanelle as he handed her two twenty dollar bills. They were at the gas station, filling up for their long trip to Florida. "Bring me a Gatorade, too. And a pack of Newports. Shorts in a box."

"And why am I getting gas again? The needle is damn near kissing the F. We could've stopped later."

"You must'a forgot how I roll, Ma. You know I only ride on a full tank," Desmond insisted. "Now, take your sexy ass in the store and pay so we can get going."

Chanelle nodded as she sauntered towards the store. It was blazing hot from the Atlanta sun, and the weather was expected to get worse by three o'clock. It was a stark contrast from the cooler weather she'd experienced in North Carolina around this time of the year. Chanelle didn't even realize it could get this hot in April. Pulling down her Michael Kors shorts as she felt them rising up, Chanelle entered the store with all eyes on her.

Walking with the stride of a model in her Giuseppe Zanotti heel-less platform pumps and wearing the smile of Miss America, Chanelle already knew that she would garner a lot of unwanted attention, but it was the price to pay for beauty.

"Damn, shawty, what yo' name is?"

Chanelle wrinkled her nose in disgust at the lanky man

standing in front of her attempting to holla. She didn't even bother to dignify him with a response as she continued to the back of the store to fulfill Desmond's request for a Gatorade. She could hear the man calling her stuck up, but she could care less what his gap-toothed ass thought. Grabbing herself a bottle of water, she made her way back up to the front of the store.

"Is this all for you today, ma'am?" the cashier asked.

"Let me get a pack of Newport shorts in a box and whatever's left over, just put it on pump five."

"May I see your ID, ma'am?"

Chanelle frowned. "Are you serious?"

"Yes, ma'am. Store policy. Anyone looking under eighteen has to be carded."

"Yeah, and I'm well over eighteen, sir. I'm twenty-four to be exact."

"Sorry…store policy."

She'd left her driver's license, as well as her purse in the car. Chanelle wanted to tell him to forget about the cigarettes, but knew that Desmond would probably flip out if she did.

"I'll be right back." Blowing her breath angrily, she left her merchandise on the counter and stomped out the door. What she saw when she got outside had her in hysterics. "Desmond! What the fuck are you doing?"

One of her suitcases was already propped against the gas pump and Desmond was in the midst of pushing her other bag next to it. Upon hearing her voice, he quickly dropped her last bag and rushed to get inside of the car.

Despite the fact that she was wearing six inch platform sandals, it didn't stop Chanelle from running towards him like she was Sonic the Hedgehog. "You bitch ass nigga!" she yelled before her face twisted into a painful expression. Seconds later, she lost her balance and toppled painfully on the pavement.

Laughing, Desmond started the car and tossed her purse out of the window. "Fuck you, bitch!"

He rolled the window down with a smirk and threw up

his middle finger. He didn't see the point in splitting seven hundred thousand with her when he could have it all for himself.

Desmond's greed outweighed any feelings he had for Chanelle. Besides that, how could he trust a bitch that would set up a nigga she'd been with for five years? She'd played the role so easily with JaQuez. It made him wonder if she'd lied about all the stories she'd told Desmond about him. For all he knew, JaQuez was innocent and Chanelle was nothing more than a scandalous gold digger. It was probably just a matter of time before she got over on him, too. But Desmond would be damned if he was got the same way.

"You got me fucked up!" Chanelle screeched, her voice revealing the pain of Desmond's treachery.

Tears stung her eyes, but Chanelle knew that she couldn't sit there looking pitiful. Seeing her chance as the Jaguar idled, waiting for traffic to clear a few feet away, she regained her composure. Quickly, she removed her shoes and took off in the direction of the car. Her legs were on fire, but she wouldn't give up. She *had* to get her money. She'd worked too hard to just let Desmond drive away with her earnings.

Desmond looked startled when he saw her at his window, but then shook his head and turned his attention back to the traffic.

Chanelle pulled on the door handle violently, but it was locked. Taking one of her heels, she banged on the window repeatedly. "Open the fucking door!"

Desmond laughed into her face before yelling, "You better let go, Chanelle. I ain't playin' with your ass!"

"You're gonna have to kill me, nigga! You ain't leaving with my shit!"

By now they'd gained the attention of everyone at the gas station. People were standing outside wondering what the hell was going on, but Chanelle didn't care. She continued to scream and curse at Desmond like a jealous lover.

Noticing that he was finally able to merge out with the

traffic, he gave Chanelle one last warning. "I'm tellin' you. You gonna end up gettin' hurt."

"Open the fucking door!" she yelled again, ignoring his words of caution. "I want my money!"

Desmond shrugged. "I warned you."

With that said, he pressed on the gas, leaving Chanelle in a heap on the ground. The motion from the car threw her down face first, but that still didn't deter her from screaming like she'd just lost a loved one.

"Muthafucka!" she wailed.

As tears strolled down her face, she felt crazy as hell after the scene they'd just caused. Watching Desmond merge back onto I-85 and honk the horn infuriated her even further. "Fuck!" Chanelle screamed one more time before burying her face in her hands.

As crazy as it looked, she sat in the middle of the gas station entrance for nearly ten minutes, alternating between yelling obscenities and crying. Chanelle couldn't believe that Desmond had actually left her with virtually no funds and no transportation. She let out another scream, not caring that people were giving her odd stares. They had no idea how much money she'd just lost. If they did, they probably wouldn't blame her. Chanelle wanted to shout until her lungs hurt.

Got damn, you can't trust niggas for shit! She figured that since they had history, and since he'd never done her wrong, that Desmond wouldn't screw her over. Now, she was regretting her decision. This ordeal even had her wondering if she should've just stayed with JaQuez. He'd done a lot of messed up things to her, but she never had to worry about not having a place to stay or money in her pocket.

What the hell am I supposed to do? Chanelle thought bitterly with her head buried in her hands. *Wait. He left my purse.*

Excitedly, she rushed back over to her luggage that was still propped up against pump five. She rummaged through her purse, but was shocked to find that Desmond had cleared out all of her credit cards and money. The only thing left was her driver's license. She still had the forty dollars Desmond had given her for gas, but what the hell could she do with that?

Greedy muthafucka. Why…why…why did I get myself into this shit? Chanelle wanted to keep screaming, but knew that wouldn't change her situation. She barely had the energy to move. She was drained emotionally and physically. *Think, Chanelle, think! What the fuck are you gonna do?* She snapped her fingers, cursing herself out for not thinking of it before.

She pulled out her iPhone and wasted no time dialing Desmond's number. She probably should've been trying to call someone for help, but instead she wanted answers. She couldn't understand why he would do that to her. She'd been nothing but good to him. Hell, she even looked past the fact that he was overweight and deemed unattractive in most women's eyes. Now, Chanelle wished that she'd taken her mother's advice from long ago.

"What?" Desmond answered with slight agitation in his voice, interrupting her thoughts.

"You better come back with my fucking money!"

He snickered. "You just don't get it, huh? You ain't gettin' shit. It's a wrap, baby girl."

"You sorry piece of shit! How could you do this to me? I trusted you!"

"*No,* you didn't. You were already paranoid that I was gonna dip out with the cash, so go ahead with that bullshit. You're just gonna have to charge it to the game," Desmond said nonchalantly.

"Charge it to the game? I'll be damned! You better bring your ass back here!"

Chanelle continued to scream obscenities in his ear, even after she knew that he'd hung up. Repeatedly she dialed his number back, but eventually he turned it off. But that still didn't deter her from leaving voicemail after voicemail.

Finally, Chanelle stopped as the realization of her situation dawned on her. She was stranded in another city with only forty dollars. It wasn't nearly enough for a hotel and she had no idea where the hell she was.

What am I gonna do? Her cell phone battery was dying and her charger was in the car, heading to Florida. Chanelle knew that she had to use her last call wisely. Taking a deep breath, she dialed a number that she hadn't used in months.

"Hello?"

"Hey, uh… Loretta," Chanelle greeted cautiously, not really knowing how to address her mother anymore.

"Who is this?"

"Chanelle."

"Oh…what the hell do you want? Aren't you the same person who stopped taking my calls almost four months ago?" her mother reminded. "So, why the hell are you calling me?"

"Wait! Don't hang up, please!" Chanelle yelled quickly. She used her last ounce of pride to get her next words out. "I really need your help. I need you to Western Union me some money. I'm stranded in Atlanta."

"Stranded? How the hell did that happen?" Before Chanelle could answer, Loretta cut her off. "Actually it doesn't even matter because it won't make a difference. What makes you think that I have money to send?"

"That's why you still sleeping with random niggas, right? For money?" Chanelle asked rhetorically, already knowing the answer was 'yes'. "I would hope…"

"You better watch your damn mouth. I'm still your momma," Loretta interrupted. "You're right. I do have money, but last time I checked, it's *my* money. My *hard earned* money that I lay on my back to get, so why the hell would I give you any?"

Chanelle's irritation was starting to show, but she had to tread carefully. If she said anything wrong, her mother wouldn't waste any time denying her request. "Momma, you don't understand. All I have to my name right now is forty dollars."

"Oh, so I'm 'Momma' now?" Loretta mocked. "I told you to quit chasing after them men. I'm pretty sure, without you even telling me, that you're stranded in Atlanta because of chasing after some nigga for *love*. Wake up and smell the coffee, Chanelle! Love doesn't pay the bills and it sure won't get your ass out of this mess you're in. Money over love, Chanelle. You can't *ever* go wrong with that mindset. I've been telling your ass for years to use 'em for what they got, not fall in love with 'em. Now, look where love got you!"

Deep down, Chanelle had to admit that Loretta was halfway right. Her philosophy of using men was something that she'd tried to teach Chanelle, but she never agreed with it. Love was the one thing that Chanelle craved. She was rarely shown any affection due to Loretta being more hung up on chasing after niggas with fat pockets. It wasn't until Chanelle met Desmond that she found what she desperately longed for. Or so she'd thought.

"Do you see what I've been trying to teach you all this time? I tried to tell you, but you didn't want to listen," Loretta continued.

After her recent dealings with JaQuez and Desmond, Chanelle was really starting to understand and agree with her mother's viewpoint. Men were better served as 'sponsors' than 'lovers'.

"Look, can you just do me this one favor? You ain't never did shit else for me and I ain't never asked you for anything. What's the big deal?" Chanelle asked.

"How easily you forget. Do you remember the last time I asked your ass for some money to help pay my rent when one of my dudes couldn't come through? Do you?"

Chanelle bit her lip to keep from screaming. "No, I don't."

"You told me to stop calling with my bullshit." Bitterness laced Loretta's words. "I still can't believe you were acting like that over some shit that didn't even belong to you. That was JaQuez's money...not yours!"

"Are you serious? That was months ago! Plus, you lie so much I wasn't sure if you were just trying to play me," Chanelle spoke. "Look, my battery is dying. Just send me the money and I'll pay you back!" she yelled urgently.

Loretta chuckled. "I'ma tell you the same thing you told me. Hell no!"

Click.

$FIVE

"Ma'am, I'm very sorry, but there is no loitering here. I'm gonna have to ask you to leave the premises," the store clerk told Chanelle timidly.

"Are you fucking kidding me? Didn't you just see what happened out there?" Chanelle demanded.

After being disappointed over her mother's lack of interest in her well being, she picked up the suitcases off the ground then walked back inside the store to debate her next move. To make matters worse, her phone was dead. She would've even taken a risk and used JaQuez's phone if they hadn't thrown it out on the side of the road right before they got to Durham.

It was hotter than fish grease outside, so naturally it made sense to figure things out in the cool, air conditioned building. Chanelle had wandered down the aisles for almost ten minutes without purchasing anything and apparently it was starting to get to the clerk.

"Ma'am, if you don't leave, I'm afraid I'll have to call the police and have them escort you off the premises."

"Seriously?" Chanelle asked in disbelief, not believing the extremes the Arabian looking man was willing to take. "Well, fuck you then and fuck this store, too!"

With one long sweep of her arm, she knocked down all the automotive and household goods on the top shelf. "I'll give you a *real* muthafucking reason to call the damn police!"

The man quickly picked up the phone as Chanelle stormed out of the store. Even though a few people gawked at her, no one dared to say anything about her outburst. Chanelle knew that she didn't need those types of problems, but needed to take her frustrations out on something.

"Stupid ass," she cursed, trudging up the sidewalk. Chanelle didn't know where she was going, but knew that she had to get out of the heat.

"Excuse me, shawty, you a'ight?" she suddenly heard a voice say.

Chanelle quickly looked to her left with an evil scowl. "Do I look alright?" she asked the man who was cruising alongside her in a cocaine-colored S Class Benz.

The handsome stranger threw his hands up in surrender. "Damn, shawty. I'm just askin'. Look, if you need a ride somewhere or somethin', you can roll wit' me. I'll take you wherever you need to go."

Without giving her a chance to reply, he eased out of traffic and into the parking lot by the sidewalk. Seconds later, he hopped out of the car and walked towards Chanelle, reaching to take her bags.

"Look, I'm good on that ride," Chanelle lied.

She wanted to get in badly, but after her recent ordeal with Desmond, she wasn't in the mood to be bothered with some slick talking dude. Not to mention, he didn't look trustworthy.

This nigga is putting on a 'good guy' act, but I bet the moment I get into his car, he's gonna try to kidnap me or some shit.

Chanelle knew that she was probably reaching in her assessment, but if there was anything she'd learned in the past twenty-four hours, it was that niggas couldn't be trusted.

"Is somebody comin' to get you?" he asked, looking at her bags. He was obviously puzzled by the fact that she was walking alongside the road in six-inch heels lugging two suit-cases. "Or do you need to call somebody?"

Shit...I don't have anybody to...

Immediately, Chanelle thought about her friend, A'mya, and wondered why she hadn't thought of her sooner. They'd been friends all throughout high school, but after graduation, A'mya moved out of state to attend Clark Atlanta University. Still, they kept in touch every once and a while. Chanelle knew that she was probably going out on a limb expecting A'mya to help her, but she'd always been kind-hearted, although a bit ditzy.

However, just as quickly as the thought came to mind, Chanelle suddenly remembered their last conversation. A'mya had mentioned moving to Las Vegas with some dude and get-ting married several months ago and they hadn't spoken since. But Chanelle knew that wasn't A'mya's fault. She'd reached out to Chanelle on several occasions, but with Chanelle so busy try-ing to keep up with JaQuez, she'd yet to return any of her friend's calls. Chanelle doubted that she even remembered A'mya's number by heart, but decided to take a chance anyway. Besides, there weren't many options to choose from.

Maybe A'mya can send me some money, especially if the man she married is loaded like she claimed he was.

"Yeah. Can I borrow your phone?" Chanelle asked the guy.

"Sure," he obliged, handing over his iPhone before giv-ing her some distance to speak privately.

404-612...Chanelle dialed slowly, hoping that she had the right number. If not, she would probably have to take up the man's offer for a ride. *But where in the hell would he take me,* she thought cynically, again remembering that she had no exact destination at the moment.

"Hello?"

"Hi... May I speak to A'mya, please?"

"This is she," the woman answered timidly. "Let me

guess, you've been sleeping with Rallo and you just felt the need to call and tell me that shit. Well, let me tell *you* something, bitch, *I'm* wifey and *I'm* not going anywhere!"

"What the hell are you talking about?" Chanelle asked confused. "A'mya this is Chanelle."

"Oh my goodness! Hey, girl! I didn't recognize your voice or the number. What's been going on? I haven't heard from you in a long time! You know I tried to call you a couple of times, but you never called me back. How have you been? I'm just taking it day to day. I…"

"Listen, A'mya," Chanelle finally interjected, knowing that if she didn't hurry and speak her piece, A'mya would keep going. She had a tendency to ramble on. "I didn't call to make small talk. This is serious. I'm stranded in Atlanta and I was wondering if you could wire me some money."

"Where are you?" Her voice took on a concerned tone. "Do you need me to come get you?"

"You're still in Atlanta? I thought you moved to Vegas with…"

"Girl, *puh-lease* don't even mention that loser or that crazy ass foolishness again! That's what I was calling to tell you. It turns out he had a wife and kids! I had to get the marriage annulled even though we weren't really married since his ass was married to someone else. Can you believe that nigga had the audacity to…"

"A'mya! Let's talk about it when you get here. It's hot as hell out here and I'm on somebody else's phone."

"Well, where are you?"

"I'm uh…" She turned to her Good Samaritan. "Can you tell my friend where we are?"

He nodded before taking the phone and giving A'mya instructions. Seconds later, he hung up. "She's on Memorial, so it'll only be a few minutes before she gets here. Do you want me to wait with you? You can sit in my car if you want so you can get out of this heat."

He'd noticed the sweat beading down Chanelle's fore-head and the way she fanned herself with her hand.

"I'm good," she huffed. "Thank you for letting me use your phone, though."

Despite the tempting offer, Chanelle didn't want him to get the wrong idea. Sure, he was cute with his caramel-coated skintone and lashes that would make several women jealous, but she wasn't about to let herself get caught up with another man so soon.

"A'ight." He shrugged before running a hand through his long dreads. "Just be careful, shawty. It's some crazy mutha-fuckas out here."

With that last word, he hopped into his car and pulled away just as quickly as he'd come.

"I hope A'mya hurries her ass up," Chanelle mumbled to herself. "I look real fucking desperate right now."

She was grateful to have a place to go, but not consider-ing the circumstances. *I wouldn't be in this shit right now if I hadn't robbed JaQuez... But maybe if I would've shot Desmond's bitch ass too while we were there...* She smiled. *Yeah... Greedy muthafucka. I should've known better.*

"I told you to quit chasing after them men. You use 'em for what they *got,* not fall in love with 'em. Now, look where love got you!" Loretta's words echoed in her mind.

"Maybe your scandalous ass is right," Chanelle thought out loud.

If she'd been more focused on their pockets instead of their heart, she wouldn't be in this predicament. *But I'll be damned if I let another nigga get over on me again though. That's for sure. Now, I'ma be on some fuck niggas, get money type of shit.*

Perhaps that should've always been her motive all along, but Chanelle had always been searching for love. Growing up, she always had material possessions, thanks to her mother's countless sponsors, but love seemed like something unattainable. It was all that Chanelle ever wanted since her mother was always caught up with a man and barely paid her any attention. Because of that, it didn't take much for Chanelle to fall in love easily and that trait was what had gotten her taken advantage of time and time again.

Not anymore, she vowed.

"Chanelle, is that you, girl?"

Breaking out of her thoughts, Chanelle's frown faded when she saw A'mya sitting in a dingy, older model two-door Honda Civic. She'd never been so happy to see her friend and for the moment, she didn't even mind being seen in that car.

A'mya squealed giddily as she jumped out of the car and hugged Chanelle tightly. "You look good, girl!"

"Thanks," Chanelle responded half-heartedly, trying to mask her feelings about A'mya's appearance.

Her girl had definitely let herself go. Her once perfect size eight figure was now more comparable to a smaller version of Jill Scott's character in *Why Did I Get Married?* and her clothes were ill-fitting. Makeup was caked on her face, making her appear older than her twenty-four years. However, the one thing that hadn't changed was the one deep dimple on the right side of her face and adorable cleft chin.

"And what are those shoes, girl? I love them!" A'mya gushed, admiring Chanelle's whole ensemble. "Did you get them from Shoe Land?"

Chanelle wrinkled her nose. "What's Shoe Land? These are Giuseppe's. I ordered them from Bergdorf Goodman's. These are thousand-dollar shoes." She hoisted her bags into A'mya's trunk before heading to the passenger door, only to discover it wouldn't open.

"Sorry, girl, the handle is broken," A'mya said, leaning over to open the door. "Those shoes are cute, but I bet you could've gotten the same pair from Shoe Land for twenty-five bucks."

"I highly doubt that," Chanelle responded snootily.

She finally took a moment to really survey A'mya's car and couldn't help but frown. With torn leather seats that exposed foam, a huge gap where the radio should've been, and stains all over the floor, Chanelle continued to turn her nose up in the air.

Suddenly, beads of sweat formed on her forehead. "Please tell me your air conditioner works." Chanelle quickly noticed that all the windows were down.

A'mya smiled. "Actually, it doesn't. I think I need some Freon."

Chanelle quickly shook her head. "Damn, girl... I thought you were doing better than this."

"What do you mean?" A'mya asked, the smile instantly wiping off her face.

"I mean, no offense, but I just didn't expect you to be driving this. What happened to your Acura?"

"You know what, Chanelle, you're still the same, and you haven't done anything except complain since you got in," A'mya said with much attitude. She reached across Chanelle to open the passenger door. "How about you complain about having to stand on the curb? Get the fuck out."

$ SIX

Chanelle's eyes were as wide as saucers. "I... I... didn't mean..." she stammered.

"I'm just kidding," A'mya said with a huge smile before her expression returned solemn. "But seriously, Chanelle, stop being so bourgeois! Bessie may be a hoopty, but at least I have *something* to drive. Be a little bit more appreci..."

The ringing of A'mya's phone interrupted the lecture as she placed a finger over her lips and checked the caller ID. "Don't say a word. Hello?"

Chanelle sighed and sunk back in her chair. A'mya was right. Beggars couldn't be choosers. She would be stranded if not for A'mya and her hoopty. Still, it made Chanelle wonder what A'mya's house looked like. If her car reflected her living conditions, then she was worried.

"I'm on my way with your cigarettes now, Rallo!" A'mya yelled. "Calm down! Traffic is real bad." She was quiet while listening to the caller speak. "And, baby, I... Hello? Hello?" A'mya pulled the phone away from her face and frowned, noticing that the call had been disconnected.

"And who was that?" Chanelle asked looking at her friend in surprise.

"Girl, that was Rallo. That's my baby," A'mya cooed as though she hadn't just been annoyed with him. "I had to lie to him because he gets so damn cranky about those stupid cigarettes."

"Oh really?"

"Yeah, I mean, we bump heads sometimes, but we love each other."

"Rallo? It sounds like he's at least, fifty," Chanelle replied with a huge grin.

A'mya smiled, too. "I mean he is older than me, but no where near fifty."

"So, he's the guy that's apparently sleeping with other women."

A'mya looked at her confused. "Why do you say that?"

"Did you forget how you answered the phone when I first called?"

"Oh yeah… that. It's just some girls from work who play on my phone. Nothing serious."

Chanelle wasn't convinced and she wasn't going to leave it alone either. "A'mya, I've been there enough to know that if bitches are calling your phone talking about your man been giving them the dick, nine times out of ten, it's true." She didn't give A'mya a chance to answer. "So, why are you still with him? For the money?"

"What do you mean?" A'mya questioned incredulously. "We love each other." She shot Chanelle a side eye. "Don't judge me when I say this, but I met him about two months ago and we just clicked." She shrugged. "It's definitely not because of his money because Rallo got laid off from his job right before we met. He gets unemployment, but I'm taking care of things until he gets his feet back on the ground."

"Are you fucking kidding me?" Chanelle couldn't believe her ears. She knew that A'mya had asked not to be judged, but she had to slap some sense into her. "If you had niggas paying for pussy in the first place then you wouldn't have these problems! You gotta quit being a doormat. Every single dude you get with is always 'hard on his luck' and always ends up leaving you the moment they get some money!"

"I'm not a prostitute, Chanelle. I see Loretta is rubbing off on you." A'mya frowned momentarily. "Rallo is different. He's older so..." A'mya paused as she pulled off and merged into the busy traffic. "You know Justin, the dude I was gonna move to Vegas with, he was around our age, so I think he was just immature and that's why things ended up like that."

"I can't believe you're still being so stupid, A'mya. I really thought you would've grown up and gotten some sense after we graduated."

"Whatever, Chanelle! If you're doing so well and you know better, then why am I here picking your ass up from the curb? Where's JaQuez? Did he leave you here?" A'mya was on a roll. "If my memory serves correctly, he was doing you dirty, but you *still* stayed with him. So, you have no right to judge me!"

Chanelle was quiet, hating that she'd confided in A'mya about JaQuez. She always disliked when people threw things back up in her face and refused to let anyone make her look stupid.

"For your information, I finally woke up. I left his ass and decided to move here to get away from him *for good*. But some idiots robbed me and jacked me for my car!" she lied. "And I damn sure wasn't gonna call JaQuez and ask for his help after I left him!"

"Oh my God Chanelle, I didn't know!" A'mya apologized. "You need to file a police report. What county were you in? Right here in Fulton?"

Chanelle sighed. "I don't know and fuck the police. Those niggas are probably long gone by now." She wanted to borrow A'mya's phone so that she could call and curse Desmond out again, but didn't want her in her business.

"Well, you can stay with us for as long as you like," A'mya offered.

"*Us?*"

"Yeah. Rallo lives with me, but I have two bedrooms so

don't worry about that."

Chanelle instantly had mixed feelings about that, but when they turned into a dilapidated apartment complex several minutes later, her thoughts about Rallo were the least of her worries. She looked as several people stood outside talking, while kids ran around in the street, completely disregarding the cars trying to get through.

"You live here?" Chanelle asked.

"Yeah. It's not much, but I'm trying to save money to start my own business. I'm the shift manager at McDonald's for right now and it pays pretty good. Eleven dollars an hour. I could probably hook you up with a job, too, if you're interested!" A'mya chattered on excitedly.

What the hell happened? Chanelle wondered. A'mya seemed to have a promising future when she left for college. With a heavy interest in Marketing, she was supposed to be the head of someone's corporation by now, but instead she was living one step above the projects and working at a fast food restaurant.

It was A'mya's insistence to chase after some no good nigga that promised her with a dream of marriage and being a housewife that caused her to drop out after completing nearly three years of school.

A'mya pulled into a parking space in front of her building. "Now, when we get inside, just let me do all the talking, okay?"

Chanelle nodded, although not fully understanding why A'mya felt the need to explain herself to a freeloader. Hoisting her bags out of the trunk, she walked behind her friend.

"Well, this is my home," A'mya told Chanelle as she unlocked the door. Seeing the look on her face, she added, "It isn't much, but we all have to start somewhere."

Well I'll be damned if I start here, Chanelle thought just before plastering a fake smile on her face. "No. Thank you, A'mya."

She didn't want to appear ungrateful, and couldn't really complain since she'd been offered a place to stay. But the inside looked even worse than she imagined. The furniture looked straight out of a Rent-A-Center and the smell of garbage was almost unbearable. An oversized bag was placed right next to the door and Chanelle could've sworn she saw a dead roach peering out from underneath it.

"Who the fuck is this?" a man asked from the sofa as he eyed Chanelle up and down.

"Rallo, please don't talk like this in front of company," A'mya begged through clenched teeth. "Here are your cigarettes." She tossed him a pack of Kool's before turning to Chanelle. "This is Rallo."

Rallo was a big man with plenty of muscles. His skin was as dark as midnight and with his emerald green eyes, he reminded Chanelle of a panther. He was laying on the sofa in his boxers and a dingy wifebeater. A can of beer sat beside him on the floor and inwardly Chanelle had to shake her head.

A'mya is better than me because ain't no nigga gonna be lounging on my shit while I'm busting my ass, she thought. *Last time I checked, it's a man's job to take care of his woman, not the other way around.*

"Hey, I'm Chanelle. How you doing?" she managed, attempting to hide the repulse in her voice.

"I'm straight." He sat up then looked back at A'mya. "Let me holla at you real quick."

"Girl, I'll be back," A'mya said, following him to the enclosed kitchen, which really wasn't very far from where Chanelle sat on the sofa.

It wasn't long before she could hear the two of them arguing, with Rallo complaining about having people in *his* house.

"It's my house, too, Rallo! Last time I checked, you don't pay any bills up in here! All you do is gamble your shit away!" A'mya shouted back, fed up with his attitude. "And she's my friend!"

"You better watch yo' damn mouth, A'mya, before I pop you in yo' shit! Don't be tryna show out cuz we got company!"

Ignoring his comment, A'mya redirected her attention back to Chanelle as she exited the kitchen. "Chanelle, you can put your stuff in the coat closet over there for now. I have to clean up the guest room a little first." Excusing herself, she walked down the hallway, leaving Rallo and Chanelle in the room alone.

He kept staring at her as Chanelle tried to hide her uneasiness. The look in his eyes wasn't one of disgust, but more of desire. She could feel his gaze still fixed on her as she placed her bags into the closet as A'mya directed.

"Where you from?" Rallo asked gruffly.

"North Carolina."

"What part?"

"Raleigh." She really wasn't interested in the small talk.

He nodded. "That's how they make 'em in N.C., huh?"

Chanelle stared at him in disbelief, shocked that he had the gall to try and hit on her. He didn't even bother to hide his growing erection, instead placing his hand inside of his boxers and stroking it.

"Are you serious right now? So, you're really gonna just sit there and disrespect me *and* your girl like that?"

"What the fuck are you talking about?" he asked, never removing his hand.

Just as Chanelle was about to excuse herself from the room, A'mya's voice reverberated from the other room.

"Rallo! You left the damn toilet seat up again! Is it too much that you clean up after yourself, please?"

"Your ass always complaining about something!" he growled before flashing Chanelle one more glance and heading to the bathroom.

I'm gonna make sure I lock my door every night, Chanelle thought as she rolled her eyes. She could hear the cou-

ple still arguing despite her turning up the TV to tune them out.
The thin walls did little to mask their argument and despite
them being in a different room, Chanelle could still hear them.

Rummaging through her bags, Chanelle pulled out her
cell phone charger and quickly plugged her phone in. She
smiled widely as the Apple symbol appeared on her screen, in-
dicating that it was charging. She couldn't wait to hit Desmond
up again, not to mention Loretta. She appreciated A'mya's hos-
pitality, but she definitely wasn't trying to stay any longer than
necessary. Her mother would come around eventually. Chanelle
was sure of it.

I still can't believe that nigga is dead, she thought, hating that her thoughts had gone back to JaQuez. He'd been on
her mind a lot. She felt guilty, but whenever she thought about
all the wrong he'd done to her, it immediately disappeared. *His
ass didn't deserve to live.*

No sooner than her phone powered back on, the notifica-
tions instantly start appearing. Chanelle could see that she had
several voicemails and a couple of text messages. It was rare for
anyone to blow up her phone, so she quickly hit the voicemail
button.

"Hey, Chanelle, it's Mimi. Where the hell are you? Are
you okay? I heard some shit went down with JaQuez and I
wanted to see if you were good. Is it true? People are saying
he's dead. Hurry up and call me back."

Chanelle rolled her eyes as she pressed the delete button.
Mimi was her cousin. They weren't that close so she figured
that she'd just called to be nosey. She wasn't really concerned
about Chanelle's well-being.

As soon as she heard Mimi's voice on the second message, Chanelle hit the delete button again without even bothering to listen. On top of the fact that they were far from 'buddy
buddy', Mimi was a huge gossip queen. Her business would be
out on Capital Boulevard, 440, and 540 if she even breathed so
much as a word to her.

Suddenly, the shrill sounds of her phone ringing inter-rupted her thoughts. The number had a 336 area code which Chanelle recognized as Greensboro. She'd seen the number several times before and knew exactly who it was even before she picked up the line.

"Hello?" she asked with an attitude.

"Is this, Chanelle?"

"Who is this?" Her heart pounded as she asked the ques-tion and her pulse quickened.

"This is Tiffanie. I know you don't know me, but…"

"Bitch, I know exactly who you are," Chanelle spat. "JaQuez's lil' jumpoff from Guilford County."

"Look, can we just be grown about this?" Tiffanie asked with slight agitation. "JaQuez was supposed to come over to see his son the other day, but never did." She cleared her throat. "It's unlike him to break a promise. I was hoping that you could let me know what's going on with my son's father."

Hearing the last words come out of Tiffanie's mouth in-furiated her. Chanelle felt as though she was rubbing that fact in her face. "Bitch, if you were *that* important you wouldn't have to call me for fucking answers. And how the hell did you get my number anyway?"

"Is that really a question? Or did you honestly forget the way you used to call my phone harassing the shit out of me back when me and JaQuez first started messing with each other? I changed my number, but I saved yours." Tiffanie blew into the phone loudly. "I told him to leave your ungrateful ass alone. He promised me that he was done with you. Now, it's funny how all of sudden he just fell off the face of the earth."

"You can't put two and two together? JaQuez wouldn't leave me, especially not for some young trick that didn't even graduate high school!"

"You don't know shit about me *or him,* for that matter. JaQuez is a great man and an even better father. He has *never* broken a promise to us. Not for you, not for anyone. We were his world."

Tears stung Chanelle's eyes and laced her words. "Fuck you, JaQuez and your bastard ass son!" Without another word, she hung up and hurled the phone across the room. A couple of seconds later she could hear it ringing once again. It was most likely Tiffanie, but she had nothing else to say to her.

Tiffanie's words chorused in Chanelle's subconscious, taunting her. Was what she was saying true? Was he actually considering leaving her for Tiffanie? It didn't matter now, but Chanelle could see that she'd definitely underestimated how deep JaQuez's feelings for Tiffanie had been. *If* she was actually telling the truth, that is.

But he was talking about marrying me, Chanelle thought. *He was coming home to me…* Thoughts of business trips and drops that he had to make filled her brain. Had he been seeing Tiffanie as frequently as she claimed? She'd never get the answer for sure, but it was a resounding 'yes' to her. That belief alone actually made her glad that he'd been killed.

Whap!

The loud sound knocked Chanelle out of her thoughts as she looked up and turned towards the hallway. Rallo was exiting the bathroom and A'mya was still on his heels. Her face was flushed and her hand rested on her cheek.

So, not only is he trifling, but this nigga be putting his hands on her, too, Chanelle thought incredulously. She could put two and two together and knew that the sound had been one of A'mya getting slapped. As if that wasn't bad enough, A'mya continued after him begging Rallo to stay. Chanelle could only look on in pity at the scene unfolding.

"Rallo, please, baby. Where are you going?"

"Don't worry about it. You act like you don't want me in this muthafucka, so I'll bounce then."

Chanelle chuckled. "Where the hell is your broke ass gonna go?" she mumbled to herself.

Rallo looked in Chanelle's direction briefly as he continued to button up his collared shirt. A'mya was right on his heels, grabbing his arm, but he kept pushing her away violently.

"Nah. A nigga can't even relax in his own damn house without his bitch naggin'. I told you the other day that I didn't want that girl. She don't mean shit to me!"

"Wait!" A'mya started again, tugging on his shirt.

"Back the fuck up for real, A'mya, or I'ma hit yo' ass again!"

"I wish you would!" Chanelle yelled, jumping to her friend's defense. She was no longer able to keep quiet.

Rallo stared at Chanelle with a grimace before returning his attention back to A'mya. "You better check your fuckin' friend. She gonna get yo' ass whipped," he responded. "I want her ass out of here by the time I get back!" he announced with a loud slam of the door.

A'mya was completely embarrassed. "I'm so sorry you had to see that. And don't worry about what he just said. This is my place and you can stay as long as you want." She touched her face lightly.

"Fuck that nigga," Chanelle spat. "I can't believe you let him put his hands on you."

"That doesn't happen all the time," A'mya sniffed quietly. The tone of her voice indicated that she was lying, but Chanelle decided not to press the issue any further.

"So, you're just gonna let him take your car like that?" Chanelle asked in amazement.

"He has his own car," A'mya sniffed. "That silver Oldsmobile Cutlass I parked next to. I'm just so tired of him doing this to me. I know they say men only do what you allow them to but..."

"Then stop being a fucking doormat. Stand up for yourself sometimes." Chanelle rolled her eyes. "Ain't no dick good enough for me to take that shit anymore!"

"Please...You stayed with JaQuez for years, didn't you?"

"It was a *money* thing, not a *dick* thing," Chanelle added.

A'mya shrugged. "Well, Rallo's oral game is out of this world and don't get me started on the sex…"

"Please don't." Chanelle's face crinkled with disgust.

"And I'll be damned if he gives it to another chick! Let's follow him," A'mya suggested suddenly, grabbing her keys off the kitchen counter.

"Are you serious?"

"You said not to let him walk all over me and that's exactly what I'm doing! I wanna follow his ass and see where he's going. It better not be to that bitch Tasha's house either!"

$SEVEN

"I can't believe him!" A'mya said as they sat in her hoopty, watching Rallo enter the strip club after paying the bouncer.

She and Chanelle had wasted no time tailing him. Thanks to the many traffic lights that had slowed him down, they were able to catch up with him pretty quickly.

"So, he has money to gamble at those dumb ass poker games he goes to and waste at the strip club, but his ass can't ever help me pay the bills!" A'mya continued to complain, banging her hand against the steering wheel.

"That broke nigga has the nerve to gamble?"

"Hell yeah, and he does more losing than winning, too."

Chanelle just shook her head, glad that she no longer had to deal with that kind of bullshit. She could hear the hurt in A'mya's voice despite the front she put up. With a day filled with nothing but drama, she was tired and wanted to get some rest, so Chanelle wasn't about to sit outside like two detectives all day.

"Come on then. Let's go and ask him."

"W-what?" A'mya stuttered. "I hadn't planned on going inside."

"So, you were just gonna follow his ass here and not do shit?"

"Well, I was gonna let him know when he came home…"

"Get out the damn car," Chanelle commanded as she rolled her eyes and opened the door. "You gotta check his ass. That's the only way he's gonna learn."

Who am I kidding, she thought. Chanelle had checked JaQuez on a daily basis and it didn't do shit but encourage him to keep his game a little tighter. Either way, she wasn't trying to hear A'mya's mouth for the rest of the ride back to her house. She'd gotten an ear full already and was tired of hearing about her relationship drama.

"It's a ten dollar cover charge, ladies," the bouncer informed them as they walked up.

"C'mon, daddy, surely you can let us in for free," Chanelle said to him seductively. Although it was only ten dollars, she didn't have the slightest bit of money to spare, and certainly wasn't going to waste it getting into some strip club.

He licked his lips as he eyed Chanelle, taking in her bottle-shaped figure. He saw naked women everyday, but he still valued a fine woman when he saw her. "Alright, sexy, I'll let you in this time."

"Thanks, boo." Chanelle smiled appreciatively before walking in with A'mya in tow.

"Ay, lil' mama you should try dancing. You got a banging ass body," he called out from behind them.

Chanelle grimaced. Dancing at a strip club was something that she had never entertained. Honestly, she looked down on stripping. She knew that the job entailed much more than just taking off your clothes for a group of horny men. Fucking and sucking random niggas for a couple dollars wasn't something that appealed to her.

"Pretty Kitty is so degrading to women," A'mya said when they entered. She looked around the room with a frown on her face. "I don't know how they can just 'do something strange for a little piece of change.' They say it pays well, but nobody could *ever* pay me enough to do that! The worst thing a woman could do next to being a prostitute. Bunch of home wreckers with fake ass bodies."

A'mya was still rambling bitterly, but Chanelle had to admit that the money did sound appealing. Before, she could be choosy, but when she thought about it, what other options did she really have? Chanelle wasn't qualified to do shit. She didn't have a college degree and she'd just barely graduated high school. The only jobs that she was suited for was waitressing or some low paying cashier job, neither of which sounded attractive. Stripping was her last choice, but it was easy money.

Just because those hoes suck dick for a few extra tips don't mean that I have to, she reasoned.

Chanelle looked around the club, taking in its lavish décor. It looked new and had two full-service bars. Big lights shined directly on the stage and two poles were in the middle of it. Big TV screens were all around the club displaying drink specials and the name of the current stripper performing. The lighting was low in certain parts and a VIP section was upstairs overlooking the stage. She'd noticed a couple pool tables and a few enclosed rooms that were probably utilized for conducting business.

This definitely ain't no Player's Club type shit, Chanelle nodded in approval. The club appeared to be classy and all of the girls looked top notch. She could see that the owner obviously took a lot of pride in maintaining the club's reputation. *I'd fit right in,* she thought. Still, she wasn't sure that she had the nerve to take off her clothes in front of a bunch of strangers.

"There he is!" A'mya shouted as she pointed in Rallo's direction.

He had the biggest grin on his face as a dark chocolate beauty with a pink Nicki Minaj wig gave him a lap dance. Rallo was so into it that he didn't notice A'mya and Chanelle walking towards him.

"Have you lost your fucking mind, Rallo?"

He frowned, gazing up at her nonchalantly. "A'mya, what the hell are you doing here?"

"No, I should be asking you that question!"

"You was trippin', so shit…" Rallo shrugged. "I decided to come up here and blow off some steam."

"Oh really? So, you never have money to help with the bills, but you can help these homewreckers pay their bills, right?" A'mya shouted, slapping Rallo's Falcon's hat off of his head.

"Calm the fuck down A'mya, for real!" he yelled back, obviously embarrassed as he picked his hat up off the floor.

"Is this where all your unemployment checks are going along with that poker shit?" Her voice raised a couple octaves. A few other patrons had taken notice of what was going on and some were paying more attention to them than the girls dancing.

Rallo was embarrassed noticing the small crowd, "Take your ass home now!" he bellowed while waving them off.

"I'll catch up with you later, Rallo," the stripper said, addressing him with a smile. "You're a little preoccupied right now."

"Nah, you ain't gotta go, Hershey," Rallo quickly disagreed.

"Yes, the fuck she does!" A'mya barked as she stood in front of him with her hands on her hips. "As a matter of fact." With one swift move, she snatched the twenty dollar bill from the front of the stripper's bra. "I'll be taking that."

"Bitch, are you crazy?" Hershey yelled, attempting to swing at A'mya. She narrowly missed her when Rallo stood between the two women, increasing their distance.

"Don't do that shit," he barked as Hershey lunged for her again. "She's pregnant!"

Chanelle's eyes widened twice their normal size. *You gotta be fucking kidding me,* she thought. *That's why A'mya looks like she fell off.* She nodded her head knowingly. It was all starting to make sense, but she wondered why A'mya left out that important piece of information before.

Hershey grinned. "You know what? Y'all obviously need it more than I do. Keep that lil' twenty dollars, boo boo."

"This is nothing to us, sweetheart," A'mya tried to front, now dropping the bill on the floor. "I make good enough money without having to whore around for it."

"Only a broke bitch would say that. Besides, that's not what I heard," Hershey responded with a smile dancing on her lips. "Rallo says that you're busting your ass working for Ronald McDonald." She laughed as a few of her girls chimed in.

A'mya turned to Rallo with her face almost as beet red as it'd been earlier when he'd slapped her. For the moment she'd forgotten all about Hershey. She was more concerned about the comments made. "So, you've been telling these…these…" A'mya was so angry that she could barely get the words out. "Hoochies about me!"

Rallo stared at A'mya dumbfounded, unsure of what to say. "I… uh…"

"You got some fucking nerve! Your unemployment checks are only a hundred and thirty dollars a week! Nigga, you ain't making but a little over five hundred dollars a month!"

Let that nigga know, Chanelle cheered silently, glad that her girl was finally growing a backbone. *Bout time she woke up.*

"And you spending it on this ugly ass hoe," A'mya continued her tirade, turning back to Hershey.

"Bitch, please. You *wish* you looked like me." Hershey tossed the wig over her shoulder. "Just remember, your nigga was spending his last on *me*," she pointed out, then walked away.

A'mya turned back to Rallo. "I can't believe you!" She wiped the water from her eyes. "I'm so tired of your shit. I want you out of my fucking house!"

"Yes," Chanelle found herself uttering out loud.

Rallo waved her off. "A'mya please calm down...you just mad right now."

"Y'all need to either keep it down or get out," the bouncer informed the duo.

"*I'm* leaving, but *he* can stay because he damn sure ain't coming home with me!" A'mya yelled before spinning on her heels and walking towards the door.

"Baby, come on!" Rallo jogged after her, still pleading.

"I can't believe that busted bitch!" Hershey commented to a few of the other strippers. "I make two stacks in a night and she probably don't even make that shit in a month!"

Chanelle had started after A'mya, but after hearing Hershey's revelation, her ears perked up at the sound of money. "Hey, can I talk to you for a second," Chanelle called towards Hershey.

"What's up?" Hershey questioned. She looked at Chanelle suspiciously.

"What's it like working here?"

"I mean, it's good money and you can meet a lot of niggas with deep pockets." Hershey scanned Chanelle up and down, admiring her frame. "You thinking about dancing?"

"No, I was just asking," Chanelle answered quickly. She still wasn't sure if this was something she really wanted to do and felt embarrassed having even inquired about it.

Hershey smirked. She was familiar with that line and decided to call her out. "Look, ain't no point in faking. Fuck what you might've thought, this is *damn good* money. The only bitches turning they noses up at this shit is bourgeois ass broke hoes who probably work at Wal-Mart or some shit." She let out a chuckle. "Now, I don't know about you, but I don't give a fuck about what no broke bitch think. While they shopping at Thrift Stores, I'm shopping at Saks and Neiman's. You feel me?" Hershey said. "If you change your mind, just come back and see Triniti. She's the house mom." With that last word, she strutted off, leaving Chanelle plenty to think about.

"Excuse me, lil' mama," the bouncer greeted Chanelle. "But your homegirl out there wants you."

Chanelle had almost forgotten about A'mya and why they were there in the first place. Dismissing her notion to strip, she headed out the door.

I must've lost my damn mind to actually consider doing that shit.

Moments later, Chanelle's cell phone rang and she answered it absentmindedly, figuring that it was A'mya calling. "Hello?"

"You scandalous ass bitch!"

Chanelle instantly gasped hearing the voice on the other end. A part of her wanted to hang up. "Rob?"

"Yeah, bitch. I believe you have something that belongs to me," he said sarcastically.

"What are you talking about? I don't have shit of yours," Chanelle retorted in a small voice. The fact that her location was unknown made her feel safe, but she was still on edge. *How does he figure I had something to do with it? Did somebody see me leaving? There's no way that JaQuez survived, so who was Rob's source?*

Rob was JaQuez's boy and business partner. He was a big dude, both in body mass as well as his reputation. Chanelle couldn't help but fear him as she'd witnessed his wrath before. Rob was a brutal ass nigga. She believed that he got off on torturing others. Truthfully, she thought that he was *worse* than JaQuez and neither were anything to laugh at.

"Oh, but I think you do… over a hundred and fifty grand of my money. You may have thought that you were just makin' off with JaQuez's dough, but that was some of my shit, too. You can bet your life that you're gonna pay me back every fuckin' penny."

"Rob, I really don't know what you're talking about," Chanelle said as she started a fake sob. "All I remember was this big nigga with a mask on coming in the bedroom when me and JaQuez were having sex. He held us at gunpoint and tied us up while he went to get the money. But JaQuez got aloose and went after him. Then I heard a gunshot and the nigga came back up, stole some of our jewelry and then knocked me the fuck out."

Chanelle's words became choked with tears. She paused for dramatic effect as she pretended to recompose herself. "When I woke up, I was untied and JaQuez was dead. I ran because I was scared. I don't know who he had beef with, but I didn't want them to come back and kill me, too."

Rob was quiet before chuckling to himself, "Damn. You're exactly the trifling, deceitful ass bitch I thought you were."

"I…"

"Well, I heard otherwise, so that means your days are numbered, bitch," Rob interupted. "You think you're not gonna pay for what you did to my man. Trust me…I'm gonna find you. I put that on everything."

$EIGHT

"Can I get some extra ketchup? Oh, and some extra napkins? I don't see the honey mustard in here either."

Stifling her attitude, Chanelle reached back into the bucket to give the woman more condiments.

"Thank you," the lady smiled genuinely, before frowning when she closed the window and turned away.

"I can't do this shit!" Chanelle complained for the thirtieth time that day and she was only two hours into her shift.

Just as A'mya had promised, she'd hooked her girl up with a job at McDonalds and Chanelle was miserable. She'd worked there for a week, but today was her first day working the drive thru. Honestly, Chanelle didn't know how she'd managed to last over the past seven days. She hated the stupid uniform that they had to wear, she hated getting paid only $7.25 an hour, and most importantly, she hated smelling like burgers and fries when they got home.

Chanelle had never worked a day in her life and she wasn't sure how long she could last. Being with Desmond and JaQuez had definitely spoiled her because both had insisted that she didn't work. She had no desire to either, with the exception of running her boutique. Chanelle was fit to be a boss, not somebody's flunkie. Hell, a pampered housewife at the very least. She'd go back to that lifestyle in a heartbeat if she could.

Dealing with the customers and all their needs was a different thing all together. Everything about the job irked her. Chanelle already knew that she wasn't built for this and the experience only solidified the fact. If someone told her that she would be working at McDonalds until she qualified for retirement, she would commit suicide before her shift even ended. She didn't understand how people could spend the rest of their lives doing something that they hated. Then again, she could.

Out of necessity.

Each day that she got dressed and rode with A'mya to work, she would curse Desmond out mentally. Much to her dismay, he'd since gotten his number changed so tracking him down had really hit a dead end. The thought of him partying on South Beach every night and balling out of control with her money infuriated Chanelle every time she thought about it.

"I'll be working here for a fucking year before I can get any money saved up to move out," she said sullenly.

"No cursing on the front line, Chanelle," A'mya advised her in a pleasant, but strict voice.

A'mya was another aspect of the job that was slowly, but surely getting on her nerves. Her persona at home and at work was completely different. At work they were no longer 'friends'. A'mya had made it very clear that she was her boss and wouldn't treat Chanelle any different from the other employees. Chanelle had to clean bathrooms and wipe off countertops just like everybody else, which caused her to resent A'mya a bit.

"Whatever," Chanelle mumbled as she handed a customer her order along with a caramel apple sundae.

As the young woman reached her hand out to accept her dessert, Chanelle couldn't help but notice the sparkling Lady Royal Oak Audemars watch on her left wrist. The Gucci shades protecting her eyes weren't hard to pick out either. Looking at the woman made her sick because she was a mirror image of what Chanelle *used* to look like.

Money.

"You know what, boo, these fries ain't nowhere near fresh," the women commented in a syrupy sweet voice. "I told the girl at the other window that I didn't want salt on my fries either. And this coke has ice in it when I specifically requested none."

Taking the bag, Chanelle rolled her eyes. "You'll have to pull up."

The women laughed, noticing Chanelle's annoyed expression. "It ain't my fault you gotta work here. Don't take that shit out on me, boo."

Before she could reply, the women had parked her car a few feet away as instructed.

"That bitch don't know who she's fucking with," Chanelle muttered attempting to calm down as the next customer arrived at her window. *I got something for her though.* She had no intentions of telling anyone that the women's order was incorrect. She could sit there and wait until Chanelle's shift ended for all she cared.

"Chanelle, there's a car parked out front. Is she waiting for something?" Malika, one of her coworkers, asked.

"Fuck if I know. She's probably just tryna make sure her order is right." Chanelle shrugged it off and continued to serve the rest of the customers. There were no issues until ten minutes later when she heard the woman's voice at the front counter.

"I'm trying to figure out why the hell I haven't gotten my order yet!" the woman barked at A'mya, who attempted to calm her down.

"What order would that be, ma'am?" A'mya asked, confused.

"Y'all gave me some cold, stale ass fries and then there was ice in my coke and I said I didn't want any!"

"I do apologize about the inconvenience, ma'am. I will surely rectify this issue for you."

"You better because I told that girl at the window ten

minutes ago about my order. I have shit to do!" She placed her hands on her hips. "Now, I want my food in less than a fucking minute and I expect that smart mouth ass bitch from the window to bring it to me."

The woman didn't give A'mya a chance to respond before stomping out of the establishment just as quickly as she'd come in.

A'mya spun on Chanelle quickly. "Can I have a word with you, Chanelle? Malika, take over the window."

"Look, that lady had a bad attitude and I had to check her ass," Chanelle answered nonchalantly, already knowing what she'd called her over for.

"Chanelle, this is your *job*. Customer service! We have to remain professional regardless of the customer's attitude. You're a grown woman. I shouldn't have to explain this to you," A'mya sighed before handing her the bag of fresh fries and a drink. "I'm gonna have to write you up for this later."

"Are you serious? So, you're gonna write me up because that bitch was disrespectful?" Chanelle asked.

"Look, Chanelle," A'mya started with clenched teeth and lowering her tone so that no one else could listen on. "I'm being real lenient with you. If you were anybody else I would've already fired you. The least you could do is show some gratitude." She paused, waiting for Chanelle's response, but she didn't get one. "After you do that, you can go on your fifteen minute break and cool down."

Chanelle sighed and rolled her eyes, feeling like a scolded child instead of a grown ass woman. She didn't even bother to argue with A'mya. The conversation was going nowhere and the sooner she dealt with the customer, the sooner she could get to her break.

Chanelle dragged her feet out the door, already anticipating that this wouldn't go well. Exiting the building, she had to shake her head at the car the girl was pushing. A diamond white Mercedes-Benz SL65 AMG convertible. She knew the exact model by heart seeing as she'd asked JaQuez for one several times, but he kept putting it off.

"Here you go," Chanelle said with an attitude as she handed her the bag.

"Took your ass long enough." The woman turned to her passenger as she pulled out a fry, inspecting it to ensure it was up to her standards. "Miserable ass bitches. How you gonna be mad at somebody else cuz you work a shitty job? And then be mad at me cuz *you* can't make the food right?"

"Backwards as hell," the passenger chimed in.

"Look, do you want your drink or not?" Chanelle asked impatiently, tired of the girls sidebar conversation while she stood there looking stupid holding her cup in the heat.

"Girl, if I was working here, I'd be mad, too," the passenger continued, the both of them obviously ignoring Chanelle, "Especially seeing you with this bad ass Benz."

"Bitch please, I'm used to pushing Maseratis. This Benz ain't shit!" Chanelle retorted. *These bitches just don't know. I'm far from a bama bitch.*

The woman scoffed before looking around as she took the drink out of Chanelle's hand. "Is that right? Because I sure don't see a Maserati in the parking lot. You must be pushing them in your dreams because right now, the only thing you're pushing is sodas under the damn machine. Thirsty, bitch."

In one quick toss, the contents of the woman's cup landed all over Chanelle, leaving the front of her pants and shirt drenched.

"Bya-tch!" the women shouted as she quickly drove off.

Chanelle was so livid she just stood there, shaking with fury. Never in her life had she been disrespected. *Do I have a sticker on my forehead that says 'Sucker' or some shit,* she wondered.

Everybody seemed to be trying her lately. Either that or she was being served with a big dose of karma. *After all the fucked up shit JaQuez did to me why am I the one getting pun-*

ished? She shook her head. *Fuck it. What the hell I got to lose that I ain't lost already?*

She was fed up with all of it, and knew what she had to do.

Storming back into the restaurant, Chanelle garnered a few stares due to her soaked uniform and the way her sneakers squeaked across the floor. If she hadn't already made a commotion with her entrance, without a doubt everyone noticed when she slammed her headset down in the middle of the floor.

"What happened?" A'mya asked concerned. "Here." She placed the car keys in Chanelle's hand. "I don't have any extra uniforms in the back, so you can go home and change. I have a spare one there you can use. I'll give you a little extra time on your break, so you can go change."

"You really think I'd come back after this?" Chanelle huffed as she shoved the keys in her uniform pocket. "You got me fucked up, A'mya." She raised her middle fingers at everyone from her coworkers, to the customers. "Fuck you. Fuck you. And fuck you, too. I'm out!"

Chanelle could hear the excited chatter of the patrons and her former coworkers as she exited the restaurant. *Glad I could be the highlight of their boring ass lives,* Chanelle thought as she hopped into the car. She could see A'mya running out after her, but Chanelle quickly pressed down the gas and sped out of the parking lot to avoid another pointless conversation. Nothing A'mya could say would make her change her mind about what had just happened.

Feeling her phone vibrate in her pants' pocket, Chanelle pulled it out and answered without giving the screen a second glance. "Fuck McDonalds, A'mya. I told you I'm not doing that shit."

The voice on the other end laughed, obviously finding humor in her statement. "Damn. That's what you're doing nowadays? I thought you would've been smart enough to snag another baller by now."

"Loretta?" Chanelle asked, pulling the phone away from her face to check the caller ID. *I've got to start looking at this shit beforehand,* she thought. "Now, you can call me, but every time I call you, your phone always goes straight to voicemail. What's the problem? Is your phone turned off? Did one of your sponsors cut you off again?"

"Not hardly. I got your messages, I've just been ignoring them. Just in case you haven't noticed, you're not really my top priority."

Chanelle shook her head at her mother's confession. She couldn't believe that Loretta could be such a heartless bitch at times. For all her mother had known, Chanelle could've been staying in a cardboard box alongside Peachtree and Pine at the homeless shelter.

"It sounds like you need to get your hustle on if you're working at damn McDonalds. I mean, that shit is embarrassing for a girl on your status," Loretta continued. "Don't they pay like two dollars an hour?"

"Seven twenty-five," Chanelle quickly corrected.

Loretta laughed. "Same thing. You might as well be working for free. Remember, Chanelle, *nothing* in life is free and a woman should *never* be."

"Anyway, what do you want?"

"I wanna know what the hell happened with you and JaQuez?"

Chanelle instantly became alert. "What do you mean? Why are you asking me that?" she inquired, waiting to see what information Loretta could give her. Chanelle knew that the streets were really buzzing by now. Not to mention, she continued to ignore both Mimi and Rob's phone calls. "We just broke up."

"Yeah? Well, it's pretty ironic that he got shot and was found dead inside his house the day after you called me, talking about you're in Atlanta."

Chanelle suddenly became nervous, wondering what her

mother was trying to get at. While holding her composure, it was time to put on an innocent act. "What? Are you serious? Oh my God! Not JaQuez…Not my baby!" Chanelle paused for a second, then let out a few fake sniffles. "I can't believe this! Why would somebody do that?"

"That's what I'm trying to find out. So, you mean to tell me you didn't know nothing about this?"

"No, I don't. Why are you asking me questions like you're a damn cop…like I had something to do with that shit?"

"Why are you so defensive?" Loretta questioned. "Besides, even if you did, I wouldn't blame you. His ass deserved it for all of the dirt he did. Stingy muthafucka." Loretta was obviously still bitter about the fact that JaQuez never gave her any money. "I was just wondering why you didn't tell me."

"This is my first time hearing about it," Chanelle lied.

"I thought one of his little workers would've called and told you something by now."

"Nope."

"So, why are you in Atlanta again, and who did you go down there with?" Loretta probed.

"It's a long story."

"Well, you sure don't sound too distraught for this to be your first time hearing about it. I thought you were in love with that nigga and shit?" Loretta suddenly began to slur, as if lost in a memory.

"I am… I was…" Chanelle stammered. "It just doesn't feel real to me yet. Are you sure he's dead?" She tried to hide the hopefulness in her voice, but Loretta caught it.

"That's what I heard," Loretta slurred again before letting out a loud burp.

"Have you been drinking?" Chanelle asked, ignoring the question.

Alcohol had always been one of Loretta's favorite things, coming second after money, and way before Chanelle. Sometimes she even wondered if Loretta even loved her. It was a bad way to think, but she could never tell. Chanelle could count on one hand how many times she'd been told 'I love you'. It was sad, but she had long gotten over it.

"Me and uh…" Loretta snapped her fingers, trying to recollect her memory. "Aw hell, I don't know that nigga's name, but he's paid out the ass though. We been sipping on a lil' bubbly."

"It's crazy how you're forty-three years old, but you still carry on like you're my age." Chanelle shook her head in mock shame. "Look, is that all you called me for? To ask about JaQuez? If so, let's end this conversation here. I don't wanna hear shit else unless you're gonna wire me some money."

"Oh boy…where did the tears go so soon?" Loretta chuckled. "Well, you better listen to this Chanelle. I heard JaQuez had a lot of money on him before he was shot, and all the money is gone."

"So what? Niggas get robbed and killed every day. Especially dope boys. That's nothing new." Chanelle was on edge at hearing her mother's words. She was still trying to keep her cool, even though she was nervous as hell.

"Anyway, word on the streets is that Rob is looking for the person who shot Ja'Quez. Got a big ass bounty out, too."

"And?" Chanelle asked. "Why are you telling me?"

"I'm just saying, smart ass," Loretta said, matching Chanelle's tone.

Chanelle paused as she got back into character. "I wouldn't kill JaQuez… I loved him," she added softly for effect.

"Well, I just thought I'd let you know." Concern laced her words as her voice softened. "If you *did* have something to do with it, I'd watch my back. His boys are out for blood."

$NINE

"Damn, lil' mama, I didn't expect to see you back here so soon," the bouncer at Pretty Kitty greeted.

"Me either," Chanelle mumbled under her breath.

She'd been so sure that she was never returning, but her awful day gave her a change of heart. Loretta's words of "wisdom" echoed in her mind as she passed Pretty Kitty on her way to A'mya's apartment, prompting her to go change clothes before doubling back to the club.

Being back on top was most important to her and she couldn't attain the results she wanted making minimum wage. Even if it meant sacrificing her self-respect, she would do what she had to do for a bigger payout. Besides, how bad could stripping be? Chanelle already knew she had the body for it and could actually dance. There was no doubt in her mind that she would make good money. Her plan was to work for a few months or so, then chunk up the deuces and work on starting her boutique.

"You finally gonna take up my offer and start dancing?" the bouncer inquired.

"Y'all hiring?" she asked.

"Shit…We should be. I know they wouldn't pass up on a dime like you. Just holla at Triniti."

"Thanks," Chanelle smiled as she walked in and scanned

the club.

Despite the fact that it was daytime, it was still pretty packed. All the women that Chanelle saw walking around seemed to be just as bad as she was although she could tell a lot of the women had undoubtedly invested in ass shots. She hated needles so she was glad that her backside was naturally voluptuous.

"So, you came back, I see." Hershey smiled as she approached Chanelle. "Got tired of them bullshit ass jobs, huh?"

"Where's Triniti?" Chanelle asked, ignoring her. She didn't feel the need to explain herself to anyone.

Hershey pointed to a corridor located at the furthest end of the club. "Last door on the left."

"Thanks," Chanelle replied as she headed towards Triniti's office. Despite her pep talk earlier, she still sucked in a deep breath, not believing that she was actually going to go through with it.

Think about the money, she kept telling herself. *The more money I get, the closer I am to opening up my boutique.*

Chanelle exhaled a deep breath as she approached the door and tapped softly. She couldn't make out what had been said, but she cracked the door open anyway, figuring she'd been granted access. However, when she opened the door, it was a different story.

Chanelle stood there like a deer in headlights watching the show that took place. The woman she assumed to be Triniti was laid back on top of the desk with her legs wide open while a man crouched in front of her, feasting between her legs as though it was his last meal.

Quickly, Chanelle closed the door before rushing off. She tried to be quiet, but her Prada heels clicked loudly on the tiled floor. Looking back, she didn't see anyone coming after her which immediately made her feel silly for damn near running away.

What the hell were they gonna do? Kill me or some-

thing? Chanelle laughed it off as she took a seat at the bar. But she kept her eyes trained on the hallway, deciding that after the man left she would try again.

"Can I get you anything?" the female bartender asked as she leaned over the counter.

"No, I'm good."

Chanelle felt like she could use a drink, but refused to pay ten dollars for one. Back in the day, that was chump change to her. Now, considering the fact that she was still holding onto the forty dollars Desmond gave her, proved that it was too rich for her blood.

A'mya had been nice enough to let Chanelle stay with her rent-free and was more than generous with groceries in the house. On top of that, they always had freebies from McDonald's to eat, whether breakfast or dinner.

I can't wait to see what my bullshit paycheck is gonna look like, Chanelle thought.

"What the hell are you doing here?"

Chanelle looked up and frowned when she saw Rallo standing in front of her. "I guess this is where you've been spending your free time now that A'mya dumped your ass."

Rallo raised his middle finger at her. "You don't know shit because we're getting back together. Or didn't A'mya tell you?" he asked smugly. "Just in case you haven't noticed, I got that bitch wrapped around my finger."

All Chanelle could do was shake her head. "Then why the hell are you here? I thought you would've learned the last time. I'm sure it had to be hard sleeping at some flea bag motel."

He smiled, letting the words roll off his back. "What's up with you? You strippin' now?" Rallo looked her up and down seductively, slightly licking his lips.

Chanelle rolled her eyes. "Trust me, boo, you couldn't even afford to *watch* me strip if I was."

"I beg to differ." He pulled out his wallet, revealing several hundred dollar bills. "Just won this shit in a poker game."

"You really are a sorry ass nigga, you know that? A'mya could use that money. Not to mention, you're trying to hit on her friend."

"Well, she ain't gettin' none of it."

Chanelle shook her head again as she stood up to leave. She couldn't stand to be in his presence anymore. Some things he did reminded her too much of JaQuez and it made her sick to her stomach.

"You crazy as hell if you don't think I'm not gonna tell her. I let you slide the first time."

Rallo grasped her wrist tightly, twisting it backwards and pulling her roughly towards him. "You ain't gonna say shit to her. Know why? Because if you do, your ass won't have any place to stay."

"Everything straight?" an unfamiliar voice asked.

Chanelle turned, surprised to see the man she saw in Triniti's office minutes before. If it hadn't been for his distinctive YSL outfit, she wouldn't have known. The Usher Raymond look-a-like stood there until Rallo released his grasp.

"Yeah. Everything straight," Rallo answered as he took off in the opposite direction.

"Thanks," Chanelle mumbled to the stranger, slightly embarrassed remembering how deep his head had been buried inside the woman's treasure box.

The man only nodded before giving Chanelle a smile and walking off.

No sooner than she'd broken off her gaze with him, a woman with a cinnamon complexion and long, black curly hair walked up towards her. Her eyes were slanted and cheeks were high, just like a high fashion model.

Oh my God. I know this ain't the bitch who threw that soda on me earlier, Chanelle thought heatedly. She stared at her. *Hell yeah, that's her.* All Chanelle could do was shake her head because she had an awful feeling that the woman was

Triniti. *I have the worst fucking luck.* She looked at the many glasses on top of the bar instantly wanting to retaliate.

"Who the hell are you and why were you spying on me? *Nobody* is allowed back in my office," the woman huffed.

"Let me guess, you're Triniti, right?" Chanelle asked in disbelief. She hadn't gotten much of a glimpse at her face when she was in the office, so it came as a shock. *This must be how the bitch can afford that kind of lifestyle.*

If Chanelle had to call it, she'd probably say that Triniti was mixed with Korean or another race rooted from Asia. Standing tall at five feet, eight inches, her hands were on her hips and her face always displayed much attitude.

"Yes, I am" she replied. "Were you…" Triniti stopped mid sentence, then looked Chanelle up and down with a slight smirk. "Hold up, you're that bitter bitch from McDonalds." Moments later, she let out a laugh that reminded Chanelle of some type of exotic bird. "What the fuck are the chances?"

"I prefer not to be called a bitch if you don't mind," Chanelle responded.

"Wow, you clean up really well. You're far from the basic chick I thought you were. And let me guess, you came here to make some *real* money, right?"

Chanelle wasn't feeling her cocky, overly arrogant demeanor in the slightest. Triniti had already humiliated her one time today, so she wasn't gonna allow it to be done again. "You know what? I'm good on that job actually." She turned to leave, but Triniti's next set of words stopped her.

"So, you're gonna let some small shit like that get in the way of you making some real money? You must like working at McDonalds making minimum wage?"

"No, but."

"No buts. Never let your personal feelings get in the way of your money," Triniti schooled. "That's rule number one and if you follow that, I promise that you'll be successful here. Follow me."

Surprisingly, Triniti's words stuck out to Chanelle. She had a point. Pretty Kitty was one of the hottest strip clubs in Atlanta. She would be a fool to pass up the potential job offer. Not to mention the money.

Doing as told, she trailed behind Triniti.

"Next time you come back here, knock first," Triniti warned, narrowing her already slanted eyes as she opened the door to her office.

"I did knock," Chanelle protested. "Maybe you should lock the door next time if you're trying to sneak around."

Triniti smirked. She decided to give her a pass this time only because she knew that Chanelle would be a good asset to the club.

"Just don't let the shit happen again." Triniti walked around Chanelle slowly, looking her up and down. Inspecting her like a piece of meat at the butcher's shop, it made Chanelle extremely uncomfortable, but she was still confident.

With measurements of 36D-26-38, *Shawty is a Ten* by The Dream was the song that summed Chanelle up perfectly. Her clear, unblemished skin further asserted her dime piece status. She was bad without even having to recruit the assistance of MAC products. The five inch Valentino heels made her ass sit up just right and the sheer leggings she wore put her fat camel toe on perfect display.

Slowly, Triniti nodded her head in approval. "Have you ever danced before?"

"No."

A smile graced her lips as she nodded again. "Fresh pussy...You'll be a hot commodity then."

"I'm not fucking no niggas. Let me put that out there right now," Chanelle snapped. "I don't know how the fuck y'all get down in ATL, but I'm not with that shit."

"Cool out, baby girl." Triniti threw her hands up in surrender. "It's just an expression. Broads that's been dancing all their life start looking rough and worn out. You still got that fresh look to you. Pretty Kitty prides itself in having the baddest bitches this side of the south and I'd say that you definitely fit the credentials."

Chanelle beamed, although she'd expected to hear that. "Thank you," she replied modestly.

"You take shots?" Trinti asked, patting her own butt.

"Ass shots?" Chanelle asked with a screwface. "Hell no."

Triniti nodded once again. "Strip."

"What?"

"If you can't strip in front of me, then how can you expect to do it in front of a bunch of men?"

Chanelle didn't know why she hadn't been expecting this. A part of her was just hoping that the skin-tight clothes that she wore would be enough. She figured that she may have to dance a little, but didn't even consider having to get butt naked. She was glad that she'd worn her best Le Perle lingerie underneath.

"You're definitely bad," Triniti complimented as Chanelle removed all of her clothes. "Niggas gonna love your lil' ass. So, when can you start? Tonight?"

"N-not tonight," Chanelle stammered nervously as she quickly slipped back into her clothes. Although she'd mustered up the courage to apply for the job, that was all she could manage for the moment. "I…uh… got something really important to do later on."

"That's fine. I'll see you tomorrow at nine then." Instead of voicing it as a question, it came out more as a command. "There are a few things I need to run down with you tomorrow about how shit goes. Tipout and other shit like that. Wear something sexy, too. A costume or lingerie is fine. Oh, and think of a name." Triniti frowned, realizing that she didn't even know her new dancer's government name. "By the way, what's your real name?"

"It's, Giselle," she said quickly. Lying was starting to become second nature for her. She figured she was safe in Atlanta, but still. This bitch didn't need to know her God-given name.

"Okay, Giselle, I'll see you tomorrow." When she started for the door, Triniti suddenly stopped in her tracks. "One more thing." She narrowed her perfectly arched eyebrows and her voice took on a colder tone. "What happened in this room, stays in this room, so don't go running your mouth about what you saw tonight with me and that guy."

It came out more like a warning with an underlying threat, than a request. Chanelle didn't miss the undertone, but shrugged it off. *Who the hell would I have to tell and who really gives a fuck?*

"I'm not a snitch, sweetheart."

Chanelle shook her head as she trotted out of the office and back into the club. Just looking around and seeing the dancers had her close to rethinking her decision. Each time she thought about how much her life had changed, Desmond came to mind. To get information about his whereabouts, she'd even tried calling his mother, but her number had been disconnected. Any ties she had to him had been severed. But if she *ever* got the chance to link up with him again, the consequences would be dire.

$TEN

Triniti smiled as she heard her ringtone go off. Without even having to look at the caller ID, she knew who it was. *Va Va Voom* by Nicki Minaj was reserved for only one person in her address book.

"What's up, Trap?" she asked, picking up the phone. She hoped he couldn't hear the smile in her voice.

"Can't sleep and I knew yo' ass would be up," he joked.

Triniti looked over at the clock. It was almost three in the morning and although the club closed around four, she decided to get off early tonight. Besides that, she was waiting on Ali to come through as promised to finish what they'd started earlier. He was nearly thirty minutes late, but she wasn't worried about it. Her attention was focused on the conversation she was currently having and she secretly wished that Trap was coming over instead of Ali. She'd been in love with Trap ever since she was fifteen when he first started working for her older brother, Maurice, selling drugs when they lived in New Orleans. Her feelings for him were unreturned, but she couldn't help that she was in love with him.

"Look, I just got so much shit on my mind." Trap replied.

Although they'd been out of New Orleans for about seven years, his accent was still present. Triniti's was a little less prominent, coming out mainly when she was mad.

After Maurice was locked up, serving a twenty-five to life bid, Triniti was practically alone in the world, their mother was strung out on the same poison that made Maurice a living and eventually died from an overdose. Her sperm donor had been just that, dipping out on her mother before she was even born. Trap wasted no time stepping in to take care of Triniti as a thank you to Maurice for all he'd done for him with no hesitation. In preparation for Hurricane Katrina, they relocated to Atlanta and made it their new home.

Although she was now grown, she and Trap were still close even though things weren't like she wanted. It seemed that no matter what, he wouldn't snap out of viewing her as 'Maurice's kid sister' and claiming it would be disrespectful to get with her. Triniti didn't believe that, *especially* since Maurice never told her that he had an issue with it.

"Like what?" she asked, wondering why he was hesitant.

Just as Trap started to explain, her doorbell rung. Without a doubt it was Ali, and she was halfway surprised at how quickly he'd arrived. Triniti hated to interrupt their conversation, but she couldn't let Trap know who was at the door.

"Who comin' through your spot this late?"

"It's uh… Starr from the club. Her man put her out and shit, so I told her she could stop by," Triniti responded.

"Oh yeah?" Trap didn't sound convinced.

"Trap, please." Triniti rolled her eyes. "Who you think is at the door then if it *ain't* really Starr? A trade?" she asked, reverting back to their New Orleans lingo.

"What do you think? I *know* it's some nigga," he answered dryly, knowing that she was insulting his intelligence.

"Why do you care if you don't wanna be with me anyway?" Triniti asked, her voice taking on a childlike tone.

Trap sighed. He hated that he'd let the conversation veer in this direction. No matter how hard he tried to convince Triniti that what happened between them months ago was a mistake, she wasn't letting up.

"That doesn't have shit to do with it. I'm still gonna look out for you," he replied.

About three months ago, Trap had slipped up and slept with Triniti. He was pissy drunk, and felt bad about it because he knew that their relationship would never go anywhere. It couldn't. Then, just a month ago he'd done the same thing, falling for her seductive skills. He'd been unable to resist after the brain that she'd forced on him. Triniti was good enough to school the challenged and he didn't even want to think about how she'd gotten that talent. After that, Trap decided that he would never let it happen again. Knowing that he wasn't going to be with her made him feel guilty and no better than the other men he warned her about.

"Just admit it, Trap. Stop denying it. You love me and I love you!"

The doorbell rung again and Triniti knew that if she didn't hurry and answer it, Ali would start calling her name. Still, she couldn't end this conversation until she got some answers.

Unfortunately, she didn't have a choice when Trap signaled the end of the conversation. "I'll holla at you later. I bet *Starr* is tired of waitin' for you," he said sarcastically.

Before Triniti could reply, he'd already hung up the phone. She knew that he was pissed, so she decided to call him back after Ali left.

"Whassup, baby girl?" Ali asked, as she finally opened the door. "Took you long enough." He embraced her, cupping her soft ass cheeks.

"You," Triniti responded eagerly, placing a hand on his hard package. "Now, let's finish what we started earlier."

"Ay, chill for a lil' bit." Ali moved away from her hand and headed towards the sofa. "I wanna talk for a minute."

Triniti raised an eyebrow as she followed him to the living room, "Talk about what?"

"Us. What the fuck are we really doin', Triniti?"

"What do you mean? We fucking. Nothing more, nothing less. Ain't that what you wanted?"

Ali sighed as he stared at her. "I mean, in the beginnin', yeah. But now, a nigga tryin' to settle down and shit." He responded. "This shit ain't gettin' old to you?"

"No. I think our arrangement is pretty good so why fuck it up with a relationship? You know I ain't looking for that right now," she countered. *Not with you anyway,* she thought. "Besides that, you know Trap ain't gonna go for that shit."

"Fuck that nigga!" Ali spat. Triniti narrowed her eyes at him as if to say 'Watch your mouth' and he raised his hands up in apology. "No disrespect, but we got our own lives to live. I know that's like your brother and he my nigga and all, but ain't no other man gonna tell me how to handle my shit."

"Ali, you acting like you didn't know that what we were doing was wrong in the first place! You work for Trap! You know how he is about shit! Me and you is some shit he ain't having!"

Ali knew that Triniti was right. From day one, Trap had made it clear to all of his workers that Triniti was off-limits. He knew how grimy his boys could be and didn't want her caught up in that kind of bullshit. Trap had always told her to look for a white-collar type of dude, anything *but* a hood nigga. Still, she was attracted to bad boys although her main focus had always been on Trap. She and Ali were never supposed to hook up and honestly, she'd never even looked at him in that way before. However, that all changed one night after having a big argument with Trap at the club. Pissed off, he asked Ali to take her home. Angry, and already fucked up off several shots of Patron, Triniti didn't give a fuck about anything Trap said. She slept with Ali as an act of defiance.

Ali rationalized it by saying that as long as Trap never found out, they wouldn't have any problems. Triniti vowed not to do it again and felt guilty each time she looked at Trap, but that feeling soon wore off. The women that Trap slept with would only justify her decision and fuel her to continue sleeping with Ali. The fact that he was easy on the eyes and good in bed didn't hurt either. She wasn't thinking about his money because she had her own, but at the same time, his money was nowhere near as long as Trap's. Ali was making play-play money compared to him.

Ali nodded. "I know, but I'm just sayin'. I'm not gonna live my life followin' the rules of the next nigga. Fuck that shit."

Originally, he'd only slept with Triniti because he'd been dying to get a sample of her goodies. But as time passed, he found himself falling for her and noticing things about her that he'd never paid much attention to before. He started seeing her as more than just a piece of ass. She was actually pretty intelligent with a bout-her-business type attitude. She was on her grown woman and he admired that about her. She was just the type of woman that he'd want to wife one day.

Dismissing Ali's conversation, she began removing her clothes. She didn't care to hear any more of his nonsense. All she wanted to feel was him inside of her.

"Damn, girl," he cursed, admiring her frame.

"C'mon, baby," Triniti purred seductively as she spread her legs and dipped one finger inside of her honey pot. She licked her sweetness off her finger and motioned for him to come closer.

Ali wasted no time unbuckling his pants and putting on a condom. He couldn't wait to be inside of her. Her pussy was like his second home and he never wanted to leave. His motto had always been that there was no pussy like new pussy, but Triniti had him rethinking that notion.

"Shit," Triniti muttered as she leaned over the side of the sofa and threw it back at him.

The sound of their skin slapping together and the feel of Ali's strong hands on her hips turned her on even more. All she could imagine was Trap behind her, taking control of her body like he did before.

"Throw that pussy back!" Ali commanded as he sped up his pace and smacked her on the ass. He plunged deeper into her sugar walls and they tightened against his girth. "Man…you got that good shit."

"You already know," Triniti boasted before Ali delivered another deep stroke, causing her to squeal. "Oooh shit…" She could feel her eyes rolling to the back of her head. "Fuck me, Trap!" When she felt Ali stop mid-stroke, Triniti turned back around and frowned. "What did you stop for, nigga? You was almost there."

"Bitch, you must be crazy." He pushed her away from him forcefully, causing her to land awkwardly on the sofa cushion. Ali threw the condom on the floor, then got dressed.

"What?" Triniti asked, sincerely confused at his sudden change of behavior. "Nigga, who the fuck you calling a bitch? And you better keep your hands off me!"

"No! Who the fuck are you callin' Trap?" Ali pulled his Dickies up and began fastening his belt. "You musta lost yo' fuckin' mind."

Shit, Triniti thought. It was routine for her to picture Trap giving her the business instead of Ali, but she'd never slipped up like this. "You're imagining things," she tried to convince him.

"Do I look like some simple minded muthafucka?" Ali waved her off. Her words had really fucked with his pride and on top of that, he was tired of always being in Trap's shadow. Triniti had done more damage than she'd thought.

"Ali! You're tripping! Come on, let's talk about it," she begged. Triniti hadn't gotten a chance to cum yet and he was good for giving her at least three orgasms. There was no way she was just going to let him walk out.

"Fuck that! If you want that nigga, then don't call me." Ali walked towards the front door and slammed it, causing a few of her pictures to fall off the wall.

$ELEVEN

"Man, I can't believe you're really going through with this," A'mya commented for damn near the hundredth time since Chanelle informed her about the stripping job.

"Look, I need to make some *real* fucking money. Not that play-play McDonalds shit. What choice did I have?" Chanelle questioned with a frown as she sifted through the racks at Victoria's Secret for a second outfit. It was her first night at Pretty Kitty, and she was nervous and excited at the same time.

"Just because the restaurant industry wasn't the right fit for you doesn't mean that you couldn't have done something else." A'mya rolled her eyes and shook her head. "Just to let you know, I'm still pissed about the way you left me hanging yesterday. I broke my neck getting you that damn job, and you go and curse everybody out. It was embarrassing."

Chanelle sighed. "Do you have to keep bringing that up? I already told you how sorry I was, but you're crazy as hell if you thought I was staying there."

"I could've gotten you a job at the Applebee's." A'mya smiled. "They tip pretty well and you wouldn't have to lose your self-esteem over some dead presidents." Seeing the unimpressed look on Chanelle's face, she shrugged it off. "But I guess after all you've been through and that ritzy lifestyle you're used to, I know you definitely could use the money."

Chanelle wasn't quite sure how to take her comment so she didn't respond. A'mya almost sounded sarcastic, but it could've been her imagination playing tricks on her. She didn't care what her friend thought. She was focused on nothing more than getting the money for her boutique. Everything else, especially how someone *else* felt about it, was the least of her concerns.

Walking through Lenox Mall and seeing her favorite stores had Chanelle infuriated, knowing that she just couldn't go in and spend a couple of stacks. She refused to window shop and put herself through that kind of torture, so she briskly walked past any store that she'd normally be tempted by.

The one thing that made her feel a little better was that she still *looked* like money. Her royal blue, oversized Hermes Birkin bag hung in the crook of her arm and her white Givenchy skinny jeans clung to her like a wetsuit. Christian Louboutin peep-toe sling backs adorned her perfectly manicured feet. Chanelle's ensemble cost nearly six thousand dollars, but she only had two hundred dollars in her wallet thanks to her brief stint at McDonalds. There was no future in fronting, but she wouldn't be fronting for long.

"So, tell me more about that dream," A'mya prodded with concern. "You should have seen your face. You were sweating like you'd just run a marathon. What happened?"

Chanelle had been praying that A'mya would have left well enough alone when she'd dismissed it the night before. She didn't feel comfortable discussing the details. She knew A'mya would probably judge her. She was afraid of her best…and maybe *only* friend, viewing her differently if she told the truth.

"A'mya," Chanelle's voice rose a few decibels. "I told you it was nothing."

"It didn't sound like nothing. It made me wonder. What *really* happened between you and JaQuez because that was one hell of a nightmare?"

"I told you that we just broke up. Nothing exciting. Nothing different from a regular breakup."

"Well, I've never heard of someone having a nightmare after just a simple breakup. I mean you literally woke me up. You kept yelling out, *please don't hurt me, JaQuez. I'm so sorry. I didn't do it. I wasn't the one who hurt you.* Then you started screaming."

Chanelle just shrugged her shoulders when A'mya looked as if she wanted answers.

"So, how did y'all break up? What did you do that you're so sorry for?"

"A'mya, I don't wanna talk about it, so can you stop asking questions?" Chanelle snapped. She wasn't mad at her friend for all the questions, but more so mad at herself for damn near admitting to a crime beyond her control. "It was just a stupid dream, so please drop it."

A'mya nodded her head, but her expression was unconvinced. It was clear that she wanted to speak more about it, but left it alone.

"Speaking of breakups," Chanelle started, shifting the conversation away from herself. "I still don't understand why you let Rallo come back after that stunt he pulled at the club."

Chanelle really believed that A'mya was getting rid of Rallo for good after all the shit she talked, but she should've known better. He had A'mya's mind gone and Chanelle was sure that when Rallo left, it would be on his own accord.

"He's the father of my child, Chanelle," A'mya said, taken off guard by how the conversation had changed. "What did you expect me to do?"

"Grow some balls! What will he be contributing to your household? Nothing! He's using you and you're too dumb to see that. He'll probably leave you the moment the baby's born. I don't know why you want to have that baby so bad." She desperately wanted to tell A'mya about Rallo hitting on her at the club, but the way she was defending him, Chanelle chose otherwise.

"Just because you're bitter about JaQuez burning you and treating you like shit, now you wanna go on some sort of vendetta to use men for their money, doesn't mean that I have to!" A'mya replied, growing louder than she intended. A few people stared in their direction, but most minded their business. "What gives you the right to look down on me and my relationship? All you see is the negative!"

"Look," Chanelle sighed, trying to contain her anger. She wanted to tell A'mya a few things, but the fact of the matter was that she was still dependent on her for the time being. She couldn't risk A'mya trying to kick her out over hurt feelings. "I'm just trying to look out for you. That shit with Rallo, I've been there done that."

"And I appreciate your concern, but I'ma need you to just stay in your lane from now on. You haven't even been here long and I'm tired of you judging my relationship with Rallo already."

"Fine. I'll wait for you outside," Chanelle responded as she walked out of the store. She had to distance herself before things got even more out of hand.

It looked like A'mya was getting ready to apologize once she realized Chanelle was offended, but she could keep her apologies. Chanelle was over it.

She stood outside with her arms folded and her 'bitch-face' on, but that still didn't discourage an ugly, acne faced dude from hollering at her. He seemed too old to be going through puberty.

"Ay, what's good, shawty?"

"Hello," Chanelle replied in a dry tone.

"I'm Eyes. What's yo' name?"

Chanelle turned away from him, not caring about how rude she may have looked. She just wanted this clown to leave her alone.

"You gonna act like you can't hear me?" the guy barked

as he jerked her arm, pulling her towards him. "You ain't gotta be rude and shit. Bourgeois ass bitch. What's yo' fuckin' name?"

Chanelle was in shock. She'd never had a stranger put his hands on her before. "Nigga, you better get your filthy hands off me!" She attempted to yank away from his grasp, but his hold was firm.

"What the fuck you gonna do about it?" He pulled her small frame closer to his body. He reeked of stale Black and Mild's and cheap alcohol. She could barely breathe. "You *can't* and you *ain't* gonna do shit."

Chanelle couldn't believe that no one attempted to come to her aid. She was right in front of the store and noticed that a few passersby were gawking at the scene in front of them, but no one came to her defense.

"If you know like *I* know, you'd better get yo' fuckin' hands off her," a male voice said.

Eyes turned toward the voice and released Chanelle from his grasp. "Damn, Trap, this you?"

"Yeah, nigga," the man replied as he pulled her close to him, but at a respectable distance. "You straight, sweetheart?"

Chanelle flashed Eyes a dirty look before turning back to her savior. She couldn't help but smile widely when she realized that he was the same guy that had come to her rescue and let her use his phone when Desmond left her stranded. He looked even better than she remembered.

He stood at six foot three and his caramel coated, muscular build looked edible. His dreads were tied up in a ponytail and a fitted 'A' cap sat atop his head, cocked to the side. She was impressed by the clout he had, along with the Yacht-Master Rolex, watch on his left wrist. Chanelle wasn't sleeping on the Gucci jeans sagging from his waist and the rare Air Yeezy's on his feet either.

Despite the shit that she was talking to A'mya only minutes ago, Trap's appearance had her star struck for the moment.

She'd forgotten everything.

"Yes," she finally managed to say.

Trap turned back to Eyes. "Apologize, nigga."

"My bad, man." He threw his hands up in surrender. "I don't want no problems."

Trap nudged his head towards Chanelle, "Nah. Apologize to *her.*"

"I'm sorry, shawty," Eyes mumbled, before balling his hands up in his pockets. "My fault, Trap. I ain't know this was you."

"Even if she wasn't, nigga, don't ever put yo' hands on no female! That's some punk ass shit."

Eyes nodded before trudging off in the opposite direction.

Trap reached for Chanelle's bags and handed them to her. "Here you go."

"Thank you."

"No problem." Trap stared at her again, "You sure you straight? It seems like every time I run into you, you in some shit, ya heard me." He chuckled, trying to make light of the situation.

"I know, right?" she joked. "Where you from, 'cuz you talk just like Lil' Wayne's baby momma?" Chanelle hadn't missed his accent by a longshot, but she wanted confirmation.

"Yeah, I'm from N.O., but damn, you didn't have to say I sound like a female." Trap laughed again, revealing a perfect set of teeth. "You never told me yo' name either."

"Oh. It's Princess," Chanelle answered quickly, giving him her middle name. She didn't know why she was lying about it, but didn't feel the need to tell him *all* of her business. "And you're Trap, right?"

"Yeah. That's what they call me. You tearin' it down, huh?"

"What?" Chanelle asked confused until he nodded towards the bags in her hand. "Oh, yeah. Trying to find some things for work."

"Where you work at?" Trap raised his hand in surrender, recalling how guarded she'd been during their first encounter. "If you don't mind me askin'."

"At the uh…" Spotting a woman walking past with some pink scrubs on gave her the quick answer she was looking for. "Grady Memorial. I'm a nurse."

Trap nodded, impressed with her career choice before feeling his phone vibrate and checking a text. "Ay, look, I'm 'bout to head out so…"

"Why don't you take my number just in case I end up in some more trouble?" Chanelle flirted as he handed her his phone.

She quickly stored in her new number from the prepaid phone that she'd just bought a few hours ago. Chanelle was done with all the harassing calls from Rob. So far she'd only given the number out to Loretta and A'mya.

"Damn, I ain't seen one of them in a minute," Trap said, referring to her tiny flip phone.

Chanelle looked down. "Oh, well I lost my other phone, so this is just a quick replacement." *I need another iPhone bad. This shit is embarrassing.*

"Cool. I'll hit you up, a'ight?" he responded. Honestly, Trap hated that he had some business to take care of because he was actually enjoying his conversation.

Chanelle nodded. "A'ight." She watched as he swaggered off, admiring the way his clothes hung off him. Trap was fine, no doubt about it, but that didn't mean shit. He was probably still like every other nigga…not worth a damn.

"You got what you wanted, I see."

"What?" Chanelle asked with a frown. She hadn't noticed that A'mya had finished up her shopping and was standing right next to her with a big grin on her face.

"That man you were talking to was Trap, right?" A'mya exclaimed.

"Yeah," Chanelle replied, trying not to sound enthused. "How do you know him?"

"*Everybody* knows Trap. You said you wanted a man with money and you found one. He owns a few businesses here in Atlanta, but it's just a cover up for drugs. I heard he doesn't play around…"

A'mya was still rambling on and on about how she had better watch herself, but Chanelle tuned her out.

I think I just found another come up, she thought.

$TWELVE

"You ready?" Triniti asked as she peeked inside of Chanelle's dressing room later that night.

Chanelle nodded her head slowly as she stared back at her reflection in the mirror. She wore a sexy red and leopard two piece lingerie set. The bottom was frilly in the front, but the back was nothing more than a tiny string that was suffocated between her voluptuous ass cheeks. The push up bra served its purpose, giving her more than ample cleavage. Chanelle could tell that Triniti was impressed as she nodded her head in approval.

"Them niggas gonna go crazy over your lil' ass! You nervous?" Triniti inquired.

"A little," Chanelle admitted.

"There ain't no reason to be. Hell, the shit is simple. Just put on a good show and you'll have them eating out the palm of your hand."

Chanelle nodded, but she wasn't completely convinced. All she could see was her busting her ass courtesy of all the baby oil she'd rubbed into her skin. The dancing would be easy, but having so many eyes on her at one time was nerve wrecking. The more she thought about it, the more she doubted herself. The confidence that she normally had was now lacking.

I can't do this shit, she thought, feeling puddles forming in the palms of her hands. *I don't know what the hell I was thinking.*

"You'll do fine," Triniti chimed in as if hearing her thoughts. "Just remember what Hershey showed you. Even if you forget that, just twerk your ass and they'll make it rain." Triniti flashed a big smile as she handed Chanelle another shot glass full of Patron. It was her third that night and she hoped that the effects would kick in soon. Judging from the petrified look on her face, Chanelle would probably freeze the moment she stepped out and the music started.

"You shaved and shit right?"

Chanelle frowned. "Of course. What kind of a nasty bitch do you take me as?" She downed the glass before frowning again at the taste. "That was nasty as hell."

"It works though. You'll thank me later." She shrugged. "He-Man will be out there to scoop up your money so you can perform without stressing over it."

"He-Man?" Chanelle questioned.

"He's one of the bodyguards here. Along with picking up your money, he also makes sure that none of the niggas try to get out of hand, of course. They go crazy over the new strippers…" Triniti's voice trailed off as if she remembered something. Finally looking up from her temporary daze, she smacked Chanelle on the ass. "You ready?"

"Yeah," Chanelle whispered, feeling her body tingling.

Perhaps the liquor was finally working. Taking one last look in the mirror, she quickly applied some lip gloss and body spray. She could hear her song starting up and the DJ announcing that it was time for Sparkle, her stage name, to come out.

Moments later, Chanelle strutted out in her four-inch heels to the smoke-filled stage and was amazed at all the people in the audience. She'd been told that Pretty Kitty was a popular spot, but she hadn't expected this. There had to be at least a hundred men or more in there and it was only a weeknight.

The men whooped and hollered as Chanelle began dancing to Tyga's, *Rack City*. The liquor had done exactly as Triniti had promised and she felt herself becoming more at ease. As the song went back to a verse, Chanelle slowly and seductively began pulling off her top. She covered her nipples coyly just throwing her bra into the audience. As money started to rain on her, she couldn't help but smile.

Maybe stripping ain't so bad, Chanelle thought as she arched her back and removed her thong. Spreading her legs wide, she gave the men more than an eyeful and tossed her g-string to the crowd. Chanelle had to refrain from shaking her head when she saw a man catch it and bring it to his nose to sniff the crotch area.

The song was almost over, but the money wouldn't stop coming. The liquor had her feeling herself...literally. Chanelle couldn't help but to close her eyes momentarily as she remembered the way JaQuez used to put it down. He was a sorry ass boyfriend, but she couldn't deny that he had skills in the bedroom.

"Shit," she moaned, allowing her fingers to dip into her valley.

Oddly, the men's cheers encouraged her to continue, and there was no shame in her game. Chanelle wasn't sure what had come over her, but the bills flooding the stage assured her that she was doing something right.

As the orgasmic feeling washed over her, a smile graced Chanelle's face. She hadn't felt this good in a long time. And she for damn sure hadn't expected it while stripping. For some reason she just felt free and her body was on fire each time she swept her fingertips across her curves. It was a feeling that she'd never experienced in all of her twenty-four years.

Hearing the last chorus come on, Chanelle positioned herself near the edge of the stage. As the music changed, she got on her hands and knees, clapping her ass to the beat.

"Got damn!" she heard a man yell out. But when she felt a tongue on her most private area, she immediately froze up.

Chanelle quickly snapped out of her trance and wasted no time slapping the man.

"Nasty muthafucka!" she shouted over the music. She then turned to He-Man, giving him the evil eye for failing to do his job. *Security my ass,* she thought, remembering Triniti's words. She was further pissed when He-Man took his sweet time walking over and didn't even bother to kick the man out. Instead, they were talking and dapping it up like old friends.

Shaking her head, Chanelle stomped off the stage. Her body still felt on fire and she was sweating profusely. She hadn't noticed until looking at herself in her vanity of their dressing room. The room was small, but semi-private. Only she and Hershey shared this particular room and Chanelle was thankful. She didn't want anybody in her face right now.

"Hey, Sparkle," Hershey greeted as she pulled back the satin fabric that served as the door. "He-Man out here with your money. How much you want me to tip him for you?"

"Tip that Suge Knight looking muthafucka? *Please!*" Chanelle grimaced. "That muthafucka can't seriously be thinking I'd tip his ass. He ain't do shit!" She nodded her head as she mulled it over. "You know what? I got a tip for his ass. Tell him to do his job right the next fucking time and I might tip his ass a dollar!"

Hershey grinned, but disappeared back out of the door. After a minute, she returned with Chanelle's bucket of money. "Look, you don't *have* to tip the bouncers, but since you're new and you're not one of the top girls yet it's a good idea to tip them niggas. They can be just as bad as some of the females here."

Chanelle rolled her eyes. "What the fuck is he gonna do?" She waved Hershey off. "I ain't thinking about that nigga. If I don't have to, why the fuck would I share my profits? I need every dime I can get." Eagerly she snatched the bucket from Hershey and peered inside. The bucket looked pretty full so she could only imagine how much she'd made. Chanelle remembered at least one hundred dollar bill and a couple of twenties.

"Tonight is usually one of our slower nights, but on nights like this where you got out of town niggas in the house, you can get more," Hershey explained. "It's usually popping on the weekend and Pretty Kitty Wednesdays… It's like our version of Magic City Mondays back when they was the shit."

"So, this club is pretty hot, huh?"

"Hell yeah. We thought we had some competition when they started talking about opening *'Diamonds of Atlanta'* last year. Shit. I even thought about going over there to strip, but a lot of shit went down there. That shit is cursed. It used to be *Body Tap, Whispers, Stacks ATL…* A lot of stabbing and shooting and shit popped off around there! DOA—Dead on Arrival, bitch!" Hershey joked. "It's nice as hell in the inside though. You know my nosey ass had to check it out."

Chanelle half listened as she quickly counted the bills, making sure to turn them all in the same direction. She was meticulous when it came to her money. It was a habit that JaQuez had gotten her into when he first started letting her count up his cash.

"Oh yeah?" Chanelle asked, disinterested.

She appreciated the fact that Hershey had been forthcoming with giving her the dirt on who to stay away from and who tipped the most, but she talked too damn much. She was a stark contrast from how Chanelle imagined strippers to be. She heard they were catty and bitchy when it came to new girls, but Hershey wasn't. That didn't mean that she trusted her though. She was sure that Hershey had some sort of angle.

"Yeah. The VIP room is all glass and…"

"That's bullshit!" Chanelle interrupted as she finished sifting through the wads of cash. "I can't believe this!"

"What's wrong?" Hershey asked, taken aback by her outburst.

"This is only three hundred dollars!"

"Shit. I made more than that on a slow night." Hershey shrugged. "I thought them niggas loved you, but I guess not. Shit happens sometimes."

"Hell no! I *saw* a nigga throw down some hundreds," Chanelle insisted. "But ain't shit in the damn bucket but some ones and five dollar bills!" She jumped up and counted through the money again. When Hershey erupted into laughter, she stopped her count. "What the fuck is so funny?"

"You!" Hershey shook her head. "That nigga He-Man got yo' ass!"

"What the fuck do you mean he got me?" Chanelle hoped that she heard Hershey incorrectly.

"That's what I'm taking about," Triniti said, entering the room unannounced. She didn't bother to knock, knowing she was coming in either way. "Them niggas loved you! I told you that they would! That E pill did the damn thang! Now, you need to get dressed and go do some lap dances."

"E pill? As in ecstasy?" Chanelle had momentarily forgotten her money dilemma, instead focusing on the fact that she'd been drugged. "Are you kidding me?"

It was all making sense to her now. The electrifying feel of her touch, the inhibition... All the time she knew it had to be something more than the alcohol that had her feeling that way, but she would've never guessed that her drink has been spiked with a pill.

"You mad, but it worked, didn't it?" Triniti asked nonchalantly. She wasn't fazed by Chanelle's reaction in the least bit. She'd expected it, but knew that she would thank her later. Without it, Triniti knew without a shadow of a doubt Chanelle would've frozen up. "I only gave you half of a pill so chill out."

"I can't believe this shit! First, I'm damn near molested and that sorry ass He-Man doesn't do shit about it; second, this nigga stole some of my money; and third, you tryna turn me into some fucking drug addict. Bitch, there ain't no way of knowing what the fuck that pill got in it!" Chanelle thundered.

"Now, somebody better pay me my shit so I can get out of here. I'm done!"

"You're so damn dramatic." Triniti rolled her eyes. She was used to this reaction, so it didn't faze her one bit. The girls could call her whatever, but they couldn't call her broke. "Ain't shit happen to you except you got paid for putting on a damn good show. So, what the hell are you talking about paying you? If anything, *you* owe me."

"It's like this; either you bring that swollen looking muthafucka in here to gimme what he owes me or *you* are gonna reach in your damn pocket and give it to me," Chanelle demanded, clapping her hands together at each syllable. If it was one thing that she didn't play about, it was her money. She'd been fucked over once by Desmond and wasn't about to let that shit happen once again.

"No, bitch," Triniti started, finally losing her cool, "It's like this: If you don't chill the fuck out and watch how the hell you talk to me, you won't get shit. I don't play that disrespect. Now…" She exhaled. "If somebody took your money, I'll handle that but you ain't gonna snap at me like it's my fault. You should *never* let money out of your sight."

"She thinks He-Man took some of her money because she didn't make as much as she thought," Hershey explained.

"Are you kidding me?" Triniti asked. She shook her head. "I'll go get him and we'll figure it out."

"You better do something," Chanelle muttered under her breath. Folding her arms, she tapped her feet anxiously awaiting He-Man's arrival.

I can't believe that nigga! Don't they pay his broke ass good enough, she wondered.

A few minutes later, Triniti and He-Man appeared in the doorway.

"He-Man, did you take some of Sparkle's money?" Triniti asked referring to Chanelle by her stage name. The two stood in the doorway as Chanelle bore a hole in He-Man's head with her stares.

"Seriously?" He looked over at Triniti with mock disappointment. "I don't have to fucking steal."

"Negro, please!" Chanelle jumped up from her seat. "I know I saw a hundred and some other big faces! It wasn't just all ones and fives, nigga!"

He-Man shrugged. "I didn't see that. I picked up everything I saw on the stage." He shook his head before giving Chanelle a pitiful look, "I know you probably expected more, baby girl, but you can't try to pin that shit on me. It's your first night. You'll do better next time."

Triniti nodded in agreement. "That pill probably fucked up your vision a little."

"See? And I didn't even know you was rolling," He-Man commented innocently. "That shit ain't no joke. You can imagine shit sometimes."

"Like hell I did," Chanelle mumbled.

"I'm sorry you feel that way. Even though you ain't tip me, I *still* brought you back all your money. It's all love over here, lil' mama."

"Thanks, He-Man," Triniti said, dismissing him. The moment he left the room, she turned her attention back to Chanelle. "You need to have your facts straight before you go accusing people of that kind of shit. I can't believe I called him in because you *think* you shoulda gotten more money."

"I didn't think!" Chanelle was ready to bust a blood vessel. "I saw the shit."

"Yeah, okay." Now, it was Triniti's turn to wave her off. "Anyway, I'm gonna need seventy-five since you came around eleven. The tipout goes up fifteen dollars every hour."

"How fucking convenient." Counting it out slowly, Chanelle reluctantly handed over the money. *Two hundred and twenty five dollars,* she thought bitterly.

Chanelle just knew that she would be making at least a thousand dollars a night, three if she was lucky. Even though

Hershey had said it was a slow night, she knew that couldn't have been completely true. From the many men in the audience, it looked like a full house to her. *I wonder how much I had before that muthafucka stole my shit.* Chanelle wasn't buying his innocent act for a second.

"Anyway," Triniti continued ignoring her comment, "If you go back out there and do some lap dances, you can probably hustle up a little more. Niggas love that one-on-one shit."

"Fuck that!" Chanelle spat. "I can't and ain't gonna do this shit!"

Triniti rolled her eyes. She'd heard that line before and after seeing all the money that Chanelle managed to hustle without even touching the pole, there was no way she was just going to let her leave.

"It wasn't that damn bad and you know it. Besides, what else are you gonna do if you leave here? Go back to flipping burgers?" She was something like a pimp when it came to keeping her girls in line. She would always convince them that they had nothing else going for themselves.

Most of the time it worked.

The allure of the fast money was too much to resist. Even if a girl decided to leave, within a day or two, they would be back, begging for their job. She knew that Chanelle would be no different.

"I don't give a fuck." Chanelle wiggled into her tight Seven jeans. "Please believe that I can find some other way to get money. I was getting money before I came here and I'ma get to the money after I leave." Chanelle was lying through her teeth, but didn't want Triniti to think she was indebted to her just because she'd given her a job.

"If that were the case, you would've never stopped by my office in the first place. Who you fooling, Chanelle? Me or you? You need me more than I need you, baby girl, cause I'm gonna get money regardless." With those last words, Triniti exited the room.

Chanelle flipped the bird at her, then blew her breath angrily. "This bitch."

"Look, I know it's fucked up," Hershey started, breaking the silence. "But you can't make that amount of money in a day at any other job even though you got ripped off by He-Man."

Chanelle's eyes grew as wide as saucers. She couldn't believe her ears. "You mean to tell me that you knew that he stole my shit but you had the fucking hush mouth when Triniti was in here?"

Hershey shrugged. "I ain't no snitch. Besides that, you wasn't getting your money back even if I did. That's just how the game go, baby girl." She sprayed herself with enough *Guilty Gucci* perfume to trigger an asthma attack before continuing. "Just tip that nigga next time. You ain't gotta kiss nobody ass, but try to keep muthafuckas on your good side or you'll have more nights like this. Triniti be knowing the shit, but since it don't interfere with her money, she don't really give a fuck."

Hershey lowered her tone and looked around as if they weren't the only two people in the dressing room. "And I heard that when He-Man does that shit, he gives her a cut so she'll go along with it. But hey, you gotta take the good with the bad. Tip that nigga and you won't have these problems next time."

Chanelle looked at her in disbelief, not believing what she was hearing. "So, basically you're telling me what…that I shouldn't trip over it?"

"Yup. Charge it to the game."

$THIRTEEN

"Whassup?" Trap greeted Triniti loudly as he waltzed into the strip club around two o' clock in the morning. There was only an hour left until closing, but the club was still booming with loud music, rowdy patrons, and seductive dancers.

"What's up, boo?" she asked with a smile then hugged him tightly. "I'm glad you decided to stop by. Most times I can't even beg you to come here. I ain't never seen a man who doesn't want to see tits and ass every night."

"You know I ain't trippin' off that shit, Triniti. I've seen more than enough pussy in my lifetime."

Trap owned Pretty Kitty and used it primarily as a means for cleaning up some of his drug money. Since Triniti had a degree in business, he allowed her to manage the place. Other than that, he didn't really have any interest in it. He was rarely ever there, preferring to occupy his time with more important ventures. He let Triniti handle pretty much everything. In fact, if one didn't know any better they would've thought it was her club. Not to mention, Trap trusted her. He knew that she would do whatever was in the best interest for the club. She would handle it the way he would and he for damn sure didn't have to worry about her stealing any money. Trap paid her heftily anyway so there was no reason to.

"Yeah, I came to pick up tonight's profits instead of you

bringin' it to me." He surveyed the club and nodded his head in approval. Everything seemed to be runnin' smoothly. "And I wanted to come check out that dancer you was tellin' me about."

Triniti kept bragging about the bad ass dancer she'd recruited and begged him to come and see her. Not only did Triniti want his approval, but she always busted her ass to try and please him.

Triniti nodded her head in response as she led him to the back office where the safe was held. "Her name's Sparkle. Pretty ass redbone, but she had an incident with that nigga Tommy. He touched her and she went berserk."

Triniti conveniently left out the ecstacy pill that she'd slipped her. She knew that Trap didn't like for her to have drugs there, but it helped a lot of the girls do their best. She would never turn down any strategy to make more money. The men loved that extra freakiness, and Triniti loved that extra money.

"Damn," Trap commented. "That's fucked up."

"If that wasn't bad enough, she accused He-Man of stealing some of her money and shit."

"He probably did," Trap snickered. When they arrived in the back room, he stood patiently as she unlocked the safe.

"I haven't counted down the safe yet so I can't say how much we made, but we did really good for it to be one of our slower nights."

"It's ai'ght. Me and Ali got some shit to do, and I wouldn't have had time to come back through."

"You know I could've dropped it off to you," Triniti answered sincerely. She had no problem doing anything for Trap.

Trap frowned. "Yeah, I know, but I hate when you have that much money on you. Niggas wouldn't hesitate to rob a female, so I need to stop puttin' you and my money at risk like that. Maybe I need to come pick up the money more often or at least have Ali do it."

"You know I can hold my own," Triniti insisted.

Trap smiled.

"And you said Ali came with you?" Now, it was Triniti's turn to frown. She hadn't spoken to him since their last sexual encounter. She'd tried calling him several times, but he never picked up the phone. "Where is he?"

"Outside smokin' a blunt. He was actin' like he ain't wanna come in and shit. I told that nigga he might as well come in and get a drink. That nigga been actin' weird as hell lately." Trap laughed before continuing, "Let me find out he done started fuckin' with another one of the strippers again and they beefin'."

"I doubt it." Triniti folded her arms. "Who cares though?"

"Well, something is up with that nigga cuz he's always the first one that wanna come through." Trap eyed her suspiciously. "You know anything about it?"

"Please," Triniti blew her breath angrily. "Why the hell would I know anything about Ali? He ain't my nigga!"

"Damn, it was just a question. Why are you so defensive?"

"I'm not," she huffed.

"Shit. Let me find out y'all got some shit to beef about," Trap joked.

"Anyway," Triniti decided to change the subject, "What business y'all gotta handle tonight?"

"Looka here, you know what I told you. The less you know, the better off you'll be. If any shit should *ever* pop off, you'll be safe cuz you really won't know anything."

Triniti pouted and crossed her arms. She hated how Trap always kept her out of the loop. She could understand his reasoning, but didn't want to be the last one to know shit either. "Nigga, I'm from the ninth ward!"

"No, that's where you were born. Your ass was raised in Gentilly. You forgot who you talkin' to? False claimin' ass," he joked. Triniti didn't know much about struggling or any of that hood shit. Her brother Maurice had kept her sheltered for most of her life. "Seriously though, you don't need to concern yourself with it, ya heard me?"

"Whatever," Triniti replied when she noticed Ali walking through the door.

"How much longer are we gon' be here?" Ali asked, not even bothering to speak to Triniti. She didn't exist as far as he was concerned. Not after what she'd done. It was the ultimate blow to a man's ego.

"Damn, nigga, you don't see my sister right here?" Trap noticed Ali's attitude, but he didn't care. He'd been brought up in the days where you always spoke, especially when you were walking in on a conversation.

"What's up, Triniti?" Ali mumbled. He finally looked her directly in the eyes. His look conveyed what his voice didn't. His desire for her.

"Was that so hard?" Trap asked sarcastically. Feeling his phone vibrating, he pulled it out and checked the caller ID. "Ay, let me get this right quick." He looked back and forth from Ali to Triniti. "Y'all gonna be straight alone?"

"Why wouldn't we be?" Triniti asked surprised.

"Shit. Y'all the ones actin' weird as fuck," Trap responded before dismissing himself quickly, leaving the two of them alone.

Ali stood awkwardly near the door with a huge scowl on his face. It was obvious that he didn't want to be bothered, but Triniti didn't let that deter her from speaking.

"Hey, Ali…" she started cautiously, acknowledging him.

"Man, don't say shit to me. You know that shit you did was foul."

Ali had hoped that their stop to the strip club would be a quick one, but it was obvious that Trap had other plans. On top of that, he hadn't been looking forward to running into Triniti again. To say that he was bitter about the name mix-up was an understatement.

"I said 'sorry', nigga," Triniti snapped. "You still salty about that shit?" She wasn't trying to talk about that anymore. In her opinion, Ali needed to man up.

"Fuck this," Ali responded as he started out of the room.

"Wait," she called out, grabbing him by the arm, "You didn't tell Trap about it, did you?"

To Triniti, Trap spoke as though he knew something was going on between the two of them. *This nigga better not be fucking up our agreement!* If it ever got out, Trap would never want to mess with her. That should've been enough for her to stop, but a girl had needs. If Trap wouldn't fulfill them, somebody had to. Ali was a decent stand in.

Ali stared at her as if she was crazy. "What the fuck do you think?" He searched Triniti's face and saw that she honestly thought it was a possibility. He laughed sarcastically and shook his head. "I didn't tell him shit. Now, get the fuck out of my way." Ali snatched his arm away from her and continued down the hallway headed for the bar.

"What the fuck is going on with y'all?" Trap asked as he passed by Ali and walked into the office. He'd noticed the tension in the air and wanted some answers.

"I don't know what that nigga problem is," she lied, "And I don't give a fuck."

"I can't tell. Both of y'all look on edge and shit. It shouldn't be no bad blood between family." Trap eyed her curiously. "Or did some shit pop off when he came through the other night?"

"W…what?" Triniti stammered, wondering if Ali had lied to her. "You can't be serious!"

Trap chuckled. "I'm just fuckin' with you, girl. Calm down."

"Nah. You calm down, nigga." Triniti tried to regain her cool and flip the conversation in her favor. "Besides even if he was blowing my back out, would you be mad?"

Trap immediately frowned. He hated to hear her talk

about things like that. "Watch your mouth, Triniti."

"Nah. Answer the question." She refused to let up until she got a response out of him.

"Are you fuckin' that nigga, Triniti?" Trap asked her seriously, searching her eyes for an honest answer.

"You answer me first."

Trap shook his head. "Triniti, you're twenty-five years old. You too damn old to be playin' childish ass games."

"Please." She rolled her eyes in her typical manner. "You're too old to not know what you want! The shit is so obvious! What are you afraid of?"

"I ain't afraid of shit," Trap denied. "Look, if you fuckin' with Ali, that's yo' business, but that nigga ain't no good."

"You contradictin' yourself." Triniti folded her arms. "If he ain't no good then why you got the nigga on your team?"

"The way Ali handle his bitches and the way he handle business is two different things. Do you wanna be baby momma number three for that nigga?"

Triniti frowned at the thought. "Like I said, we don't have shit going on so you may as well quit with the lectures."

"Yeah. Ai'ght." Trap wasn't convinced, but he wasn't about to argue with her all night about it. He already knew that Triniti would do what she wanted regardless.

"You don't have to worry about that because I only want you," she cooed, stepping closer to him and invading his personal space. "Wasn't it good to you last time?"

Triniti's hands made their way down to the fly of his jeans and massaged the area gently. As she started to tug on the zipper, Trap jerked away from her as though her touch was poison.

"Triniti, we supposed to forget that shit ever happened, remember?" Trap reminded her sternly. "It shouldn't have happened. It was a mistake."

"Mistakes only happen once. We've made love on three

different occasions."

"We fucked," he corrected her. "It's a difference." Trap tried to ignore the pain in her eyes from his last revelation by turning away from her. "Look, I gotta go."

Triniti's eyes welled up with tears although she'd fought hard not to. Hearing him say what she'd long suspected had her emotional. "Trap, you was the nigga that took my virginity back when I was eighteen," she hissed through the tears that were now running like a faucet.

Trap sighed. "Don't do this, Triniti." He tried to wipe her tears, but she slapped his hand away.

"The first nigga and *only* nigga that I let in my heart," she continued with a shaky voice. "You can rationalize it any way you want by calling it a mistake or whatever the hell, but I know the truth."

"Oh yeah?" he asked, narrowing his eyebrows. "If you felt that strongly about a nigga then you wouldn't be sleepin' with Ali, right?"

Triniti could feel her heart drop to the pit of her stomach. She couldn't believe that Ali had actually told him. She opened her mouth to object, but Trap spoke first, silencing her with an index finger and a smile.

"You can fuck whoever you want, Triniti. You ain't got to feel guilty about the shit."

"But I'm not fucking Ali!" she lied. "And how you gonna act like you don't care when you keep bringing it up?"

"Chill out," Trap told her in an attempt to get her to lower her voice. "It doesn't matter whether you are or not. It doesn't change anything." Trap sighed. "And I just brought it up because I hate when people lie to me."

"I'm not lying!" she insisted. "And what do you mean 'it doesn't change anything'? Anything like what? Us?" Triniti searched his eyes for an answer, but couldn't find one.

Hot tears unwillingly ran down her face. "What's wrong with me?" Her voice shook, "Tell me why you don't love me

then! Tell me why you won't try! You don't even consider us!"
Triniti slapped her hand against her chest for emphasis. "What
the hell is wrong with me?"

"Nothing is wrong with you, Triniti," Trap assured her.
"And I do love you." He kissed her forehead softly and wiped
away her tears. "Just not the way you want me to."

$FOURTEEN

"Six thousand dollars," Chanelle said as she counted up the money she'd made in the course of four weeks.

It was a small amount in comparison to what she was used to as JaQuez' wifey, but this was money she'd earned on her own. That fact alone made her proud despite the demeaning way that she made it. Honestly, it wasn't even as bad as she thought it would be. She wouldn't make stripping a permanent career choice, but the fast money was addicting.

Chanelle had already put down a deposit for a nice apartment in Norcross, but it wouldn't be ready until the end of May. She'd wanted to live in the heart of the city, but she would save money staying in the outskirts…money for her ultimate goal.

Chanelle counted down the days on a daily basis because she was more than fed up with living with A'mya and Rallo. They were always arguing or getting into physical fights. That was until they had makeup sex. Rallo and A'mya didn't give a damn where they did it. Like the old *112* song stated, *they would do it anywhere*.

She once caught them making love in the kitchen. As if the view wasn't disgusting enough, the fact that they were doing it in the middle of dinner being prepared was unsanitary!

Since then, she made it a point to *always* eat out. Needless to say, she couldn't wait to get the hell out of there.

Everything was coming along, but she still had to get a car. She'd been trying to save as much as possible in order to score a lower down payment. Besides that, she knew that her lack of credit would be a major obstacle in securing a car at a luxury dealership. Chanelle could've easily gotten a little raggedy car, but she was a bad bitch and expected to push a whip that represented that title to the fullest.

Chanelle was quickly making her way towards being one of the top girls at Pretty Kitty due to her knack for working the pole. She wasn't afraid to experiment and always came up on something innovative. Because of that, she was seeing a big payoff. Work had gotten easier, and she hadn't had any more issues out of He-Man. To this day he still denied that he'd stolen any of her money, but she knew otherwise. He even had the audacity to ask her out on a date but of course, she turned him down. On top of the fact that he was ugly *and* sneaky, his paper wasn't long enough.

"It's only a matter of time," Chanelle murmured to herself as she clicked the internet icon on her new laptop. Going into her favorites folder, she selected the link labeled 'Chanelle's Chic Boutique'. It was a piece of property that was located on John Wesley Dobbs Avenue. It was nearly 2400 sq ft. If that location didn't work out, Chanelle also had her eye on a smaller spot at Atlantic Station.

The sound of Chanelle's cell phone going off disturbed her thoughts and she smiled seeing Trap's name on the caller ID. Now *he* fit the description perfectly of the type of man she was looking for.

"Hello?"

"Whassup, beautiful?"

"Hey, Trap," Chanelle greeted seductively.

"How you been? A nigga ain't heard from you all day and shit."

"I know. I've been real tied up with work," she half-lied.

Chanelle still kept up the façade of being a nurse who worked the graveyard shift. There was no way that she was going to tell him that she was actually a stripper. It was none of his business anyway. To help keep up the story she even bought a pair of scrubs and wore them when they went out on their two breakfast dates.

Even though Trap had been in and out of town, Chanelle smiled at the fact of her and Trap talking everyday since meeting at the mall that day. He even texted her all throughout the day to see how she was doing. It was sweet and thoughtful, but Chanelle knew that most men were this way in the beginning. After a while it would all fly out the window. However, it *did* let her know that he was interested and that was all the ammo she needed.

"I can respect that, but maybe you can take off for just one night and come chill with ya boy. I'm tryin' to go out on a date at night this time," he said with a slight chuckle.

"I don't know," she responded.

"C'mon, you gonna make a nigga beg? I ain't used to this shit," Trap joked, but was serious at the same time.

He'd never had a woman refuse a date with him, if anything they were throwing themselves at him before he even discovered their name. Women like that were already categorized as smuts in his book. Chanelle both surprised and intrigued him by the way she wasn't readily available to him.

He wasn't used to a female like her. She looked like a video vixen, but carried herself like a lady. The fact that she took her job seriously was also admirable. He loved a woman that didn't need a man for anything.

She giggled, loving how sexy he sounded when he said 'baby'. "I'm sure you have plenty of other females that you could take out."

"I'm not gonna lie to you. There are other females I *could* take out, yeah. But is there another female that I *want* to take out? Nah, I'm tryin' to spend time with you."

Chanelle had to give it to him, his words almost sounded sincere. He was definitely trying. "All right," she relented, then looked at the clock. It was 7:05 p.m. "You can pick me up. Just give me thirty minutes."

After giving him directions, Chanelle placed her money neatly inside of a jewelry box that she kept in the middle drawer of the dresser. Arranging her clothes neatly on top of the box, she closed the drawer softly. She didn't think that Rallo or A'mya would mess with her things, much less steal from her, but she still wouldn't leave it out in the open to tempt them. The lock on her door further ensured that there would be no issues.

Satisfied with the setup, she rushed to the bathroom to get ready. She had to ensure that she was on point. Chanelle could tell from Trap's swagger, along with his bankroll, that many women were undoubtedly dying for his attention, so she had to stand out.

Just as she prepared to turn the knob on the bathroom door, Rallo waltzed out with only a towel wrapped around his waist. He stood staring at her for a moment while Chanelle frowned.

"Excuse me," she said rudely, pushing past him. Before he could say anything else, she'd closed and locked the door behind her.

"Stank ass, bitch," she heard him mutter before the bedroom door slammed.

Chanelle didn't care what he said about her. The disdain they had for one another was mutual. While she'd never been anything but courteous to Rallo, she suspected that he'd overheard a conversation she'd had with A'mya about him. It was that or A'mya told him about their conversation at the mall a few weeks prior. Either way, it didn't matter to her.

She smiled at her reflection and applied another coat of her MAC 'Pink Friday' lipstick. She ran a comb through her long locks then blew a kiss at the mirror, satisfied with her appearance.

I work them long nights, long nights to get a payday. Finally got paid, now I need shade and a vacay... Big Sean rapped on her ringtone.

Chanelle looked to see Loretta's name on the caller ID. Briefly she thought about sending it to voicemail, but in case she'd heard some new developments about Rob she relented and answered the line.

"Yes, Loretta?" she asked impatiently.

"That's some greeting for your mother," Loretta said, feeling slightly offended.

"Well, if your mother put money and men over you, you'd probably answer the same way," Chanelle retorted.

"Listen…That's what I called about. I have two thousand dollars for you if you still need some money."

Chanelle's eyes immediately perked up at the sound of the word money. "Really?" One part of her wanted to decline and tell her to keep her measly money. But a bigger part of Chanelle knew that even the smallest addition to her stash would bring her that much closer to her goal of getting a car and becoming a business owner.

"How are you sending it? Western Union?" she questioned.

"Well actually, my boo James is in Atlanta on a business trip so he said that he could meet you somewhere to bring it to you."

Chanelle rolled her eyes. "James? I've never heard that name before, so he must be your latest trick."

"Look, he's taking time out of his night to bring you this money. At least be appreciative! It was his idea in the first place," Loretta snapped.

"Oh wow. So, you can't even think to help me out on your own. You're certainly deserving of 'Mother of the Year', don't you think?" she asked sarcastically.

"Look, Chanelle, you keep talking shit and I'll tell him

never mind."

She grew quiet at her mother's request, giving Loretta the okay to go ahead, "James told me that you could meet him at the Ritz-Carlton in Buckhead. He said he'll be checking in by eight. He'll be driving a silver Audi A7 with South Carolina plates. I'll just give James your number so that he can..."

"Don't give my number out to no strange nigga!" Chanelle protested. "I'll just call you if I need anything."

"Fine, Chanelle." Loretta paused. "I love you."

Chanelle was quiet. Not knowing how to respond, she disconnected the line instead. Those were the words that she'd been dying to hear from her mother for as long as she could remember, but Chanelle just couldn't bring herself to say the same.

"What time does A'mya get off?" Rallo yelled the moment she exited the bathroom.

"Nine!" Chanelle shouted back. *Shouldn't you know,* she thought, shaking her head.

"You heading out?" Rallo eyed her up and down lustily. He was still only wearing a towel and only inches away from her personal space.

He couldn't help but notice the way her jeans accentuated her onion booty and how her cleavage seemed to spill out of her tank top. The six inch Chrissy Lou Asteroid Spike-Toe pumps she wore only increased her sex appeal.

Rallo could feel his dick hardening. He'd snuck to see her perform at the club a few times before and he had to admit that she was bad, but the fact that she was his ol' lady's friend had stopped him from pursuing her any further...that and Chanelle's bad attitude. Still, the apparent camel toe in her J. Brand jeans had him reconsidering.

"You bad as hell, you know that?" Rallo asked, licking his lips.

"Does A'mya know that?" Chanelle countered with a roll of her eyes.

"She can see, can't she?"

"Watch it, nigga." Chanelle hadn't had any problems from him since the incident at the strip club, but this was also their first time alone since. Chanelle had been avoiding him like AIDS if A'mya wasn't home. She would even try to stay out and hang with Hershey if she knew Rallo would be there.

"I'm watching it alright..." He grabbed for her hand, pulling it toward his towel.

Chanelle pulled her hand back quickly. "Don't try me, Rallo." She narrowed her eyes. "I promise you'll regret that shit."

Rallo stared at her silently, no doubt contemplating whether or not it would be worth it. The serious look in her eyes let him know that she wasn't playing. While he wanted to sample Chanelle's goodies, the timing wasn't right. A'mya's break was approaching and she usually came home and brought him some food. He wasn't trying to get caught.

Rallo nodded his head slowly. "You got it...for now. But believe me, you gonna come up out of those panties sooner than later." He gave her one last fleeting look as he retreated back to his bedroom and closed the door.

Chanelle stared in the direction of his room with a baffled expression. She was glad that he'd decided not to act on his impulses. There was no way she would've been able to overpower his bulky ass. She grabbed her studded Alexander McQueen clutch and sauntered out the door. She was going to wait for Trap outside just in case Rallo changed his mind.

No sooner than she'd stepped out the door did she notice Trap's Bentley Coupe parked out front. His car stood out, not only because it was expensive, but because all of the other cars looked like they belonged in a junk yard rather than an apartment complex.

Realizing that, Chanelle was instantly embarrassed. He'd never been to the apartment before and she was worried that his impression of her would change. *I should've met him somewhere. Now, he's gonna think I'm some kind of gutter bug looking for a come up.*

She looked back at the apartment with a scowl. Rallo was peeking out from the blinds and wasn't even trying to be discreet about it. On top of that, it seemed like everybody outside had gathered around Trap's car like the hood celebrity that he was.

"Excuse me," Chanelle said with a frown as she pushed past the spectators and hopped inside of the European luxury car.

"Hey," Chanelle greeted before noticing Trap was holding a conversation with one of the corner boys. She waited impatiently as they spoke and heaved a sigh of relief when they finally did a hoodshake and the man walked off.

"Whassup, baby? My bad about that." Trap leaned over the middle console to give her a hug and quick kiss on the cheek.

"That's okay."

"Ay, Trap! When you gonna put me on?" a young boy asked with his hands up in the air trying to catch Trap's attention. He stood in front of the car with a toothpick hanging out the side of his mouth. "I'm tryna get like you, my nigga!"

Chanelle rolled her eyes. *Will these broke ass niggas get lost?* She was tired of the thirsty looks the females were giving Trap as well. They walked in front of the car slowly, switching their asses exaggeratedly, hoping to catch his eyes. Chanelle made a face at them. *Like he would pick bummy hoes like y'all when he's got a dime like me riding shotgun. Bitch, please.*

"I'll holla at you later though, man," Trap told the young guy. "My girl gonna start trippin' in a minute."

"That's whassup," the boy nodded before backing off.

Trap rolled up the window and proceeded to back the car up as people scurried out of the way, allowing him space but still admiring the expensive vehicle.

"Well, aren't we Mr. Popular?" Chanelle commented,

hoping that she sounded easygoing.

"I guess." Trap shrugged. "The whole hood just fucks with me cuz I show love."

Chanelle frowned at the word 'hood' and her mind went back to her initial thoughts about him picking her up. *I don't want him to think I'm like these bitches.* "I'm just staying here with my friend for the time-being until my condo is finished. I'm having it remodeled."

Trap looked at her like she was crazy, puzzled by the information she'd volunteered. "Say what?" He didn't believe that he'd heard her correctly.

"I just wanted to let you know this isn't my house."

"Look, shawty, it ain't no big deal. I was born in the projects and this, compared to where I came up, ain't shit. So, whether or not you really live here or not is irrelevant. I would never judge a female by something so petty like where she stays at. We all gotta start out somewhere." Trap smiled, thinking about his own come up. "What matters is that you workin' towards some shit and you shootin' for somethin' higher. Ya heard me?"

"Yeah," Chanelle agreed nervously.

"Just relax, you can be yourself with me. No flexin' or any of that other fake shit. I'm tryin' to get to know you, not all this material shit."

"I hear you talking," she stated, unconvinced.

"I'm serious. Shit. When I was younger, I didn't care about what a girl had up here," Trap tapped the side of his forehead with his free hand. "But I'm older now and honestly, I can get pussy anywhere. That's some shit that ain't hard to find. A female that got shit goin' for herself, who got some real goals, now that's a little harder to find. Now it's just a bunch of scandalous bitches lookin' for a come up off a nigga's money."

"Perhaps you just attract the wrong kind of females," Chanelle replied.

Trap shrugged before glancing in her direction. "You

probably right. But not anymore, right?"

Chanelle smirked. "Not anymore." She adjusted her seat slightly. "So, where are we going?"

"A little restaurant called 'Beulah Mae's'. It's on the east side."

Before Chanelle could reply, she felt her phone vibrating. She'd gotten a new text message from her mother: *James is at the hotel. Have u already left?*

Chanelle wasted no time hitting her back: *I'm on my way now.*

"Trap, can you do me a really huge favor?"

"Depends," he joked. "Nah. For real. Whassup?"

"I need you to take me to the Ritz Carlton in Buckhead."

He looked puzzled by her unusual request. "Say what?"

"My stepfather wanted me to meet him there since he's in town." The lie flowed naturally off her tongue. "Just really quick, please? And I promise you won't have to meet him or anything. I don't really have a way to get around since my car is still in the shop." It was another one of the many lies she'd told Trap about her life.

Trap smiled. "Yeah, sure no problem."

Chanelle returned the smile graciously. She was glad he was there just in case James tried any funny shit. She'd been tried by one of her sponsors before and vowed to never let it happen again.

The ride down I-75 was pretty quiet, except for the loud bass thumping from his speakers. But Chanelle didn't mind at all. Her thoughts were focused on getting the money from James so she wouldn't have been much of a conversationalist anyway.

Twenty-five minutes later, they pulled up in the front of the hotel and Chanelle quickly texted her mother: *We're here. Right in front of the building in a Bentley Coupe.*

"You and your stepfather pretty close?" Trap asked.

"I mean…somewhat." Her tone of voice indicated that

she didn't want to speak on it any further which Trap instantly picked up on.

A Bentley??? Damn, looks like u don't need the money after all. He should be dressed in a light blue dress shirt and a stripped tie, Loretta replied.

Chanelle's eyes were glued to the front door, but James had yet to exit. A few families waltzed in and out, along with a couple of white businessmen, but nobody came over to the car. Nearly fifteen minutes had passed and she could see that Trap was starting to get agitated. So was she.

"Let me call my mom really quick," Chanelle said as she stepped out of the car. She didn't want Trap to hear the way that she was about to chew her mother out. Even bigger than that, she didn't want him in her business.

Taking a couple of steps away, she quickly dialed Loretta's number. She could barely get out her 'hello' before Chanelle began her rant. "Where the hell is this James person? We've been waiting out here for fifteen minutes and I haven't seen that nigga yet!"

"Calm down. I was just about to call you," Loretta explained, "James said he doesn't see you either. Are you sure you're in front of the building?"

"Yes, I'm standing outside right now! There's nobody but the fucking valet out here! Are you drunk again?"

"You better watch your damn tone Chanelle. I'm trying to help you out," she warned her daughter. "And who the hell is driving a Bentley? Do you even need the money?"

"Yesssss, Loretta, and the driver of the Bentley is just a friend," Chanelle responded with an agitated tone.

"Well, give me a minute. I'm gonna call James and call you right back."

Chanelle hung up the phone without another word. She paced back and forth furiously, hoping that Trap wasn't watching her in his rear view mirror. Seeing headlights bounce across the pavement, she looked in the direction of the entrance.

Maybe this is James. Maybe he's just pulling up, she thought just before her body came to a complete hault.

Seeing the familiar car made her heart nearly stop beating. It felt like she couldn't breathe as a Toledo Blue BMW 760Li slowly crept past the entrance. It had the same black Asanti rims and dark tint that she was more than familiar with.

"It can't be," Chanelle said as her eyes squinted to get a better look. "Rob? But how would he know where I was?"

As the car neared her, Chanelle took cover behind Trap's Bentley. Her legs shook uncontrollably because she was sure that the car, along with herself, would look like Swiss cheese if Rob started blasting.

"Oh my God, I can't believe this. I gotta get out of here," she whispered to herself.

Suddenly, her cell phone interrupted her train of thought and seeing Loretta's name on the caller ID pissed her off. "You lying, bitch! Are you trying to set me up?"

There was a few seconds of silence as if she'd caught Loretta off guard.

"What the hell are you talking about?"

"Where the hell is the so called James at?" Chanelle asked. She crawled out a few feet from behind the car to get a glimpse. Chanelle knew she looked stupid as hell and undoubtedly Trap would be asking her what was going on when she got inside, but she had to play it safe. Maybe Rob didn't see her.

"I was calling to tell you that he's at the Ritz-Carlton *Atlanta*," Loretta huffed. "I gave you the wrong name. It's only like fifteen minutes away James said. So, if you…"

"Naw something ain't right about this. Fuck you and that damn money!"

Click.

Just as Chanelle heard the door of Trap's car chiming, she knew he was about to get out. Not wanting him to see her hiding, Chanelle quickly stood up and jumped into the passenger's seat, ignoring the stares from other patrons as her mind raced. Could it have really been him? Did Loretta set her up? Was she just overly paranoid?

If it was *him, he would have killed my ass right then and there. He wouldn't wait.* Chanelle knew enough about Rob to know that he didn't give a damn about who was around when he handled his business. He was reckless that way. *This is Atlanta... A lot of celebrities and shit are here. That could've been anybody's car, right? But it was the exact same car. Damn, why didn't I get a good look at the license plate?*

Chanelle couldn't afford to get caught slipping. Her life was on the line and she'd be damned if she lost it like JaQuez did.

$FIFTEEN

"You sure you're okay, Princess?" Trap asked her again.

Chanelle was still shaken up from the earlier events of the night. She was trying hard to play it off though. Otherwise she would have to come clean to Trap, and she knew he wasn't ready for that yet.

"Yeah," Chanelle agreed nervously.

"You seem uptight. Plus I saw you duckin' down behind the car earlier. What's up with that? You not hidin' from your boyfriend, right, cuz I'm not dealin' with that shit. You had me about to pull out my heat when I opened the door."

Chanelle shook her head. *Damn, I guess he did see me,* she thought before answering his question. "No, not at all." She had to think quickly. "I just saw one of my nosey co-workers. Since I called out tonight, the last thing I need is for her to run back and tell my boss that she saw me all dolled up.

"Oh, well, you can relax now. You with me, you safe."

Hearing his comforting statement made her smile even though she was certain that if push came to shove, Trap would-n't make good on his word.

"This isn't as bad as I thought," Chanelle commented, looking around the cozy restaurant. "And the fact that you own it is even more impressive. Why didn't you tell me before?" She playfully punched him in the arm.

Trap shrugged before adding modestly, "I ain't never

been one to brag. But yeah, I opened it up last year and decided to name it after my grandma. A lot of things on the menu are actually made with her original recipes."

Chanelle nodded as she finished off the last of her peach cobbler. "That's sweet. I'm sure she's flattered."

"Hell yeah." Trap cracked a smile as he thought about it. "But anyway, I'm glad you made time to come chill with a nigga and shit. You know you hard as hell to get up with."

"I know you're not talking Mr. In and Out of Town." Chanelle smiled. "Since you're busy, too, I'm sure you know how it is. It gets real hectic working at Grady. But I gotta work if I want money," she responded quickly, hoping they could move off the topic. Each time they talked about her 'nursing job', she felt like he could see right through her. His gaze made Chanelle feel exposed. Oddly enough, she liked it though. "I get tired of working there for twelve hours, talking about it makes me feel like I'm back at work."

Trap raised his hands in mock surrender. "Oh nah. I don't want you feelin' like that, so I'll ease up."

Chanelle stirred her ice around her cup with her straw before taking a small sip. "You know what's funny is that we always talk about me, but not much about you. I'm starting to think you're hiding something."

"I ain't got shit to hide. What do you wanna know?" he asked casually. "You already know I don't have kids, no ol' lady. Now, you know I own a restaurant. Shit. What else is there?"

"*And* you have a Bentley and a Benz. I wanna be like you when I grow up," Chanelle joked flirtatiously. "If I knew that running a restaurant would be *this* profitable, I would've opened one myself."

Trap laughed heartily. "I mean, the shit didn't happen overnight."

I bet. "Well, whatever the case, I'm tryna get like you. I thought nursing was where the money was, but obviously not."

"Ay, everything you do is a gamble, ya heard me? You can't live your life basin' it on the next man's success cuz you never know. I *never* thought I'd get anywhere near the success I'm at now, but shit… a nigga blessed." Trap looked at her curiously, "Your money ain't shit to frown at though. What are you an LPN or a RN? My fault, cuz I forgot what you told me."

Chanelle was quiet, not remembering what the hell she'd told him. She could barely remember the difference and she didn't want to fuck up and say the wrong thing. "A umm…RN. But anyway, see, there you go again, talking about me instead of you. So, here's a question for you. What do you want for your future? Where do you see yourself?"

"That's that *Think Like a Man* shit ain't it?" he joked.

Chanelle laughed, remembering the movie. "No, it's not. So, do you want kids? Do you wanna get married?"

Trap nodded thoughtfully and rubbed the tiny hairs on his chin before he shrugged nonchalantly. "I know I want kids, but I ain't with that 'baby momma, baby daddy' shit. So, let me ask you a question."

"Sure."

"Why were you stranded that day when I first met you? I mean it was hard not to notice when you had your suitcase and shit."

"It's a long story," Chanelle answered.

"Well, I'm willin' to listen to you. I wanna know a little bit more about you," Trap said sincerely. "Plus, you can trust me."

"Well, when the time is right, and if I ever get to the point where I can trust you, then we can discuss it, but not right now."

Trap nodded. "I can respect that."

Suddenly, Chanelle's phone vibrated loudly against the table. She snatched it up quickly with a frown when Loretta's name displayed on the caller ID. *This bitch has a lot of nerve to call me after she just tried to set me up.* After hitting the ignore button, Loretta wasted no time calling right back. To that, Chanelle powered her phone off. *Fuck you.*

"So…" She smiled, then tossed the phone into her purse. "Then I guess you *do* wanna get married?" Chanelle probed.

"You wanna be my wife?" Trap asked, surprising her with his question.

"I mean… It's uh…"

Trap burst out into laughter from the frazzled expression on Chanelle's face. "I'm just fuckin' with you, shawty, but for real though, I wanna get married if I find the right woman. It's too many scandalous ass bitches out'chea." He shook his head as bitterness started to lace his tone, "Bitches deceptive as hell now. Lyin' and cheatin' and shit. That's my main thing."

Once again Trap's cognac colored eyes met Chanelle's and stared deeply into her chocolate pools. "Looka here, Princess, I don't know how far you wanna take this shit, but I'm really feelin' you." He wet his lips before continuing, "Take it how you want, but I'ma tell you right now, don't *ever* lie to me. That's the worst shit you could *ever* do to me, ya heard me?"

Chanelle nodded solemnly, halfway agreeing with all that he'd said. The fact that they both seemed to have the same background intrigued her. They both were guarding their damaged hearts carefully. For a moment she wanted to throw all caution to the wind and tell him the truth, but dismissed that thought as quickly as it had come. Trap probably wouldn't empathize with her. He'd tell her to get the fuck out and find her own ride home.

Since she'd been deceiving him from the very start, she knew it would be hard to rebound from that. How could she tell him that she wasn't Princess, the on-call nurse at Grady who graduated from Clark Atlanta and moved from North Carolina to continue her education. She was Chanelle, the woman that robbed her boyfriend to run off with her ex- lover and ended up with nothing to show for it. She was the woman shaking her ass in Pretty Kitty several times a week for quick cash. It was definitely too late for her to have this conversation with him.

What the hell would it have mattered, Chanelle thought, attempting to refocus. *The goal is not to fall in love with this nigga like you always do. It's strictly about his ends! Thinking with your heart is what got you in this fucked up predicament in the first place.*

She hated how easy it was for her to catch feelings. Just looking at Trap with his black Givenchy crewneck shirt with his gold chain swinging was enough to make her fall in love. He was so fine, so intelligent, and unlike any other nigga that she'd ever met. She couldn't remember JaQuez or even Desmond being this charming during their initial encounter.

"You're a good dude," Chanelle stated finally, almost in disbelief.

"Why you say it like that?" Trap asked, studying her curiously. "You say it like you surprised."

She shook her head. "I mean it's just hard to find a good nigga nowadays. I…"

The sound of Trap's phone ringing interrupted Chanelle's statement and he placed his hand up to signify for her to put the conversation on pause. "My bad, shawty. It's business. I gotta take this."

Chanelle nodded absentmindedly before staring back down at the peach cobbler she'd been nursing for the past ten minutes. They could've left the restaurant thirty minutes ago, but she hadn't been ready to end the date. Going back to A'mya's house was like a little piece of hell, but she didn't yet trust herself or Trap completely to go to his house. For now, *Beulah Mae's* was the safest bet.

"You said you low on cereal?" Trap asked the person on the other end of the receiver. "You want how much? Yeah. A'ight. Bet… I'm round the corner. I'll stop at the store and then head through there."

I knew this nigga was a d-boy, Chanelle thought as she ear hustled on the sly.

Trap tried to speak in a hushed tone, but while the restaurant was noisy and slightly crowded, Chanelle could hear the conversation just as clearly as if he were speaking directly in her ear. Being around JaQuez for so long, she could easily pick up that he was speaking in codes. The untrained ear would think he was referring to cereal, but she knew that one of his trap houses was low on product and Trap needed to supply them with more. *You ain't fooling me.*

Trap hung up the phone and tossed it back into his pocket. "My bad, Princess, but we gonna have to wrap this up. I gotta run a few errands."

Chanelle nodded, agreeing to go along with his game.

"You need a to-go box or anything?"

"No, I'm good."

"A'ight."

Trap wrapped an arm around Chanelle's waist as they trotted out of the restaurant. He even opened the door for her, as he'd done when they arrived.

"Thank you." Chanelle beamed as she took a seat. Admittedly, this had been her first time riding in a Bentley, but she tried not to seem so pressed. She had Trap under the impression that she was raised in the suburbs instead of the projects. She was telling lies on top of lies. While she had never had much of an accent, she'd definitely worked on expanding her vocabulary to further fit the bill of the fake persona she'd created. Go hard or go home was her motto.

Chanelle glanced at him as they rode down the highway with Maxwell serenading them on KISS104. Trap seemed like a good dude, but so did JaQuez in the beginning. Her heart longed to love again, but her mind kept chanting her new motto, over and over so that she never forgot. *"You use 'em for what they got, not fall in love with 'em."*

"So, when's the next time you gonna let me take you out?" Trap asked, breaking her from her thoughts. "Don't have a nigga waitin' so long."

He had a smile on his face, but Chanelle could tell that he was dead ass serious. It was time for her to be a little more available. The last thing she wanted was for him to possibly end the pursuit and she'd be right back where she started.

"I won't. I'll have to see what my schedule is looking like and I'll get back with you."

"A'ight," he chuckled. "I'll take that for right now." Trap glanced at her briefly. "Like I said, if you need anything, let me know, ya heard me?"

Chanelle nodded absentmindedly, knowing that if Trap knew what type of shit she was *really* into, he wouldn't be so forthcoming with his help.

Trap leaned over and gave her a kiss on the cheek. "I'll holla at you then."

Chanelle had been so preoccupied with her thoughts that she hadn't even noticed that they had reached the apartment. She nodded again. "Okay."

Her Louboutin heels clicked across the pavement as she headed to A'mya's apartment. It was only ten o' clock and although the sky had become murky and dark, it still was warm out. Hence, everybody was still chilling outside like they didn't have anything better to do. A few of the men looked in her direction on the sly, but nobody dared to say a word while Trap was still there.

Trap sat in his Bentley watching Chanelle's retreating figure. He called himself ensuring that she made it in safely and while that was part of it, he was hung up on the sway of her wide hips and the extra switch in her walk. She was definitely a dime and he was ready to stake his claim on her.

Chanelle turned back in Trap's direction and waved before going inside. A'mya's car wasn't parked outside, so she knew her friend must've been at work putting in overtime. Just thinking about it was enough to make Chanelle roll her eyes, remembering the way things had gone down.

At least I got the hell up out of there. Chanelle made

nearly three times what A'mya made in a month and worked less hours. It was the beauty of stripping although she had to admit that some nights she came home sore. Having learned a couple pole tricks had taken a toll on her. Her legs and arms were often sore, but it was nothing that an Epsom salt bath couldn't resolve.

The apartment was unusually dark, except for the light from the TV, but it brightened the room only slightly. A Drake music video was on, playing at an ear-splitting level. Rallo was parked on the sofa in his usual spot with his blanket covering him.

How can this nigga sleep through some shit so loud? "Can you cut that down?" Chanelle yelled with her hands planted on her hips. She stood on the side of the sofa, waiting, but Rallo seemed to be ignoring her. With an attitude, she snatched the remote off the coffee table and flicked the TV off.

"Stupid ass," she muttered. "Where's A'mya?"

Again Chanelle's question received no response, which further pissed her off. *Why we gotta play these games,* she thought, figuring that Rallo was feeling some type of way from their earlier encounter. A nagging feeling in the back of her mind told her to just leave it alone, for fear that he may actually act on his earlier actions, but the bitch in her wouldn't back down.

Angrily she pulled back his blanket, determined to force him to answer her, but what she saw made her realize why he was so quiet.

Rallo was dead.

$SIXTEEN

Chanelle watched with red rimmed eyes as the officers finally removed the yellow tape that had prevented entry into the apartment. The red and blue lights were still illuminating the street like fireworks and serving as a constant reminder of what just happened. The procedure had taken hours. She'd been asked question after question until she was completely drained and emotionally exhausted.

Each time Chanelle blinked, she could see Rallo's lifeless eyes staring up at her. He'd taken two gunshots to the dome. The huge hole in the side of his head was gruesome. The blood drenched his face and created a small pool underneath him, coating the pillow he'd been laying on. Chanelle had never seen anything like that before in her life.

"Well, Miss Daniels," the detective said as he handed her a cream colored business card. His name read 'Detective Lynch'. "Be sure to give us a call if you discover anything else."

Chanelle nodded her head slightly, uttering a soft, "Okay."

"Do you have another place to stay?" Detective Lynch asked with concern. "You can stay here, of course, but with the circumstances…"

"Yeah, I have somewhere else to stay. My ride is coming," Chanelle answered quickly. She'd called Trap only ten minutes prior after leaving A'mya several messages that she'd yet to return.

"Well, we'll have an officer standing outside for security until you leave. What's his or her name, so I can inform him?"

Chanelle smiled for the first time since the incident. His words made her feel more at ease. "His name is Trap."

"Does this 'Trap' have a last name?"

"No, just, Trap, and thanks for everything."

She looked around cautiously as she made her way back to the apartment. What had just occurred was enough to shake up anyone. Moreover, the question that kept echoing over and over in her mind was 'why?' Who the hell had it out for Rallo so bad to do him like that? And why wasn't A'mya answering the phone? Chanelle had gone from calling her cell phone and leaving voice mails to calling McDonald's. Neither method received any response. Apparently she'd already gotten off from work.

Did they do something to A'mya, too, Chanelle wondered as she entered her bedroom and locked the door. Laying down on the futon, she pulled the comforter around her body protectively. There were so many thoughts racing through her mind that she didn't know what to think. A small part of her wondered if Rallo's downfall had been meant for *her* instead. Chanelle couldn't forget the car that bore a striking resemblance to Rob's.

Did Loretta really set my ass up, she thought before dismissing it. *No…I didn't come back to the house so how would Rob have known where I stayed?*

Satisified with her answer, she rested her head against the pillow and tossed the covers over her head to block out the light illuminating the room. Chanelle doubted that she would be able to doze off, not that she wanted to. Police protection or not, she didn't want to stay in the apartment even a second longer than she had to. Whenever Trap came back, she would have him drive her by A'mya's job to look for her.

Hearing a faint knock on the door, she arose from the makeshift bed. *That was quicker than I thought.* Chanelle padded towards the front door swiftly and opened it. But when she saw the person on the other side, she immediately screamed and reached to close it.

"B-b-but… H-how did you…?" she stuttered before letting out another scream, hoping that someone would hear her and come to her rescue.

"Shut the fuck up!"JaQuez growled before pushing her so hard that she hit the floor. He pushed his way inside the apartment and shut the door behind him. "You thought you was just gonna leave me for dead and not have to answer for that shit! Bitch, you must've forgot what my muthafuckin' name is."

Where the fuck are the police? They said they would stay here until Trap came. How the fuck did JaQuez get through?

Chanelle's eyes were wider than the Pacific Ocean and sat frozen with shock. It was as though she'd truly seen a ghost, but he *was* one as far as she was concerned. *Desmond killed him,* she thought before taking off towards the kitchen. Chanelle figured that if she could get to a knife she could at least defend herself. She would be damned if she went down without a fight. She wasn't about to make it easy for him.

JaQuez sneered as he pulled out a gun and cocked it back, stopping Chanelle in her tracks. He had her full attention. "Did you miss me?" he asked sarcastically.

"Fuck you, JaQuez!" Chanelle yelled defiantly, but still trembled.

"Fuck me, huh? So fuck the nigga who took care of yo' broke, money hungry ass! The muthafuckin' hand that fed you!"

"No, fuck you, the nigga who beat our baby out of me, but let his fucking mistress keep hers! Fuck you, the nigga who beat my ass constantly!" she spat. "Nigga, you deserved it!"

JaQuez nodded as he stepped closer with his gun still

trained on her. He wasn't the least bit impressed by her show of insolence. In fact, it only served to fuel the flame. When he was within arms distance of her, he backhanded her roughly.

"Do you know how *long* I been waitin' to get at you?" JaQuez didn't wait for her to answer as he continued in a sinister tone. "Bitch, we gonna have a real good time. I been *dreamin'* of this day!"

Suddenly, he rushed at her, snatching Chanelle by the throat and hemming her up against the wall. JaQuez had been so rough that the cheap wall instantly dented. "Keep talkin' to me like you lost yo' muthafuckin' mind and I *swear* I'll drag this shit out until you *beg* me to kill yo' simple ass! A'ight? We got an understandin'?"

JaQuez released her slightly, allowing a tiny flow of oxygen to return to her lungs. It was enough for her to respond, and make his point.

His actions changed Chanelle's tune instantaneously as tears flowed down her face. "Please, don't do this," she cried out, completely shedding her pride and former bravado. Her behavior at that moment was much different from how it had been a month since she'd first robbed JaQuez. She wasn't the only one who realized it either.

"Nah, bitch." JaQuez shook his head. "You ain't give a fuck when you robbed me! A nigga ain't have shit after you cleared me out. Where the fuck is my money?"

"I…I don't have it," Chanelle studdered.

"Bullshit!" he scowled. "I know you ain't blow it this fast! Not 700 stacks! You got ten seconds to tell me where it's at or I swear to muthafuckin' God, Chanelle, you're gonna feel one of these bullets."

"I don't have it!" she insisted. "Desmond…the nigga with me… he took it all!"

JaQuez was quiet as he surveyed her face, checking for any traces of sincerity. Then he shook his head. He wasn't convinced. "Wrong answer." He backed away from her a couple of feet before pulling the trigger of his .45, hitting Chanelle in her calf. She howled in pain at the burning sensation. "You wanna try that shit again? Cuz I can guarantee you, we can do this the easy way or the hard way. But either way, you're gonna end up a memory."

"I'm telling you, he robbed me when we got here. I really don't have the money, but I have about six thousand dollars," Chanelle offered in-between sobs as she pressed her hand against her wound.

JaQuez shook his head angrily. "What the fuck is six thousand dollars? Bitch, that's play money!"

His expression was menacing and at that moment Chanelle knew that she was staring into the eyes of the devil. If she could've looked into the future and discovered that it would end up like this, she would've really reevaluated her 'foolproof' plan.

"Was it worth it?" JaQuez asked as if hearing her thoughts.

Chanelle didn't respond, instead praying silently to God. She was going to die tonight, she knew it without a shadow of a doubt. Now, she just wanted to ensure that her soul had a place to go when she passed. "Lord, forgive me for my sins," she finally said out loud.

"Don't pray to God, bitch, *I'm* the one in control of your life now." Without another word, JaQuez pulled the trigger, hitting her right in the abdomen.

The exact same place where he'd been shot.

Chanelle opened her mouth to scream, but blood erupted from it instead, like a volcano.

Maybe someone will hear the shots and help me, she thought desperately.

In the distance, she could hear banging on the front door and Trap's muffled voice on the other end. She wanted to believe that he could help her, but knew it was too late. She pressed her hands against her stomach in a feeble attempt to stop the bleeding, but it was no use. She wanted to call out to Trap, to warn him since she knew that JaQuez would most likely kill him, too, but she couldn't.

"Wa…" Chanelle gurgled, feeling more blood escape from her mouth as her soul start to slip away.

"Ay! Ay! Princess!"

Chanelle jerked upright instantly when she felt a hand on her shoulder shaking her vigorously. Wide eyed and startled, she looked to see Trap and a police officer standing over her.

"Are you okay?" Trap asked while searching her distressed face worriedly.

"Watch out!" Chanelle looked puzzled as she found her voice. She looked down to her stomach and examined herself. There was no bullet wound… *What the hell,* she thought.

"Watch out for what?"

"What happened?" Chanelle asked finally, realizing that she was on the futon instead of the kitchen floor.

"You were screamin' and shit," Trap said. "We had to kick the damn door down when you wouldn't answer."

The officer nodded in agreement. "Honestly, ma'am, it sounded like you were dying."

"I was," she murmured inaudibly.

$$\$$$

"Ay, Triniti, check them niggas out."

Triniti's eyes followed the direction that Peaches nodded her head in. Standing at the entrance of the club were two tall men wearing cheap suits, gumshoes, and navy blue collar shirts. Although they were attempting to look inconspicuous, both men stuck out like sore thumbs. Sure, Pretty Kitty attracted all types of customers, but years in the business had taught Triniti what to look for. Rather than making themselves comfortable at the bar or taking a seat near the stage, they stood awkwardly, scanning the club.

They were looking around for something... someone.

"I smell bacon," Triniti muttered under her breath before downing the last of her shot. She straightened her silk blouse and slipped her feet back into her studded platform Valentino pumps. "How can I help you gentlemen today?" she asked, with a smile faker than Barbie's.

"Yes," one of the men replied smoothly before flashing a badge at her and placing it back into his breast pocket. "I'm Detective Watson and this is Detective Thurmond."

Triniti eyed both men keenly. They were attractive with cocoa-hued skin and lowcuts, but she didn't fuck with police. Detectives or not, they were all the same to her. Pigs. The fact that her brother was in jail under the work of some undercover didn't make matters any better. Black cops were the worst of the worst to Triniti.

They have no fucking remorse for locking up other black men for the most trivial things. All that to suck up to the white man shit. She shook her head disapprovingly.

Detective Watson picked up on her glare and spoke up. "And you are...?"

"I'm Triniti," she answered reluctantly. "Now, how can I help you two?"

"We're looking for someone by the name of Chanelle Daniels." He reached back into his breast pocket and handed her a picture.

Triniti's face didn't reveal that she immediately recognized Chanelle. Instead, she squinted her eyes as though she was looking at a stranger. *So, that bitch lied about her name. I'm not surprised. This must be why. I oughta kill her for bringing this hot shit here.*

"I'm not sure why you thought you could find her here," Triniti finally said to the detectives.

"We're following up on a tip that we've gotten about her possibly working here as a dancer under the name of Sparkle. Surely they weren't making something like that up, right?" Detective Watson replied.

Triniti shrugged her shoulders. "People make up shit all the time. But I haven't seen her." Chanelle hadn't come to work that night and Triniti wondered if she knew the police were looking for her. *This bitch can't be bringing heat to the club. We're gonna have to talk about this whenever she comes back... If she comes back.*

"Miss this is a very serious matter. Chanelle Daniels is wanted for murder in the state of North Carolina. We have reason to believe that she killed her ex-boyfriend, JaQuez Bell, a few weeks ago."

Triniti's eyes bucked at the newfound information. He couldn't be serious. *That scary bitch killed a nigga? I don't believe it.* She shook her head. *But if she did, oh well. Nigga probably deserved it anyway. Niggas ain't shit,* she thought cynically.

Her attitude was partly due to the fact that she hadn't heard from Trap in days. In her mind, he was probably hugged up with some new bitch. It was easier for her to blame it on another female rather than take responsibility for the fact that her overbearing ways and stalker behavior had pushed him away.

Triniti cleared her throat. "Well, I'm sorry I can't be of any help to you." She was maintaining her original statement. She didn't see shit, ain't heard shit, and didn't know shit.

Detective Thurmond narrowed his eyes and finally spoke up. His voice was deep and almost sounded as though he was growling at her. "I know you don't want to get locked up for obstruction of justice, do you? We could get a warrant and search this whole fucking place!"

"Look, she doesn't work here anymore," Triniti replied firmly, refusing to let him intimidate her.

Detective Thurmond didn't look convinced and opened his mouth to speak again, but Watson held up his hand and interrupted. "Well, take my card if she should come back or if you hear something, okay?" He flashed her a charming smile before sliding it into the palm of her hand.

Triniti threw it in her Celine bag dismissively, not even bothering to read the information on it. "Have a good day gentlemen," she said before turning in the opposite direction.

"There's a reward for any information, by the way!" Detective Thurmond shouted over the music even though Triniti kept walking.

Do I look like a broke bitch? They can keep that shit. "Good night, officers," she called over her shoulder. "Don't let the door hit you on the way out."

$SEVENTEEN

***Police just stopped by the club. Raided our shit. Call
me.***

Trap frowned at the text message he'd just received from
Triniti. He'd been en route to rural Walton County with Ali riding shotgun. Now, it was looking like they might possibly have
to turn around.

Trap dialed Triniti's number and listened to her ringback
tone impatiently until she answered the line.

"Hello?" she asked with irritation present in her voice.

"What's up?" Trap greeted. "What the fuck happened?"
Trap ignored her attitude, figuring that it was due to the unex-
pected police visit.

"Nothing," Triniti answered dryily. "It's a damn shame
that I have to lie to get your ass to call me now. Nigga, we
haven't spoken in four damn days!"

"Are you fuckin' kiddin' me?" Trap asked in disbelief.
"You ain't my ol' lady! Triniti, don't you ever do some stupid
shit like that again!"

"Then don't *you* do some bullshit like ignore my damn
phone calls! You're always preaching about how we're like
family and shit. Well, nigga you're all I got right now and you
been avoiding me. Why the hell don't you ever pick up or return my calls?" Triniti demanded, hating how unwanted she

felt.

"I been busy, and I'ma holla at you later cuz I'm busy right now."

"Wait!" Triniti yelled abruptly, "The police really did come by!"

"Then why the fuck are you playin' games? Why did you just tell me that they didn't?"

Triniti became quiet.

"What did they want?" he asked.

"They said one of the dancers is wanted for murder."

"What? Who?"

"Her name is Chanelle, but we call her Sparkle," she informed.

"I don't know who that is."

"Oh, yeah." Triniti nodded her head. "She's the new dancer I wanted you to meet, but since you're never here, you haven't seen her yet. That's why you need to come around more often. How is this your club but you don't ever know shit that's going on here?"

"Triniti, that's *your* job. I gave it to you for a reason. Now, if you ain't up to it then let me know, because you can easily be replaced."

"Is that right?" she scoffed. "I doubt it."

"So, did they arrest her?" Trap rushed, eager for her to get to the point.

"No, she wasn't at work. Actually, she hasn't been to the club in a few days, so I don't know what the hell happened. But that bitch is definitely in some deep shit."

"Well, keep me updated on if they come back or what her ass has to say when she comes back to work. I can't have no police up in my shit, Triniti, so you might need to fire her ass."

"That's what I was thinking," Triniti agreed. "So, can you stop by my house later?" she asked in a more delicate tone, stripping her previous attitude.

Trap blew his breath exasperatedly. "Yeah. Maybe." He

disconnected the call before she could respond. Ten seconds had barely passed before Triniti was calling his phone again. He wanted to hit ignore, but knew that she would probably blow up his phone if he did.

Triniti was starting to act like an obsessed groupie or an ex-girlfriend and he wasn't feeling it. *She needs to fall back and play her position,* he thought. Trap knew that he was partially to blame, however. If he had never slept with her in the first place, then things would've never gotten so out of hand.

"What?" Trap barked the moment he hit 'Accept' to answer the call.

"You fucking some bitch now? Cuz you ain't never talked to me like this before!" Triniti yelled.

"That's because you never lied about something like that! Look, I'll talk to you later," he shot back.

"It *is* some bitch!"

"Chill out with callin' her a bitch, Triniti! You don't know shit about her!"

Triniti's nostrils flared. She couldn't believe her ears. She'd hoped that her assumptions were wrong, but this confirmed it. "Yeah. Whatever, nigga. Fuck you and her."

Click.

Ali shook his head from the passenger seat as he puffed on his blunt. Triniti had been so loud that he'd caught everything. Although he hadn't dealt with her since she'd called him by Trap's name, he couldn't hide the fact that he still had feelings for her. But the fact that she was so hung up on Trap further pissed him off.

It's always the wrong niggas that be winning, Ali thought sullenly. It was no surprise that he was jealous of Trap… although no one else realized it.

"What the hell is wrong with your girl?" Ali asked, faking as though he hadn't heard a thing.

Trap shook his head. "I don't even know, man, and I don't have time to worry about that shit either."

Trap turned down a lone, dimly lit road and continued until he pulled up in front of an old farmhouse. Trap killed the headlights and parked next to a gray, Chevy before exiting his vehicle, ready to handle his business.

They had a situation to tend to with one of their workers named Drew. Apparently he'd been short with his money quite a few times, but it was the first time the news had reached Trap's ears. Although Drew had been a pretty good worker up until then, Trap still had to make an example out of him. The moment he started giving someone a pass, *everyone* would figure that they could get over or accuse Trap of slipping.

There was no doubt about it, Drew would get dealt with tonight.

"I told you I could've handled this nigga earlier today. Could've saved you this drive," Ali said as they made their way towards the back of the house.

"Yeah, but I wanted to talk to this nigga myself. I can't understand why he would step out of line."

Ali shrugged. "Shit. Niggas get greedy."

"Yeah, you probably right," Trap agreed.

"That nigga been talkin' shit, too," Ali added, laying it on thick.

"Oh yeah?" Trap asked, raising an eyebrow. He wondered why Ali hadn't mentioned it beforehand. Either way, they were here now.

When Trap opened the cellar door, they stepped down into the unfinished room. Drew sat in the middle of the floor, tied to a chair with his mouth gagged. Two of Trap's other workers, SK and Phoenix, stood against the wall. They'd brought Drew to the destination as promised and waited patiently for further instructions.

After giving both of his soldiers some dap, Trap removed Drew's gag. "So, what's up, my nigga? I thought I was feedin' you well enough, but you decided to *still* cross me? You got a girl and two kids, Drew. Why would you risk that shit?"

"I'm tellin' you, man," Drew responded, unusually calm despite his predicament. "I've been set up. It's nothin' like the way it looks."

Trap raised an eyebrow. "Nigga, don't insult my intelligence. You think muthafuckas can't count? You thought nobody would notice that you was gettin' sticky fingers?"

Drew made eye contact with Trap as he spoke his next sentence. "I got no reason to steal from you. C'mon, Trap, you know this shit don't even sound right. If I been stealin' from you for months, why are they just now tellin' you?" He shook his head. "You got a foul nigga on your team but it ain't me." His eyes adjusted past Trap towards Ali, but Trap was too focused on Drew's words to notice.

"Niggas will say anything to save their own ass," Ali commented with a frown as he mugged Drew. Inwardly he was sweating bullets though. Drew was far from telling a tall-tale. He had indeed been set up, by Ali, no less.

Ali's jealousy towards Trap ran deeper than most knew about. It was something that he'd kept hidden very well. He was just waiting in the shadows for the perfect opportunity to take action. He'd always resented Trap for taking over a lot of the drug game in ATL, especially since it was Ali's stomping grounds.

He'd started out young as a runner with dreams of becoming a boss, but Trap swooped in before Ali made it to that point. Trap... an outsider from New Orleans who came and took over easily enough after flooding the city and the surrounding areas with his pure cocaine and unbeatable prices.

There was no way to compete with Trap. He paid his soldiers well, his product was potent and sold well, and it was made clear that if you weren't eating with Trap, you would starve. Ali reluctantly aligned with him and worked his way up the ranks quickly. His goal had always been clear: Knock Trap off his throne. It was just easier said than done when the men were loyal to Trap. That was the case tonight with Drew.

Ali ending up running off at the mouth about his plans, testing the waters to see if anyone else shared his sentiments. Unfortunately for him, Drew wasn't one of them. Ali tried to play it off, but Drew wasn't buying his flimsy explanation. Still, Drew said that he would pretend that he didn't hear it since it was obvious that Ali was high off something when he'd made those comments. In the end, Drew would've been better off telling Trap because Ali would be damned if another nigga possibly held his life in his hands.

Ali wasted no time calling Trap up and letting him know the fabricated situation. He'd hoped to get the approval to body Drew right then and there, but Trap insisted on speaking to him face to face and handling it. Now, Ali just had to ensure that Drew didn't throw him under the bus. There was no question in his mind that SK and Phoenix were loyal to Trap, so he would be easily outnumbered.

"You ain't lyin'. Niggas will lie their ass off to protect themselves," Drew said sarcastically with his eyes still fixed on Ali. Then he refocused his attention back to Trap. "You might want to take a second look at the niggas you keep close to you."

"What are you sayin', Drew?" Trap asked impatiently, tired of him talking in circles.

"Your boy…" was all Drew could say before Ali reached for his .357.

In the blink of an eye, he let off two slugs to Drew's chest without warning. The impact was so sudden and powerful that Drew toppled over onto the cold, hard concrete floor.

"Treacherous ass nigga." Ali shook his head. "It's niggas like him who fuck up an operation. The last thing we need is tension between us over some shit that a dead man would make up in a weak ass attempt to save his life."

Trap shook his head as he looked down at the corpse. "Nah. Wouldn't be no tension. You always been thorough as hell. Believe me, I can read niggas like a map. If you had some larceny in your heart, trust me, I'd know and you would've *been* murked. I know you got my back." He turned his attention to the other men. "Y'all clean this shit up."

Sounds like you need to get your eyes checked then, nigga, Ali thought with a grin as he followed Trap out the door. *I got ya back, alright. To load your cocky ass up with bullets.*

$EIGHTEEN

"Oh my God," Chanelle moaned softly as she clenched the fifteen hundred count Egyptian cotton sheets. Trap plunged in and out of her, gripping her plump ass firmly to ensure that she wouldn't run away from him.

This is more like it, she thought, staring up at Trap. Each time they sexed, he always ensured that she got hers and he was *far* from a one-minute man like Desmond had been. Just the thought of him pissed her off, but she couldn't help but to compare the two. Trap was truly putting it down.

"You like this shit?" Trap asked as he changed his pace, slamming in and out of her quickly before moving slowly, ensuring that all ten of his inches found its way to the bottom of her valley.

Chanelle let out a squeal before placing her hands on the headboard and throwing it at him like a quarterback. It both pained her *and* felt good at the same damn time. The euphoric bliss that she felt was one that Chanelle never wanted to lose again. The sounds of their flesh slapping together in unison and the headboard banging against the wall was another instant turn on. Her moans echoed throughout Trap's house, but luckily they had it all to themselves.

She could feel her body becoming weak and her body jerked slightly as she felt herself cum. About three minutes

later, Trap did the same before collapsing on top of her. Their
bodies were dripping with sweat, but neither one of them
minded. Trap kissed her lower back gently before rising from
the bed.

"You have to go?" Chanelle asked breathlessly before
looking over at the clock on the nightstand.

It was only about seven o' clock in the evening, but this
was his usual routine. She was used to it by now. Trap had
come clean about his position as a hustler after some good
pussy and a little pillow talk. It was something that she'd already known, but there was nothing like gaining some reassur-
ance. He hadn't made it clear the type of scale he worked on,
but judging from the lavish, four thousand square foot house in
Buckhead that he lived in, Chanelle felt it was safe to say that
he was definitely a heavy hitter.

Despite the fact that he'd revealed a lot about his personal life to her, she still hadn't come clean about her past. She
hadn't even told Trap the intricate details about her dream.
While he felt comfortable and at ease with her, she doubted
she'd ever get there with him. Even still, what had once been a
reoccurring dream had stopped all together since she'd moved
in with him. Chanelle could admit that he *did* make her feel
safe.

"Yeah," he replied from the bathroom. "I ain't gonna be
out real late though."

Chanelle could hear him rummaging around for a bath
towel while trying to fight off his fatigue. Who didn't want to
lay down after a good fuck. She never bothered to ask him to
stay home with her, although a few times she'd been tempted
to. Chanelle had to admit that she was sprung off the way he put
it on her.

Almost.

Good dick could never replace the big green faces that
she longed for. Whenever Trap left, she would constantly look
for his stash, but could never find it. Wherever Trap kept it, it

definitely wasn't in the typical spots.

The past two weeks that she'd been living with him, Trap bought her nearly whatever her heart desired, but the one thing he never did was put money directly in her hand. It made her think back to being with JaQuez, how he tried to control her with his money. Was that the reason that he never gave her no more than a thousand dollars at one time?

Chanelle would never ask, but was certainly curious. Something deep inside told her that he wasn't like that, but how could she trust her heart again? It had led her in the wrong direction one too many times. The last thing she wanted was to get burned again, figuratively and literally.

"You should go chill with your girl… A'mya, right?" Trap suggested, feeling bad about leaving her alone in the big house for hours on end.

Chanelle nodded. "Yeah. A'mya."

Things hadn't been the same between them since Rallo's death. They only spoke once briefly so she knew that she was alive, but other than that, communication had been scarce.

Trap tossed a pair of keys onto the bed. "You can take the Benz to go get her if you want."

Chanelle smiled. She'd been stranded in the house any other time that he left. The fact that he now felt comfortable enough to let her drive his car spoke volumes. She would take full advantage of getting the car, but it wouldn't be to chill with A'mya. Chanelle needed money badly and since it was obvious that she wasn't getting any out of Trap, she needed to make her way back to *Pretty Kitty*. She wasn't about to put her dreams on pause again, depending on a man to take care of her. She was thankful for all that Trap had done for her, but she wasn't about to wait until things went south before she ensured that her future was secure.

Just as she heard the water starting for the shower, her cell phone rang. Seeing A'mya's number on the caller ID, she wasted no time answering. "Hello?"

"Hey, Chanelle," A'mya greeted. Her voice was still downtrodden so Chanelle knew that she was still affected by Rallo's death.

"What's up, girl?"

"Sorry I've been so distant lately."

"Nah. You're good," Chanelle assured her. "How you been?"

"I'm okay, I guess."

"I don't wanna make it seem like it was a joyous occasion, but how was the funeral? The last time I talked to you was the day before he was buried."

"The funeral was nice. I met family members that I didn't know he had," A'mya said quietly.

"So, do you or the police have any information on who could've done this yet?" Chanelle questioned.

"Well, the police found out that he owed a few guys some money from that stupid ass gambling shit, so that might've had something to do with it. Or maybe it was somebody's husband from the many women he screwed…who knows."

"Oh…" Chanelle wasn't sure of what else to say because honestly she was relieved to hear that Rallo was indeed the intended target. She started to think that she'd just been paranoid about seeing Rob's car that day. "Can I ask you something?"

"Sure," A'mya responded.

"Where were you the day Rallo died? I called you so many times, but you didn't answer. I even went to your job, but everyone said you'd left hours ago."

"Honestly Chanelle, I was with someone else," A'mya admitted. "I met a guy at my job a few days before that, and we went out on a date that day. I didn't wanna hear your mouth about getting with someone that soon, so I just decided not to answer. I had no idea though that you were calling about that." A'mya's voice was barely over a whisper.

Chanelle quickly decided to change the subject. "So,

where are you staying at now?"

"I found an apartment off Campbellton Road. It's not too far from my old one," A'mya's voice brightened a little, but not by much. "Are you still working at the club?"

"Nah. Not really. I'm over here playing wifey," Chanelle joked.

"See, I told you that you would find love." A'mya's smile could be felt through the phone. "You're really lucky. I'm just trying to focus on how I'm going to be able to take care of my baby. I never thought that I would have to do it without Rallo."

"Are you kidding me?" Chanelle asked suddenly. "A'mya, why would you keep that baby? You're already struggling! You need to go ahead and abort it and make your life easier."

"Wow… That's all you can say, Chanelle? *Abort* it? I would've thought that the same girl who got her child *beaten* out of her would have more concern for human life. Instead of being supportive of me, you're always putting me down."

"I'm just being realistic, A'mya! You can't afford it. You're being selfish if you decide to keep it. Don't get me wrong, you'd be a great mom, but who would wanna grow up in that kind of environment?"

"What kind of environment, Chanelle?"

"You're staying one step away from the projects, you work at McDonalds and you're driving that shitty ass car. All your money goes to rent… you can't afford daycare or formula! You're gonna have a welfare baby!"

"I can't believe you would say that," A'mya sobbed, noticeably hurt.

"A'mya, I…"

Click.

Chanelle sighed before tossing her phone back onto the bed. She didn't mean to hurt her friend's feelings, but she had to start being realistic and stop living in her fantasy world. The sooner she did that, the better off she would be.

Seeing a light on her phone flash, she picked it back up. She had a new voicemail. Raising an eyebrow, Chanelle hit the voicemail button, wondering who it was.

"Chanelle!" Loretta's voice boomed. "Why in the hell have you been ignoring my calls? Listen, you have got to call me back. Please...it's urgent! If you don't, I swear that you'll regret it."

"Yeah right, bitch," Chanelle said, shaking her head. The only thing that she regretted was going to the hotel and believing that her mother would actually do something to help her out. Rallo may've been a victim of his own wrongdoing, but she still didn't trust Loretta. "Fuck you."

With those last words, she headed to join Trap in the shower.

$$\$$$

Chanelle smiled as she entered *Pretty Kitty*. The smell of money mixed with perfume filled her nose, making her eager to get started. The patrons were welcoming her back and showing her love, a few even stopping her to tell her about how they'd missed her. On top of that, the club was packed so Chanelle was certain that she could hustle up a couple grand tonight.

"Don't forget about me later, baby," one of her regulars said, sliding a ten dollar bill into her cleavage.

"You know I got you, Henry," Chanelle replied seductively as she made her way through the club and towards the dressing room.

Chanelle had barely gotten a chance to put her things down when Triniti's voice boomed in the doorway.

"Where the hell have you been for the past two weeks? You didn't call me or say shit! You're lucky I didn't drop your ass from the roster!"

"You gonna let me dance or what?" Chanelle cut straight

to the point.

She wasn't in the mood to explain herself. She just wanted Triniti out of her face so that she could hurry out. What was the point in complaining and starting shit when they both knew Triniti would never stop her from dancing. Chanelle was one of the top girls before she'd left, and judging from the earlier remarks, she still was.

"I shouldn't." Triniti's mind went back to the detectives that had been looking for her. "I don't know what type of shit you're into but don't bring it here."

Chanelle looked at her with confusion. "What the hell are you talking about?"

Triniti opened her mouth to speak, but Hershey's entrance into the dressing room stopped her, "Look, just remember that you're new and expendable." She started out before pausing at the doorway to issue one final warning, "Extra heat from the police is some shit I'm not having. Keep that in mind. I'm not going down for no fucking body." Triniti stomped off angrily and Chanelle turned to Hershey.

Chanelle stood in place not knowing how to react from Trinit's last comment. At that moment, a thousand thoughts sprinted through her mind. *Heat from the police? Body? Oh shit, did the police come here looking for me? Do they know about JaQuez?* She wanted desperately to run after Triniti and ask all those questions, but decided to wait until after the club was closed. The less people around when they discussed a subject like that, the better.

"What the hell is Triniti's problem?" Chanelle asked trying to play off her nervousness.

Hershey shrugged. "The hell if I know, girl. She's been in a terrible mood lately, but I don't really give a damn. I'm just trying to hurry up and get back out there. That nigga named Stacks is back again."

Chanelle looked at her with a confused expression. "You saying that name like I'm supposed to know who that is."

"My bad. I forgot you ain't been here. He came yesterday and, girl, that nigga got money to blow, for real!" Hershey explained as she spritzed her body with perfume. "Niggas talk about making it rain, but Stacks makes it blizzard! He ain't stingy for shit."

"Damn," Chanelle muttered as she rushed to put on her outfit for the night.

"I made about three thousand off that nigga alone yesterday. He broke us all off real nice. Especially when he get all liquored up, then he really get careless as hell. We in VIP." Hershey checked her appearance in the mirror one last time before rushing out of the dressing room.

All Chanelle saw was dollar signs as she rubbed baby oil into her skin. She hated that she'd missed Stacks the day before, but if he was paying like Hershey claimed, she could make up for it.

In less than five minutes Chanelle waltzed out of the dressing room and to the floor. Her eyes shifted up towards VIP for Stacks, but a crowd of females were blocking her view. However, it was hard to miss the dollar bills flying up in the air every second.

Jackpot, she thought. She started towards the staircase, but a hand gently pulled her in the opposite direction.

"Don't go up there. Shit. He ain't the only nigga with money," the Usher Raymond lookalike told her with a charming smile.

Chanelle returned the smile half-heartedly before looking around warily.

The man frowned. "What's the problem? You don't believe me?" He reached down into his pocket and revealed a fat wad of cash. "Baby, this Ali, I never leave the house with less than four grand in cash. Hook a nigga up with a lap dance."

"It ain't about your money, boo," she assured him. "It's just… ain't you Triniti's boyfriend? I remembered seeing y'all in her office that day."

"Hell nah," Ali responded with a frown. "That shit with me and her is old."

Chanelle didn't look convinced but said 'Fuck it'. He was paying so she was about to do her job. She couldn't help but think about Trap though, no matter how hard she tried to block him out. They were dating, and for the moment, she was living with him. If he could see her disrespecting him in the worse way, she'd be out on her ass. *I guess what he won't know won't hurt. I gotta get this paper.*

Turning around, giving him a perfect view of her apple bottom, Chanelle grinded onto him slowly and sensually. She could feel his dick hardening through his Gucci denim jeans.

"Calm down," she said with a small laugh.

"I'm good," Ali replied, hoping that his size would be enough to convince her to come home with him that night. "You need to let me take care of you."

"I already got a nigga to take care of me."

"Oh yeah?" He raised an eyebrow. "Well, if you was my shawty you wouldn't be up in here showin' off my goods for other niggas to see."

"I'd rather take care of myself."

"Miss Independent, huh?" Ali smiled.

His grin grew even wider when he noticed Triniti looking in their direction. It only lasted briefly before she disappeared to another section of the club. It was immature, but he wanted her to feel jealous. He wanted her to feel a shred of the pain he had when she'd called out Trap's name. To feel as he did when she rejected him.

"Yup. I'd rather have my own now," she stated. Chanelle turned her gaze back up towards VIP. "You know that nigga Stacks? Where he from?"

Ali laughed. "Now, how you gonna ask me about another nigga on *my* time?" he joked.

"I was just asking. Everybody's going crazy over him, but I think I'm good with you." *Especially if that whole stack is for me,* she thought.

That thought however instantly disappeared when one of the females stooped down for a couple of seconds, giving Chanelle more than a glimpse of Stacks. Her eyes grew wide and she stood still in place. Seconds later, Ali asked her a question, but she could no longer hear him. She just stared as Stacks continued to toss dollars like money wasn't a thing.

The palms of her hands quickly began to sweat and her heart rate amplified. Instead of hanging out on South Beach and partying at the club, LIV every Sunday like she thought, he was right there in the flesh.

Desmond, she thought furiously. *This fat ass motherfucker is balling out of control with my damn money!*

It was the opportunity she'd been waiting for since the incident occurred and she would be damned if she missed it.

$NINETEEN

"What the hell type of shit are you getting yourself into?" Hershey asked Chanelle with concern as she dug into her bag for the item in question.

"Damn, you nosey as hell!" Chanelle complained with a smile.

"Bitch, you been knew that," Hershey joked before pulling out her mace. "Some niggas tried to fuck with you?"

Chanelle didn't bother to answer. Hershey was a huge gossiper and although they were cool, she knew not to tell her what the mace was for. She didn't want anybody trying to convince her otherwise. Until they lost a half million dollars, they wouldn't understand shit.

"This is all you got?" she questioned as she looked at the can of mace. The way Hershey always preached about keeping items to "protect yourself from thirsty niggas", Chanelle had assumed she would at least have a knife.

Hershey shrugged. "Ay, it works for me. I ain't tryna catch a murder charge." She looked at Chanelle sternly. "Let me find out you are though."

"Good looking out, Hershey," she thanked her abruptly, hoping her facial expression didn't betray her real thoughts. She exited out of the back door stealthily. Chanelle didn't know which car was Desmond's, so she crouched behind a black Suburban with a perfect view of the entrance. It was almost closing time and most of the patrons had left, with the exception of some of the dancers and other stragglers. It had taken everything inside of her not to act a fool in front of everyone, but she kept her cool and stayed out of Desmond's sight. Instead, she plotted long and hard until coming up with the perfect plan. Armed with Hershey's mace and an empty bottle of Ciroc that a customer had given her, she was ready to get what she was owed.

Can't fall down, stay triumphant, keep on living... Stay on your toes, she kept chanting to herself.

When Chanelle suddenly heard her cell phone going off, she nearly dropped the bottle on the concrete. *Shit,* Chanelle cursed before fumbling to retrieve her phone. *I need to turn this shit off.*

"Hello?" she said into the phone, surprised when silence greeted her. "Hello?"

"C-Chanelle," the voice finally choked out with sobs.

"A'mya? A'mya what's wrong?" Chanelle asked urgently.

She wasn't quite sure what to expect since Rallo was dead. She hoped that A'mya still wasn't mourning over him, but knew that it was her duty as a friend to be there for her regardless. Their conversations had been scarce up until this point and she had to admit that she missed A'mya more than she thought she would.

"I-I..." A'mya began. "I really need you right now. My stomach is cramping up and I think I'm losing my baby. I saw some blood."

"Oh my God," Chanelle gasped. "Do you need me to call 911? You probably need to get to a doctor if you wanna save your baby. Can you drive?"

"I'm scared," A'mya cried out in a childlike tone that Chanelle had never heard. "I don't want to be alone and Mike is at work with my car."

"Mike?" Chanelle was lost. "Who is that?"

"My new boyfriend, remember?"

Damn. She actually hooked up with that nigga for real, Chanelle thought with a frown, vaguely recalling A'mya's prior confession. She still couldn't believe that A'mya had cheated on Rallo, but definitely didn't blame her. Still, the fact that Mike was borrowing her car let Chanelle know that he was just like all the rest…a loser. *Where does she get these niggas from?* Chanelle wanted to give her friend a lecture, but knew the timing was awful.

"Listen, A'mya, go ahead and call 911. You need help ASAP if you want to save your baby. I'll be on my way as soon as I can though, alright?" Chanelle was sure that probably wasn't the answer A'mya was looking for, but what else could she say? Chanelle had the opportunity to get at Desmond and she couldn't let anything get in her way. Not even her best friend.

"Please hurry," A'mya begged. "I really don't want to do this alone."

"Don't worry, girl. I'll be there."

Chanelle disconnected the call before powering it off. She didn't need any more distractions with what she was about to do. It was now or never. Do or die and she had to get back what was rightfully hers.

$$$$$$$$$$$$$$$$$$$$$$$$$

Desmond stumbled as he stepped off the last step coming from VIP. He wasn't white boy wasted, but he was definitely tipsy. On top of that, he'd snorted a few lines of cocaine before he arrived. Desmond was all about having a good time and what better way than with drugs, females, and money?

"Ay, somebody needs to call him a cab!" Triniti yelled as she looked in Desmond's direction. She'd seen him throwing back shots all night and wasn't about to feel responsible if his drunk driving ass murdered someone that night.

"I don't need no muthafuckin' cab!" Desmond slurred. "I got it, shawty."

Triniti turned to DJ Quet, "Do it anyway!"

When she took off towards the back, DJ Quet waved him off. "Go ahead, man, before she comes back wailing on me."

"Good lookin', fam," Desmond thanked as he trudged out of the door.

He'd wanted to take a couple of females back to the hotel with him, but had spent all the cash he'd brought with him. Even though he had more money at his apartment, some of the girls didn't want to go without being paid first.

Fuck it, he thought. *Tomorrow night I'll just bring more.* Desmond had never been attractive to most women, but he knew that his pockets enabled him to be treated like the king he felt he was. He didn't mind paying for pussy at all. He had it, so why not?

Desmond made his way over to his new Porsche Panamera Turbo S. He still had JaQuez's Jaguar, but there was nothing like stunting in a car purchased with your own money. It still had that new car scent and was one of the many purchases that Desmond had made after his new comeup. He was blowing money fast like there was no tomorrow.

Instead of taking the lengthy drive to Miami, he decided to stay in ATL, doubting that he'd ever run into Chanelle again. By now he was sure that she'd taken her ass back to North Carolina. His constant thought was, 'how is she gonna make it in this city alone'.

Desmond chuckled to himself as he thought about it. *Stupid bitch.*

He still didn't feel the least bit remorseful about what he'd done. If he hadn't done it, Chanelle would have. It was take or be taken. Reaching into his pocket for his keys, Desmond frowned when he couldn't find them.

"What the fuck?" he muttered.

At that exact moment, he heard what sounded like hair spray coming from behind him and his eyes began to tear up and burn. Desmond howled out in pain as he rubbed his eyes feverishly.

I should've known these niggas would start hating and wanna rob me, Desmond thought as he continued to sputter. "Help," he managed to say before coughing. His lungs felt like they were on fire. He hated that he hadn't been paying more attention to his surroundings.

"Help is here. How does that shit feel, nigga?" Chanelle asked with a smirk as she stepped closer to him.

She surveyed the parking lot to ensure that there were no witnesses before raising the bottle of Ciroc that she'd brought with her. Truthfully, even if there had been someone watching, she *still* would've done it.

Before she could bring the bottle down on his head, Desmond lunged at her wildly, causing the glass to break and drop from her grasp. The mace was burning the hell out of his eyes, but he wasn't completely defenseless. He'd dealt with mace from C.O.'s plenty of times when he was locked up. Instead of using his hands to wipe his eyes, he used them to pummel blows at Chanelle. Finally knocking her to the ground, he held one meaty hand against her throat, cutting off her oxygen supply.

Chanelle thrashed at him weakly, but Desmond's grip was strong. His three hundred pound body had shifted all of his weight onto her small frame. It was obvious that he was playing to win and she was so close to losing her life.

Just as Chanelle felt like she was about to start blacking out, she could faintly hear a voice calling out to them. It sounded like Ali, but she wasn't so sure.

"My nigga, get the fuck off her," Ali repeated before cocking his gun back to show that he meant business.

Desmond arose off Chanelle slowly, still blinking his

eyes rapidly and raising his hands in a show of surrender. "You got it, man. Chill."

Ali placed his gun back into the front of his jeans before walking over to Chanelle and helping her off of the ground, "You a'ight? What happened?"

Chanelle nodded before rushing back towards Desmond with fury in her eyes. She only managed to get one blow in before Ali pulled her back.

"That bitch is crazy," Desmond muttered.

"No, muthafucka, *you* crazy if you think I'ma let you leave with my money again!" Chanelle blasted.

"He took some of your money?" Ali frowned as he looked back and forth between the two.

"I ain't got shit of yours," Desmond chuckled as he finally located his keys. "The sooner you realize that, the better off you'll be."

"Let me go!" Chanelle yelled, twisting her wrist in an attempt to be free of Ali's hold. She couldn't let the chance slip past her again. She held so much rage in her heart for him after all that she'd been through.

"You better be thankin' this nigga," Desmond started, "Cuz you would've been a dead woman fuckin' with me."

"Oh, yeah?" Chanelle spat. Using her free hand, she reached into Ali's waistline for his gun and emptied the whole clip into Desmond's chest. She stepped closer with every pull of the trigger, ensuring that she didn't miss her target and could see the spaced out look on his face after she finished the job.

The sound of the gunshots rumbled throughout the deserted parking lot like thunder. Upon looking at Desmond's bullet-ridden corpse, she dropped the gun silently as tears cascaded down her cheeks against her will. The moment was surreal. She couldn't believe that she'd acted so impulsively. Chanelle expected to feel relieved or ecstatic, but instead all she felt was remorse and fear.

They're gonna haul my ass off to jail.

Ali's gun hadn't had a silencer on it so she knew that in no time the police would be called or someone would come out and witness Desmond's body there. From the bullet wounds in his chest and head, it was obvious that it was more than self-defense.

"Ay, y'all heard that shit?" DJ Quet asked as he stood at the entrance. He wasn't able to see Desmond from where he stood, but Chanelle still trembled with fear that he might approach them.

"Hell yeah," Ali said. "I don't see shit though. Y'all bout finished up in there?"

"Just about. Got a few muthafuckas actin' like they don't wanna leave. You know how it go!" DJ Quet shouted back before going back inside.

"Get that nigga's keys," Ali advised her immediately. He knew they didn't have much time. "And open the trunk."

Chanelle looked at him surprised, as she did as she was told. "You're gonna help me?"

Ali grinned. "Why not? If a nigga would've took my money, I would've done the same thing."

Together they lifted Desmond's body and hoisted him into the trunk. Chanelle took one long last glance at him before Ali prepared to slam the lid down.

"Wait!" she shouted suddenly. Ali looked at her confused, but Chanelle didn't bother to explain. Taking a deep breath, she began digging through the dead man's pockets.

"Damn. You coldblooded," Ali commented with a slight laugh.

I know this nigga gotta have something! When Chanelle opened his wallet, she was disappointed to find that it was void of any money. Just when she felt tears of frustration stinging her eyes, she noticed a hotel cardkey. *The W hotel, huh? That nigga has to have something there! Especially since he probably brings bitches back there.* She nodded with a smile. *Ain't nobody fucking his fat ass for free.*

Although Chanelle was sure that Desmond had probably spent a big chunk of the money, it would still be better than nothing.

"Drive the car to the other end of the lot and I'll handle some shit on my end." Ali spoke up, whipping out his cell phone preparing to get in touch with the crew that would dispose of all the evidence.

Chanelle wasted no time doing as she was told. She didn't know why Ali was helping her, but she was grateful. She wasn't ready to be locked up for the rest of her life on a murder charge. Besides, Desmond deserved it.

This Porsche is bad as hell, she thought. *I wish I could keep this shit.* She knew that doing so could possibly be suicide, even after Ali had the body disposed of. Besides that, how would she explain the car to Trap?

As she got out of the luxury whip, she caught a glimpse of her reflection. Blood stained her outfit and a few splotches had gotten onto her skin. Chanelle looked a terrifying mess. Her hair was still wild and faint, red fingerprints were visible on her light skin. Even though she had no idea if he was back or not, there was no way she could go back to Trap's house looking like that…much less the hotel.

"No worries," Ali assured her, noticing her appearance. "You can slide through my crib and clean up."

Chanelle nodded absently as she followed him to his car. She was eager to get to the hotel, but when she thought about it, there was no rush. If she waltzed into that kind of establishment looking crazy, someone would undoubtedly call the police.

The ride to his house was quiet and she was grateful that he hadn't hit her with a barrage of questions. She was sure that Ali was curious to know the backstory, but it was one that she didn't wish to confide in with anyone.

She'd felt possessed when she'd turned the trigger on Desmond, and even now she couldn't believe the callous way that she'd handled him. The money that she'd lost was still on her mind, but judging from the way Desmond was spending cash, it was probably all gone.

Less than twenty minutes later, they were pulling into his modest, single-family home in Decatur. Chanelle had been shown to the bathroom and indulged in a long shower. Seeing the blood stream into the drain eased her mind. It was as though all evidence of the night had gone down with it.

Not wanting to put back on blood stained clothes, she made her way towards the living room after getting out of the shower. Chanelle had plans on asking Ali for something to change in before making her way back to the club to get Trap's car. The next time Trap left to take care of business, she was going to burn the soiled clothes for sure.

"Can I borrow a t-shirt and maybe some sweat pants? My clothes have blood on 'em," Chanelle said as she stepped into the family room where Ali sat.

"Yeah, sure. Actually, I have some clean t-shirts and a pair of sweat pants in the laundry room. It's right down the hall," Ali told her, trying hard not to focus on the way the towel hugged her curves and the droplets of water glistening on her skin. It took everything within him not to push her up against the wall and have his way.

"Thanks." Chanelle smiled as she followed his directions.

After taking a shower, she felt much better. Now, she just hoped that Ali wouldn't end up trying her. He'd helped her out in a big way so Chanelle was sure that she would end up having to owe him *some* type of favor, but hopefully none of the sexual kind.

Ali was definitely cute, but sexing two men at the same time would make her feel like a hoe. Chanelle had done a lot of things that she wasn't proud of, but she could never stoop that low.

BAM BAM BAM!!!

Chanelle nearly jumped out of her skin at the sound of

knocking at the door.

"Who the fuck at my door like the damn police?" Ali muttered exasperatedly as he headed towards the door.

His words caused Chanelle's heartrate to go up. Could it really be the police at the door?

When she heard the front door open and the voice speaking to Ali, she knew that it was much worse.

I gotta hide, she thought frantically. *How the hell did he know I was here?*

$TWENTY

Chanelle's heart beat loudly as she crouched in a corner of the laundry room and attempted to listen in to the conversation taking place only a couple of feet away from her.

"Whassup, Trap?" Ali motioned for him to come inside, but Trap declined.

"Nah, man. I should be asking you what the fuck is up?" Trap barked.

Ali looked at him with a confused expression, trying desperately to jog his memory. *What the fuck is this dude talking about,* he wondered.

"The traphouse in the Bluff got robbed!" Trap roared.

"So, what the fuck does that have to do with me?" Ali didn't bother to mask his annoyance. *Does he think* I *robbed his ass?*

"Nigga, *you* were supposed to pick up the money and take it to the stash house off Candler Road! Did you forget?" Trap asked sarcastically.

Shit, Ali cursed. He had indeed forgotten after helping Chanelle out, truthfully, that wasn't the complete reason that he hadn't picked up the money. Ali was tired of feeling like a do-boy. Although there were few that Trap trusted to pick up the money, it was the sheer fact of the matter that *Trap* never did it himself because he was a *boss*...the title that Ali wanted more than anything. Ali figured that it wouldn't hurt anything if he did it on his time, but that theory proved incorrect.

"Because you *forgot,* I'm out over a hundred g's!" Trap continued.

"I mean…" Ali started.

"Nah, nigga." Trap held up his hand to silence him. "I ain't really tryna hear shit that you gotta say unless you gonna pay it back!"

"Nigga, you must be crazy. I'm not one of your flunkie muthafuckas! You ain't gonna handle me! Besides that, why the fuck is you trippin' so hard over a hundred stacks?"

Trap nodded with an uncharacteristic calmness. "You right. But since your memory is so bad, I'ma put you back out on the corner just like one of my flunkies so you can remember what to do the next time."

"Run that by me one more time!" Ali demanded, not believing his ears.

"You heard me," Trap replied as he turned away and made his way down the driveway towards his awaiting vehicle. "You bad for business. Since you can't handle being lieutenant, I know a couple niggas that could. Hopefully you'll learn from this."

Ali stood there furiously as he watched Trap speed out of the neighborhood. *Are you fuckin' kiddin' me?* If there was one thing that Ali couldn't do, it was return back to the block and hustle. He hadn't done that in over five years. *Who the fuck does Trap think he is? I worked too damn hard for this shit. I got to move on this nigga ASAP.*

"Ali," Chanelle called out anxiously, breaking him out of his thoughts. "Can you take me back to the club now?"

"I thought you were gonna change your clothes?" he asked, noticing that she'd put back on her bloodstained clothes.

"No, I'm good. I'll just wait until I get home," she answered quickly. She was still nervous from thinking that Trap had come there looking for her.

"A'ight. It's whatever you wanna do." Ali nodded before walking towards his garage. He found her sudden shift in behavior odd. He wondered if she was shook after hearing his conversation with Trap. "Ay, if this is about what happened just now don't worry about that shit."

"Huh?" Chanelle asked, pretending as if she didn't know what he was talking about. "Look, I just need to get home because my man has been blowing my phone up."

"Yeah. A'ight." Ali wasn't completely convinced by her explanation, but who was he to question her? He had his own business to attend to after she left.

"So, what was up with you and that nigga?" Ali prodded as he started the car and backed out of the garage.

"What nigga?" Chanelle tried to remain calm, but her nervousness showed through her voice.

"Dude from the club," he responded. "I didn't wanna ask you while it was still fresh but you owe me some type of explanation. Let me know what kind of shit you got me into, shawty."

Chanelle exhaled deeply before responding. "Well, that was my ex. When we broke up he stole this chest from me. It belonged to my grandmother and she left it to me when she died. She was never the type to use a bank, so she kept her life's savings inside. He robbed me and held me at gunpoint for it. I was left with nothing after that. He knew it, too! That's what made the betrayal worse."

Her voice lowered off as she tried to calm down. Although the majority of her story was a lie, whenever Chanelle recounted anything dealing with Desmond, she felt her anger rise all over again. She couldn't help but wonder if he'd blown through all the money or if it was stashed somewhere. Not that she would ever know now. Desmond had paid her back with the ultimate price... his life.

"Damn," Ali uttered as he shook his head. "That's fucked up."

"Yeah," Chanelle said quietly, satisfied that he'd bought her story.

Ali may have helped her out, but he was still a stranger. She wanted to believe his intentions were good, but she still didn't trust niggas. Judging from the conversation he had with Trap, Ali couldn't be trusted.

"Where you parked at?" Ali asked as they pulled into the parking lot several minutes later.

"I'm good right here," she insisted. Chanelle had parked Trap's car in the back and with them knowing one another, there was no way she could let Ali see what car she was getting into.

"Damn. What's the problem? Don't worry, I ain't gonna stalk you or some shit, shawty. I know you'll put the murder game down if I did." Ali chuckled, but inwardly he was curious as to what she was trying to hide.

"No. It's nothing like that. Trust me, I'm good."

"Look, Sparkle, I'm not gonna leave until I know you're straight. A nigga *did* save your life. If I wanted to do somethin' to you, don't you think I would've done it at my house?"

If only that was my problem, Chanelle thought. She could see that Ali wasn't going to let up so she finally pointed toward Trap's Benz. It was on the other side of the large parking lot, almost hidden from view due to the dark shadows cast over it. "Right there."

Ali pulled up beside the German car and shook his head. "This your nigga's whip?"

"Why can't it be mine?"

"Cuz I know you ain't making that much money at *Pretty Kitty*, no matter how bad you are. That's a two hundred thousand dollar car." Ali whistled. "A S65 AMG... Ain't no way it's yours."

"Well, it is." Chanelle opened her door, preparing to get out, but Ali's next words froze her in place.

"Lying ain't a good way to start off our relationship."

"Relationship?" she asked confused.

Ali nodded. "Yup. Our *business* relationship."

"How you figure we have one?" Chanelle retorted with her hand on her hip, immediately regretting her earlier actions. From attacking and killing Desmond in the parking lot to letting Ali help her out.

"How long y'all been fuckin' with each other?" Ali countered, ignoring her question.

"Who?"

"C'mon, are we really playin' this game? I know you're Trap's bitch cuz you're pushin' his whip. I've *never* seen a female drive his car before. That's how I know you must mean somethin' to him."

"What's it to you?" Chanelle snapped.

"How long y'all been fuckin' with each other?" he repeated. His question received a shrug so he tried again. "You love him?"

"It's not that deep," she muttered softly. Chanelle felt a sinking feeling in her stomach. Ali was up to something, but she wasn't sure what it was. "But I would appreciate it if you didn't mention any of this to him, especially not where I work."

"I got you, baby girl. I can understand and appreciate a woman that's all about her paper," Ali responded, then smiled. "You must've been nervous as hell when he came to the crib just now, huh?"

Chanelle decided to ignore his sarcasm. "Well, thanks for everything." She started out of the car again, but Ali tugged at her hand.

"Nobody does something for nothing, sweetheart," he enlightened her. "Now, sit down and hear me out. I think you'll appreciate what I have to say."

$$\$$

"What the hell?" Triniti mumbled under her breath as

she idled her car a few feet away from the driveway. She could-
n't believe her eyes when she saw Chanelle hop out of Trap's
car and enter his house…with a key.

When Triniti was leaving *Pretty Kitty* for the night she
noticed Trap's Mercedes leaving out of the parking lot and decided to follow him. She hadn't seen him inside of the club and
the fact that he'd come there without saying a word to her was
unacceptable. Not to mention his avoidance pissed her off. She
had been determined to get to the bottom of things, but seeing
Chanelle was a big slap in the face.

Her, she thought heatedly. *A damn stripper? And possibly a murderer.*

Triniti whipped her car around the cul-de-sac and
reached for her cell phone. While dialing, she pressed each button brutally. It was surprising that she didn't crack the screen.

The phone seemed to ring endlessly before Trap finally
picked up. "Hello?"

"You seriously got another bitch driving your car!"
Triniti went off.

"Ay, look," Trap interjected. The agitation in his voice
was strong and caused Triniti to hush immediately. "I got
robbed tonight and I ain't got time for your bullshit right now."

Click.

Triniti stared at the phone in disbelief before placing it
into her cup holder. While she understood that the robbery was
his main priority right now, she was sure the situation with
Chanelle hadn't occurred overnight. Just how long had this
been going on? Why did he pick her? And how the hell hadn't
Triniti noticed before?

Hearing her phone buzz with an incoming text message,
she eagerly lunged for it, nearly crashing into a parked car.
Where you wanna meet us at?

Triniti stared at the message with disappointment. She
was happy to receive the news, but at the same time she was
disappointed that Trap wasn't calling her back. With a sigh, she

dialed the number back.

"What's good, T?" the voice on the other end greeted her.

"How'd it go, Darrell?" Triniti asked with a smile, slightly brightening up.

"Man, that shit was easy as hell," he laughed. "I would'a never guessed that Trap would be that easy to rob!"

Darrell went on about the job Triniti had put him and his boy onto, but she barely listened. All she wanted to hear about was the money.

"How much did y'all get?"

"Shiiit…we got about a hundred and fifty thou!"

Triniti nodded with approval. She knew that Trap had thousands of dollars at his disposal, but he was still fairly frugal with his money. He was the type of person to trip over losing twenty dollars. He wanted every cent of his cash and judging from his distraught voice, getting Darrell, Vonnie, and Hakeem to rob Trap had done exactly as she'd intended.

They were three wild young niggas who were infamous jack boys. She knew that they would be perfect for the job seeing as they wouldn't run their mouth and weren't overly flashy. She didn't have to worry about it being traced back to her.

"Well, meet me on Fulton Industrial so I can get my 30% finder's fee," Triniti stated as she maneuvered out of the neighborhood.

"A'ight. Let us know if you got any other licks to put us on," Darrell told her excitedly. "We down for whatever."

"Oh, trust me…it'll be sooner than later."

$$\$$

"Where the fuck is it?" Chanelle nearly screamed in frustration as she maneuvered around the plush hotel room at the W.

Finding Desmond's room had been easy enough. His

keycard identified that he was staying at the one in Midtown and the clerk wasted no time giving her the room number, for a fee, anyway. Chanelle had been standing in the lobby plotting her next move when she overheard the young woman at the front desk complaining about her shortage in hours that week to a manager. After the manager left, Chanelle could still her mumbling about how she hated her job and wanted to quit. That was all Chanelle needed to hear, and when the clerk saw the two hundred dollars, she was given the room number without any qualms.

Finding the money was a different matter. Aside from a couple of empty liquor bottles littered across the floor and the unmade bed, she couldn't find anything else.

Chanelle had overturned the mattresses, snatched open all of the drawers, and the only thing she found was a soiled pair of panties underneath the bed.

I can't believe this shit, she thought angrily. This was her last chance at coming across the money since Desmond was dead. From the lack of clothes here, it was apparent that he had another place to stay and that would be impossible to locate. The money was just as gone as it had been when Desmond pulled off with it almost two months ago, leaving her for dead.

Discouraged, Chanelle started for the door, but not before giving the room one last onceover. *There's nowhere else it could be.*

"Fuck you, Desmond!" she screeched before heading towards the door to leave. No sooner than she'd gotten the door open, her heart nearly burst out of her chest. The color drained from her face as though she'd seen a ghost.

"Hey, is Stacks in there?" a short, thick brown-skinned girl, looking no older than eighteen asked. She was completely oblivious to Chanelle's jumpy behavior.

"Hell no," Chanelle spat with a frown.

The girl wrinkled her eyebrows up at her and started backing away slowly with her hands up. "You his girl?" When

Chanelle took a couple of steps closer to her, she quickened her pace, but ended up on the floor. "Look, I didn't know he had a girlfriend. He told me he was single and I figured..."

Chanelle started to tell her that she was far from his girlfriend, but quickly realized that this put her at an advantage. *Let me see how much she knows. Maybe she knows where he stays.* "Where did you meet Stacks and how long y'all been fucking?"

"I met him at Kamal's. I work there as a dancer. I swear there ain't shit else to it. He just was busy stuntin' in the club and talkin' about how he got it. Stacks said he could really make it rain if I came to the hotel with him and so we meet up here every night around this time."

"Do you know where he lives?" She gritted her teeth. "And you better not lie, bitch."

The girl shook her head vigorously. "We only meet here, I swear."

Chanelle frowned. *This bitch ain't no help.* She took off down the hallway without another word. *Dammit. I'm right back where I started. Still out of seven hundred thousand dollars and got a possible murder charge to go with it.*

"Fuck my life."

$TWENTY-ONE

"Hello?" Chanelle asked with annoyance.

"Damn, no love for me, huh? The nigga that saved your life?" Ali spoke sarcastically.

"I thought I was clear when I told you not to call me? What if Trap was home?" Chanelle whispered as she looked around the empty kitchen. Even though Trap had left almost an hour ago, she was still uncomfortable. She had Ali saved in her phone as 'Alisha', but that didn't ease her mind as much as she thought it would.

On top of that, Loretta had been calling her phone constantly, flooding her inbox with messages that Chanelle hadn't bothered to listen to. As far as Chanelle was concerned, she didn't have a mother. A'mya had called as well, but Chanelle was afraid to face her. After the Desmond fiasco, she'd never made it to check in on her friend and felt an extreme amount of guilt. With all the shit she'd gotten herself into, Chanelle knew that A'mya would never be able to understand that.

"Fuck Trap. It would be in your best interest to be more concerned about the person who has the gun with *your* prints on it and access to that dude's body."

Chanelle gasped slightly. *Niggas ain't shit,* she thought.

"Now, listen up. Remember what I told you about helping me set someone up?"

"Yeah," she replied reluctantly. "Just who are you trying to set up anyway and what exactly do you want me to do?" When Ali had first presented the idea to her, he hadn't been forthcoming with the details, only promising to be in touch.

"Trap."

"Trap!" Chanelle yelled. "Are you crazy? What did he do to you?" Chanelle quizzed. It seemed like anything set people off nowadays.

"Mind your own damn business," Ali snapped.

"It is my business if I'm involved," she protested.

"You just worry about playin' your part. If you fuck this shit up, expect to get *fucked*."

Chanelle was quiet as she fought with her own emotions. Her conscience weighed heavily on her heart, but she knew that she didn't have a choice. It was either her or Trap and she refused to rot in jail for the rest of her life. She could tell that Ali would make good on his threats, so it would be easier to just go along with it. She had too much at stake to just lose it all.

"I'll do this on a few conditions," Chanelle began. "That you get rid of any evidence that you have involving that night, I get a cut of the money you get from him, and that Trap doesn't know I had shit to do with it."

"Cool." Ali would let Chanelle think whatever she wanted. It would make things easier for now, but the results would be the same. He wanted Trap knocked off his throne, and it was sure to happen with Chanelle on his team. "But who said anything about robbing him? I want that nigga dead." He paused. "So, we got a deal?"

Chanelle knew that she was making a deal with the devil but nonetheless her mouth opened and responded, "Deal. What do you need me to do?" She regretted it just as soon as the words came out.

$$$$$$$$$$$$$$$$$$$$$$$

"Darrell and Hakeem, I knew y'all lil' niggas was crazy,

but not enough to fuck with me," Trap chastised before ripping the duct tape from their mouths, allowing them freedom to speak.

"Nigga, fuck you!" Darrell gurgled after coughing up a mouthful of blood.

If Trap hadn't removed the tape when he did, Darrell was sure that he would've choked on the blood. His body and face was bruised and battered, but he maintained his hard demeanor.

He and Hakeem were handcuffed to chairs in an abandoned warehouse located off Warner Street. One minute they were walking back to their car after leaving the club, the next they were being held at gunpoint and forced into a van. The cuffs were so tight that it was starting to chafe their wrists and cut off the circulation to their hands. They'd just endured several rounds, and what felt like hours of torture and Trap didn't show any signs of letting up.

"Nah, fuck y'all," Trap stressed.

When Trap learned the good news, he'd dropped everything that he was doing. Trap put the order in for them to be taken to the warehouse and pushed his Bentley as fast as he could down congested I-75. He'd felt like he couldn't reach his destination quickly enough. Trap didn't give the orders for the perpetrators to be killed because he wanted to be the one to do it. Yes, he wanted to be face to face with the niggas that had the gall to rob and steal from him.

"You know I don't play about my muthafuckin' money and you should've known that I would find out. The streets talk *especially* when there's a bounty on your head. So, why the fuck would you run your mouth just to get some pussy?"

Trap was referring to how the men had managed to get caught up. It was Ali's baby momma, Chenica, who'd made the discovery. One of her girlfriends had gossiped to her about the way Hakeem bragged about robbing Trap. He wanted to prove that he had "stacks on deck." However, his attempt to impress the girl had ended up with him being tortured and close to having his young life snuffed out like a cigarette.

"I got one more question for you," Trap said as he continued to walk around the dimly lit room with a smirk. The varying shades of light made his face appear eerie and almost satanic. His tone was even and firm. "Why the fuck would y'all be crazy enough to fuck with me?"

Hakeem's eyes were swollen, but it wasn't from crying. Trap had spared no mercy with his blows, hitting any and every inch of their bodies. He'd wanted them to suffer before he put a bullet through them, but it was one thing that he had to know first.

"Money talks," Darrell muttered defiantly.

He already knew what their fate would be. There was no point in kissing Trap's ass now. He'd known the possible consequences of his actions each time he committed a robbery and accepted it.

"You right." Trap nodded. "But this talks louder."

He aimed his gun at Darrell slowly, looking directly into his eyes. He waited to see that all too familiar look of fear. It was something that he got off on. With his boss status, he didn't get his hands dirty too often, but whenever he did, sometimes it was just like Christmas for him.

After seeing what he was looking for, Trap wasted no time releasing two bullets from his chamber and directly into Darrell's heart. The man slumped slightly before his eyes dimmed forever.

"You got any last words?" Trap asked Hakeem as he faced him.

Hakeem's back was opposite of Darrell's so he luckily didn't have to see what had just taken place, but he'd heard everything. He winced slightly before shutting his eyes tightly.

"Man, please... I got kids," Hakeem begged.

He never thought that he would resort to begging, but his best friend being murdered within arm's distance made him realize how real shit was. He thought that he could thug it out, but truth be told, Hakeem wasn't about that life. He was just a dude that was tired of being broke and jumped on the opportunity to make a quick come up. Darrell and Vonnie were the true jack boys. Hakeem was nothing but a wannabe.

Now, all he wanted to be was spared. If he hadn't blown all of his money he would've offered to pay it back.

"Then I hope that money you stole will be enough to take care of them," Trap replied coldly.

"Can't we work somethin' out? I can repay you."

"Y'all hear this nigga?" Trap asked, turning his attention to Ali, SK, and Phoenix, who were standing silently in the shadows watching the horror show take place.

SK laughed. "Hell yeah. Man, kill this nigga, Trap."

"If you promise not to shoot me, I'll tell you who put us up to it!" Hakeem hollered out quickly, praying that Trap didn't take SK's advice. It was his last ditch effort to save his life.

Trap studied him curiously, not the least bit surprised by his request. "Damn…niggas snitch real quick to save their lives."

"I got kids, man. I just wanna be there for them," Hakeem mumbled. "So, is that a deal?"

"Nigga, you could say any name," Trap spoke.

"Nah. It don't benefit me to protect them." Hakeem looked back up at Trap as best he could through his puffy eyes. "Deal?" Hakeem realized that Trap may kill him anyway, but what else could he do? He was willing to do damn near anything to keep his life.

Trap nodded slowly. "A'ight. You got it. I won't shoot you, but if the shit sounds funny, then I will."

"It was Triniti!" Hakeem blabbed quickly, hoping to make a believer out of Trap.

All of the men's eyes bucked at the mention of Triniti's name.

"What?" Trap asked.

"Bullshit," Ali murmured. He knew that couldn't be true. There was no way that Triniti would do anything to hurt her precious Trap.

Hakeem could sense that they didn't believe him so he continued hurriedly. "She told us exactly where y'all kept the money and even said that Ali wouldn't be there because he was at the club! She had everything mapped out! She told us the street, how many niggas would be inside, where to find the money..."

Hakeem was still talking, but Trap could no longer hear him. He was silent and his facial expression remained emotionless. He didn't want Hakeem to realize just how valuable the information was.

"You gotta believe me!" Hakeem shouted, uncomfortable with the sudden silence that had engulfed the room.

"I believe you," Trap said finally. *I just don't believe her,* he thought. He was still in minor shock at the revelation. He knew that Triniti was pissed about his new relationship, but to take it to these heights, that was the ultimate 'fuck you'.

Trap shook his head before turning to leave. There was nothing left to say, any other questions he had, he wanted to direct at Triniti. He wanted to hear it from the source.

"Where are you going?" Hakeem quizzed nervously, especially when he saw that the other men hadn't moved from their posts. A sinking feeling formed in his stomach and his pulse quickened as he realized that Trap wasn't going to honor their agreement. Still, he pressed on. "Ain't you gonna let me go?"

Trap stopped in the doorway. "That wasn't the deal. You said for me not to shoot you, and I'm not. I'll leave that to them."

Hakeem's screams echoed after him before he shut the steel door. Trap walked over to his car, in no particular hurry. His head was still reeling from the news. He had half a mind to go confront Triniti that night, but in his emotional state, he'd probably act irrationally.

Fuck that, he thought.

What other way was there to behave? She'd gotten three niggas to rob him and then she was still attempting to wedge herself into his life. He could bet that if it hadn't been for Hakeem, he probably would've never found out. He doubted that Triniti would ever come clean. But now she wouldn't have a choice but to do so.

"After all I did for that bitch!" he said out loud, banging his hand against the steering wheel roughly.

Trap didn't know why he'd expected more from her after all that she'd done, but he guessed that a small shard of him just wanted to believe that she was the same Triniti from years ago. Before he ruined their relationship with sex and gotten her feelings involved. Before she'd started acting like some type of psycho ex-girlfriend. Back when he could trust her with any and everything. Trap didn't understand her logic in the slightest. Hurt feelings or not, she'd crossed the line and would be dealt with accordingly.

Trap didn't hand out free passes to anyone.

$ TWENTY-TWO

"Finally," Triniti sighed while walking around her empty condo.

She'd been packing since the day before. Now, all of her belongings were finally in cardboard boxes, stacked neatly near the door. Her oversized furniture was still in place, waiting for the Mayflower movers. The eighteen-wheeler would be driving along the interstate to take her things back to New Orleans while she would be taking a one-way flight there via Hartsfield-Jackson Airport.

Triniti took one last fleeting glance around the place that she'd called home for nearly seven years. It was a beautiful condo located on Peachtree Street with a great view of down-town. She hated having to sell it, but it had to be done. She saw no point in continuing to reside there. Triniti had the money from the robbery and Trap had a new girl. She had no desire to continue working at Pretty Kitty when she'd already made enough to go off and do her own thing.

Trap wasn't aware that she was leaving yet, but he would figure it out eventually. Just like everybody else would. She didn't owe anyone an explanation. Triniti just wanted to close this chapter in her life. She'd been a fool for love, chasing after a man that only wanted her for sex. If anything, she should've went back to Louisiana after the Hurricane had passed. Trap wasn't her damn family, her brother Maurice was and with him still incarcerated at Angola, she needed to be closer to him.

And that damn Chanelle, Triniti wondered what made *her* so special to him. She tried to block out her feelings of jealousy, but it was hard to repress. Trap was the only man that she'd ever loved, so trying to get over him was easier said than done.

"That bitch ain't shit but a stripper," Triniti said to herself bitterly. "And a fucking criminal." Her mind went back to the detecives who'd dropped by the club. *As a matter of fact, where the hell did I put that damn card? I should turn her ass in!* Triniti didn't need the reward money, but why turn down free money?

Suddenly, there was a knock on her door. Triniti looked at her watch quizzically, wondering if the movers had come a day before schedule. Questioning who it was, she cracked her door slightly, keeping the safety chain intact.

"Trap," she breathed. Triniti wished that she'd looked first. She would've just pretended that she wasn't home.

"Whassup?" Trap greeted with a smile. He looked at her strangely when she didn't make a move to invite him in. "You said that you wanted me to slide through and now I'm finally here."

"That was days ago, Trap," she replied with disappointment in her voice.

He gave a vague shrug. "I been busy. But I'm here now. What? You got a nigga over here? Why you looking so jumpy?"

"I'm not," Triniti asserted with a roll of the eyes.

"So, let me in."

Triniti sighed before closing the door and removing the security latch to allow him access.

She tried hard not to stare at him, but had to admit that he looked damn good. His dreads were tied back into a ponytail and dark shades covered his eyes. A pair of True Religion jeans sagged off his waist with a money green Armani shirt.

"Damn, what's up with all this?" Trap asked as he stepped inside. The immaculate decorations that had once adorned the room were undoubtedly in the boxes that he saw piled up in the entryway. "Where are you goin'?"

"Why?" Triniti folded her arms with much attitude. "You gonna try and stop me?" she asked cynically before walking towards her sofa and taking a seat.

"Nah," he replied before making himself comfortable on her overstuffed accent chair. "Shit. I was just wonderin' 'why'. You really wanna leave a nigga?"

Triniti narrowed her eyes. "Why not? You don't need me, you got Chanelle's ass." She laughed condescendingly. "The bitch that's wanted by the law for a murder. You sure know how to pick 'em."

Trap looked at her with a baffled expression. "What the hell are you talkin' about? I don't know no damn Chanelle."

She rolled her eyes. "Nigga, you ain't gotta play dumb with me. I saw the bitch driving your car and pull up at your house. I followed her when she left the club the other night. Light-skinned with long ass hair and the stripper body?" Noticing his surprise at her revelation, Triniti shook her head in mock pity. "And you have no idea of who you're really fucking with."

"Run that shit by me again? Where are you gettin' this from?"

Triniti sighed with annoyance. "Chanelle Daniels aka the new stripper named Sparkle... the new chick that you're laid up with who you obviously don't know shit about."

A million thoughts ran through Trap's mind. He'd come over to confront Triniti about her disloyalty and now she was saying that his girl was just as grimy. Females couldn't be trusted. He realized that more and more each day. Chanelle was leading a double life and he couldn't believe that he'd been blind to it all.

"Yeah, she's the bitch those detectives came looking for that night. Apparently she murdered her ex-boyfriend named, JaQuez in North Carolina. Of all the females for you to pick, you choose the one that murdered her ex. Poor JaQuez, if he hadn't chose her grimy ass maybe he would still be alive." Triniti enjoyed giving him this wakeup call.

Murder, he thought. *What the hell?* Trap definitely didn't know who the fuck he was dealing with anymore.

"Who knows, you could've ended up the same way. I'm amazed you haven't seen her ass on the news," Triniti added, laying it on thick. To her knowledge, the story wasn't being aired on TV, but she wanted to ensure that Trap got the picture. He'd made a grave mistake in choosing Chanelle over her.

"Damn, guess you're thinkin' some bitches ain't shit, right?" Trap asked, recovering quickly from the newfound information. He would deal with the Chanelle situation when he got home. Right now he needed to get back to the situation at hand.

"Maybe you'll pick 'em better next time," Triniti said casually with a shrug of the shoulders. "If you had picked me, you wouldn't have these problems."

"Are you sure?"

"I'm positive. I would never lie to you like she did."

Trap nodded, keeping his eyes fixed on her with the focus of a cat eyeing a mouse. "Just like you probably wouldn't have robbed my ass, right?"

"What?" Triniti asked, rising slowly from the sofa. Her heart rate sped up as she realized the real reason for the house call.

"I still can't understand why muthafuckas think I won't find out about shit. Triniti, you already know how I get down so why the fuck would you put yourself in a position where you could be my next victim?"

"Whoever put my name in that shit is lying," Triniti denied, knowing that she didn't sound the least bit convincing.

But she would be damned if she admitted to it. *He probably doesn't have anything concrete on me anyway.* It was the snitch's word against hers and she'd never given Trap any reason not to believe her.

"The niggas in your camp got loose lips. I saw the call log, the text messages and all that shit," Trap lied. "I just wanna know 'why'?"

"Is that really a question?" she scoffed, no longer feeling the need to deny the allegations. When Trap made his mind up, it was hard to change. She'd been a witness to that several times. "You hurt me, Trap." Triniti's voice wavered with emotion as she willed herself not to cry, but her eyes betrayed her when she felt hot tears stinging her eyelids, causing her vision to blur. "I loved you more than a woman could love a man, but you didn't give a fuck! You treated me like any other chick!"

Trap shook his head. "It wasn't like that. I had overstepped my boundaries! No matter what, you're still Maurice's little sister."

"Are you gonna hold on to that excuse forever?" she asked angrily. "I'm a grown ass woman, Trap, if you hadn't noticed!"

"But you still act like a lil' ass girl. I mean you creepin' around with Ali and shit!"

Triniti stared at him in a state of shock. "How did you know?"

"It wasn't hard to tell, Triniti! Y'all sloppy as fuck. I seen your car parked at his house in the wee hours of the mornin' too many times. I told you not to fuck with that nigga because all my boys were no good, and you did the shit anyway."

Triniti couldn't believe her ears. She'd thought her and Ali had been fairly discreet, but obviously that thought was wrong. Her mind probably should've been in a different place, but she couldn't help herself when she blurted out. "What did it matter to you? You didn't want me!"

"I never said it mattered," Trap replied coldly. "I just knew that you weren't the female I wanted to wife after that. I knew then that you were sneaky and disloyal, but I still fucked with you." He shook his head, wishing that he'd taken action sooner. "It's only because of your brother! I promised him that I would take care of you and honestly, I felt like I owed him that."

Maurice had taught him everything that he knew about the game. It was due to his connects that Trap was half as successful as he was now. Without Maurice, he would've still been that lil' poor nigga on the block, selling candy or whatever else he could steal. Maurice saw the hustle in him and put him onto a game far more lucrative.

"But you went too fuckin' far this time when you decided to steal from me." Trap finally revealed the gun that he'd concealed and aimed it at Triniti.

"So, that's enough for you to kill me? Over a couple dollars that you could stand to lose?" She walked up to him boldly, not showing an ounce of fear. "After you let my brother take the fall for you?"

"You got a fucked up ass memory," Trap said as he kept his gun trained on her.

"Nah. Maurice told me how he killed that guy for you. He saved your life, but you still let him take the wrap!"

"Is that what that nigga told you?" Trap asked, his face distorted with confusion. It was true that Maurice had saved his life, but there was nothing that Trap could've done to prevent his arrest. Maurice's prints were all over the gun, along with a few other bodies. The fact that Maurice refused to dispose of his trusty .32 resulted in him being locked up for life.

How the hell is he tryin' to pin that shit on me, like I'm some sort of coward, Trap wondered.

Triniti's eyes were focused on Trap's. She knew that she'd gotten under his skin and her statements were actually false. She merely wanted to get a rise out of him and the opportunity to strike.

While she only weighed about one hundred and thirty five pounds, her will to live was stronger than anything else. She rushed at Trap, and her sneaky move caused his gun to fall from his grasp. Quickly, she kicked the gun from his reach as Trap grabbed her arms to prevent her from reaching down to get it. They both knew that whoever ended up with the steel would be the one leaving the condo alive.

Trap shoved her out of the way roughly before searching around the room for his fallen weapon. Triniti used that moment to her advantage, crawling quickly to the gun. It was lying partially hidden under the sofa. Her arm was outstretched as she lunged for it. However, she was unsussesful as Trap managed to grab the firearm first, then pointed at her again. Triniti wasn't gonna be able to talk herself out of this one.

"You're dead to me now," he said, just before firing one shot.

$TWENTY-THREE

Beep Beep!

Chanelle rushed over to the stove and pushed a button to stop the shrieking of the oven timer. She pulled out a beautiful batch of macaroni and cheese before turning over the steak that she cooked on the stovetop. She'd been cooking for nearly two hours, but now wasn't entirely sure why she was going through the extensive motions.

"That nigga probably gonna pass out before he gets a chance to eat," Chanelle muttered as she popped open a can of biscuits, preparing to place them in the oven next. "Oh well. They say presentation is everything."

Her eyes shifted over to the table that she'd already set. A glass of Riesling waited as well. It was the most important part of the meal. Inside she'd slipped two Rohypnol pills hoping to rush the usual thirty minute time-frame that it usually took to work. Chanelle needed Trap to be out of commission for her plan to work. It was different from what Ali had in mind, but *she* was the mastermind of this operation.

Chanelle wasn't sure how her future would pan out, but she prayed that whatever amount of money Trap had would be enough to finance *Chanelle's Chic Boutique*. She knew that Ali wanted Trap dead, but she just wanted the money. If she could save Trap, she would. He'd been nothing but good to her, but when it all boiled down to it, she was putting herself first.

Tonight was when Ali wanted to make things happen and now she just needed to call Trap and figure out how far away he was from home.

His phone rang about four times before he picked up with an exasperated, "Hello?"

"Hey, baby," Chanelle cooed seductively. "Are you on your way home?"

"Yeah. I'm about thirty minutes away."

"What's wrong?" she asked, setting the stage for her next reveal.

"All I ever asked is for someone to keep it 100 with me," Trap grumbled, "Is that too much to ask?"

Chanelle was puzzled by his statement, but figured that it had something to do with where he'd been for nearly three hours. "Well, you know that I'm always gonna keep it one hundred with you, baby. I'm cooking you a big dinner so you can relax like the king you are," she told him with a lovable voice.

"That sounds good," he said, sounding slightly more at ease. "I'll see you when I get home, a'ight?"

"Yup. I'm wearing that lingerie you like, too." Her last statement fell on deaf ears. She looked at her phone and saw that he'd already disconnected the call.

"What the hell is his problem?" Chanelle said before dismissing it.

It didn't matter anyway. Attitude or not, Trap was coming home. Quickly, she dialed Ali, needing to update him.

"What's up? You got shit straight yet?" he asked eagerly.

"Yeah. He'll be home in about thirty minutes."

"Bet. I'm on my way."

"Okay."

"Oh, and Sparkle," Ali started. "Don't try to fuck me over."

Ali meant what he told her with his earlier warning although ultimately she would end up fucked in the end, regardless. No matter what, his plan was to stage everything so it looked as though *she* murdered Trap. He needed to be able to reign over the streets without static and doing this would ensure things went his way.

"I won't," she assured him. "As long as you do what you promised for me, we won't have any problems."

"Let's hope so."

Click.

"Fuck you," Chanelle replied.

Killing Ali was part two of her plan. She doubted that he would make good on his word so she figured that taking him out would be her next move. She hoped that he didn't end up arriving before Trap or it could throw her whole scheme off.

Hearing her *K. Michelle* ringtone going off, Chanelle already knew who was calling her phone. It was Loretta. She'd been calling her non stop, but today was definitely setting a new record. She'd called at least ten times before finally resorting to sending a text message.

Urgent! Call me! Please!!!!

"I've had enough of this," Chanelle said, immediately snatching her phone off of the counter and dialing Loretta's number. "Maybe if I curse her ass out one last time, she'll stop calling."

"It's about damn time!" Loretta huffed. The phone didn't even get a chance to ring before she'd picked it up. "I was starting to wonder if you had gotten your number changed or blocked it."

"I should've gotten it changed by now, so that was my dumbness," Chanelle answered. "So, what the hell do you want? What the hell is so urgent that you've been calling my phone for weeks?"

"JaQuez isn't dead," Loretta blurted out.

Chanelle paused for a second before letting out a minor chuckle. "What the fuck are you talking about? What do you mean JaQuez isn't dead? I thought you said there was a bounty out for whoever killed him! Did you have too much to drink…again?" *Not to mention I saw that nigga die,* Chanelle thought frantically.

"That's what I thought, too, but obviously it wasn't true. Apparently he's not dead. Everybody is saying that you tried to kill him!"

"Me?" Chanelle whispered. While she didn't physically pull the trigger, she'd pulled a big enough role in his "murder" to be considered responsible.

"Yes! That's why I've been trying to get in contact with you! Why the hell didn't you call me back? I left you tons of messages!"

"Because you tried to set me up! I'm pretty sure I saw Rob's car at the hotel that day when I was supposed to be meeting this so called James. Don't you think it's a lil' weird that he would be there at the same time? That shit was a little more than a damn coincidence." Chanelle still wasn't sure if she could trust Loretta, but she was her only connect to finding out what was going on in North Carolina.

"Damn," Loretta said with disgruntlement. "I know I've done a lot of fucked up shit to you, but I would never sell you out to some nigga that I never cared for in the first place."

"Please, you would've done anything for that so called bounty."

"Are you serious? My men give me plenty of money, Chanelle. I would never turn on you like that."

"Look, just give me the details about what you know," Chanelle rushed her, wanting to know all that she could before Trap made it home.

Loretta sighed. "Apparently he's been at Rex Medical recovering for the past few weeks. You know your cousin Mimi works there and she told me that she'd seen him! Do you need money to get out of town?"

"Get out of town?" The color drained from Chanelle's

already light face. "He knows where I am?"

$$\$$$

"Hey, Triniti I need to talk to you about Darcy. She keeps taking my time slot on stage, and her ass knows I need to get out of here by a certain time," one of the dancers complained.

Normally, Triniti entertained all the drama that went on inside Pretty Kitty, but not tonight. Tonight was different. Tonight she didn't have anything to say to anyone, including some of her favorite patrons who greeted her when she first walked in. Instead, she made a b-line straight to her office without saying a word. Now that this would be her last day, they could all kiss her ass for all she cared.

She made her way over to the desk with her Damier print Louis Vuitton rolling suitcase in tow. Triniti planned on using it to store the money that she'd skimmed that week. That had been the true reason why she never wanted people in her office. She'd been afraid that they would notice the small safe in her desk's bottom drawer where she kept the 15% she took each time she totaled out for the night. A ritual she'd done since the club first opened. Since the club made thousands of dollars every night, her dishonest cut was pretty hefty. After opening the drawer, she quickly entered the combination on the safe's keypad.

"Yup. It's all here." Triniti smiled for the first time in hours as she counted up her money and stuffed it into her luggage.

She exhaled deeply before placing the keys to the club on the table, and then looked around the room, reflecting on the events that took place only mintues ago. After losing her grip on the gun, Triniti closed her eyes after hearing Trap say she was dead to him, preparing herself mentally for the blast that would end her existence. But surprisingly it never came. When she opened them back up, Trap was already heading out of the door. The bullet that Triniti just knew would end her life was lodged inside the wall behind her instead. Trap's final words were that if she ever tried to get back in contact with him, then he wouldn't miss intentionally the next time.

Triniti counted her blessings at that point. She didn't dare question his decision even though she longed to know why he'd had a last minute change of heart. Instead, she picked herself off of the floor and left only minutes after he had. She wanted to get her money from the safe and then get ghost.

Good fucking riddance, ATL, Triniti thought as she exited her former office and sauntered out to the parking lot.

Triniti disarmed the alarm to her car before tossing her suitcase into the backseat. Even though it was only eight o' clock, the parking lot was pretty full. For a brief moment, she wondered if Chanelle would come to work. The mention of the woman caused a crooked grin to form on Triniti's face as she thought about how stupid Trap looked after she'd revealed the truth about his new wifey.

"Where the hell is that damn card?" she wondered aloud. She was ready to cash in on another payday. The detectives hadn't told her how much the payout would be for the information, but she would take whatever it was.

Triniti cut on her dome light to illuminate the contents of her purse as she dug around for the business card.

"Bingo."

She smiled after seeing the card and reaching for her cell phone. Triniti had about two hours until her last minute flight to New York, so she was prepared to tell them they would just have to mail the reward once she got settled. The phone had just started ringing when Triniti heard a tap on her window.

"What?" she scowled before noticing Vonnie standing there. She rolled the window down slowly. "Von, can you hold up real quick? I'm trying to handle some business."

"Hello," a male voice answered.

"Hi, my name is…"

Before Triniti could get her name out, Vonnie snatched the phone out of her hand and threw it on the ground. The battery bounced out of the back compartment and he crushed her phone with his heavy sized twelve shoe for emphasis.

"What the fuck is your problem, Von?" Triniti looked at him wondering why he was tripping on her. They'd gotten their fair share of the money and nobody had any complaints before, so what was his issue?

"You snitched on my fuckin' boys?" Vonnie demanded.

"What are you talking about?"

When Vonnie raised his gun at her, Triniti could've pissed in her pants. She'd had a gun pointed at her twice in less than two hours and felt that her luck was running thin. With the deranged look in his eyes, there was no way he was going to let her out alive.

It was at that moment when Triniti wished she'd gone straight to the airport instead of trying to get the money. She also wished she'd backed her car into the parking spot like it normally was. Triniti glanced out of her rearview mirror briefly and saw that her car was blocked in undoubtedly by Vonnie's tinted out Ford F-150.

"Calm down, Von, and just tell me what happened." Triniti spoke slowly and as calm as she could manage with her hands up in the air in surrender.

Triniti didn't know where he'd gotten the false information, but knew that it was important to make him understand before he did something irrational. Was he really crazy enough to shoot her in the middle of a parking lot?

"Bitch, Darrell and Hakeem are dead and that shit ain't no coincidence!" he sniffed, unable to stop the tears from racing down his face. "I heard you snitched on them to save your own ass! Ain't nobody know we robbed them niggas but you!"

"How do you figure that? Y'all got plenty of enemies and why would I…"

"You lyin' ass, bitch!" were the last words that Triniti heard before Vonnie unloaded three bullets into her chest. Her body jerked back and forth before finally coming to rest on the horn.

$TWENTY-FOUR

"What?" Chanelle said, nearly jumping out of her skin. She was sure that her ears had deceived her.

"Who the fuck is JaQuez?" Trap repeated as though he was speaking to a slow-witted child. His expression was furious.

"Who?" she questioned like an innocent child.

"You heard me, *Chanelle,* or are you gonna lie and say that you didn't? That's all you seem to be good for."

Chanelle was quiet as she tried to figure out how Trap knew about JaQuez. *How the hell did he know her real name? Could JaQuez be here in Atlanta? Did Trap run into him somewhere? Oh God. What if he brought JaQuez back here with him?*

"He's my ex-boyfriend," she admitted finally.

"Bitch, you better tell me the whole fuckin' truth! Did you murder that nigga?" Trap barked as he rushed towards her, snatching Chanelle up like a ragdoll. "Do you have the muthafuckin' police after yo' ass? I don't need this shit!"

Trap always thought that he was overly cautious about covering his tracks. His eyes stayed in the rear view mirror to ensure that he wasn't being followed and he never handled the drugs directly... not even keeping any at his house. Up until this point, he'd maintained the position of being untouchable. It was a well-known fact what he did for a living, despite the businesses that he'd opened to clean his dirty money. Even with that said, the FEDS were never able to get anything concrete on him.

But Chanelle could fuck that all up with her bullshit. The last thing he needed was extra heat on him due to something *she'd* done before they'd even met. If Trap had known then what he knew now, he would've left her ass stranded on the side of the road that day at the gas station. He would've kept driving. Fuck that chivalrous shit when you had females like her. Deceitful for no reason.

"No," Chanelle replied as her eyes welled up with tears. "I don't know about any police!"

"Well, they dropped by the strip club looking for you saying that you murdered some nigga named JaQuez!"

Chanelle looked at him confused. *I thought Loretta said he was alive? But if the police are looking for me, then he has to be dead... Right? Or is Loretta working with JaQuez?* Chanelle felt like her mother was behaving out of character and that explained everything! JaQuez may have been dead, but the bounty on her head was probably in still in effect. Either way, Chanelle had to get out of Atlanta. If the police could find her, then so could Rob. That was if she could make it out alive. Trap had a death grip on her and with the look on his face, he was liable to snap and do anything.

"Who told you this?" Chanelle inquired.

"Does it really fuckin' matter? The point is that you should've been the one to tell me this shit!" Trap yelled before shaking his head. "I can't believe you've been lyin' to me the whole time! You told me that your name was Princess. You told me you were a nurse. Now, I find out that you're a damn stripper in my own muthafuckin' club!" Trap held so much disappointment in his face. "I let your scandalous ass stay in my house! Drive my whip!" He removed his hands from her shoulders and replaced them tightly around her neck.

Damn, he owns Pretty Kitty, she thought, surprised that

he hadn't caught her before. Suddenly, Triniti's comments about Chanelle bringing extra heat from the police and her not going down for a body came to mind. Now, that comment made sense. *Maybe Triniti told him.* Chanelle wasn't sure if her theory was right, but if it was, she wondered who else Triniti could've told. *Dammit.* The only bright side was that Trap hadn't told the police that he knew where she was. Then again, with the murderous look in Trap's eyes, it seemed like her ending would be the same.

She would end up losing her life regardless.

"Let me explain," Chanelle rasped as she put her hands on top of his in an attempt to free herself from his vice-like grip.

"Bitch, it's a little late for that, don't you think? What the hell reason did you have to lie to me?" That was the piece of the puzzle that he couldn't understand. If she wasn't plotting on him, there was no reason why she couldn't have been straight up with him in the beginning.

Grudgingly he released his grip, allowing her the chance to state her case.

"I didn't kill, JaQuez!" Chanelle blurted out. For a moment she contemplated lying, but didn't know how much Trap really knew. She also didn't want to risk him snapping her neck off. "But a dude that I was with…he killed him."

"Why?" Trap prompted.

"Well, we robbed him," Chanelle started slowly before continuing to explain to him quickly what all transpired. "Me and this other guy." She felt no need to tell Trap that her ex had also been her co-conspirator. "But shit went wrong and he ended up shooting JaQuez. We got the money, but then that nigga two-timed me and left me stranded here without shit. That's what happened when you helped me out on the side of the road that day. He threw my shit out at the gas station and took everything."

"So, why did you rob that nigga anyway? You couldn't

just leave him?"

Chanelle shook her head with a frown. "You wouldn't understand. He had to pay for all the shit he did to me. I took years of abuse, infidelity." She ignored his disapproving glare. "Nigga, don't judge me! You don't know my struggle!"

At that moment, he was no better than JaQuez was in her eyes. Chanelle felt that he was taking this shit way too personal.

"Females are a trip," Trap observed.

In Trap's opinion, Chanelle was the worst type of female. To him, it didn't matter what the hell JaQuez had done to her. She didn't have to rob that nigga, much less kill him. Trap was certain that Chanelle had done things that she was leaving out. It always went that way. Women were quick to shout out a man's shortcomings, but not as forthcoming with their own. He was positive they'd both done their share of dirt.

"No, niggas are a trip," she corrected. "You don't know shit about me getting my ass kicked on more than one occasion, me losing my baby, or keeping a fucking STD!"

Chanelle was way past hysterical at that point. If it was one thing that she didn't tolerate, it was anyone acting as though *she* was in the wrong. She'd done what any woman in her situation would have, right?

"Shawty, you delusional. All that shit may have happened to you and I'm sorry you chose the wrong nigga, but your thought process is fucked up. That dude ain't hold a gun up to your head and tell you that you had to stay! I'm sure of that, especially if you had time to go fuck with another man and plot on his ass!" Trap threw his hands up in the air. "At any time you could've left JaQuez alone, but you chose not to. Just like a greedy, grimy ass bitch." Trap nodded his head knowingly. "And I bet you thought you was gonna rob me too, huh?"

"No!" Chanelle denied quickly. It wasn't a complete lie, but she would be damned if she told him the truth.

"I bet you would've told JaQuez the same thing." Trap couldn't believe that everything seemed to be falling apart at

the seams. Triniti had robbed him and now Chanelle was planning on it, too. He didn't care what she said.

"Listen, you gotta get the fuck out before I catch a murder charge," Trap told her. He wasn't sure why he was sparing
her life. She was the epitome of everything he hated, but he
couldn't bring himself to do it. *Just like I couldn't kill Triniti,* he
thought. *Damn, I'm gettin' soft.*

"I have something to tell you before I go," Chanelle
said, before taking a deep breath. "Ali was planning on setting
you up."

Trap's head was spinning. It seemed like everyone on his
camp was treacherous. Everyone seemed to be plotting against
him. Tupac had said it best when he proclaimed that it was him
against the world. It was the story of Trap's life.

Niggas always gotta get greedy, he thought. *Can't be
happy with the shit cuz they too busy jockin' the next nigga's
shit.* Trap didn't know why he didn't see it before. Ali had never
said anything out of the way to him, but after their last altercation about the stash house, he should've known better. Ali's attitude towards him ran deeper than just being yelled at over his
insubordination, it was months, probably years of envy.

Trap couldn't figure it out though. There had been plenty
of opportunities to rob him before, so why did Ali want to do it
now all of a sudden? There was something that Chanelle wasn't
telling him.

"He was or he is? And how the hell do you know about
it?" Then it dawned on him. "You was gonna help that nigga,
huh?" Trap asked flatly, fighting to compose himself. The more
he learned about Chanelle, the more he despised her. He
thought that Triniti had crossed the line, but Chanelle took it to
a new level.

"Ali told me that if I didn't help him that he was going
to tell you about me working at the strip club," she admitted
softly. She'd deliberatlly left out the part about Desmond. "But
I always planned on telling you. Regardless of how you feel

about me now, I couldn't do you like that after all that you've done for me."

Chanelle deserved another Academy Award for her latest performance. She sounded so sincere that she almost believed herself! In all honesty, she could give two fucks about Trap now. She was furious at his treatment of her. If it wasn't for the fact that she needed him to save her own ass, she wouldn't have said shit. *And to think I almost fell for this nigga!*

It didn't matter, Chanelle just needed Ali out of the way. No body, no murder was the name of the game. She knew that Trap would waste no time killing Ali and one loose end would be tied. The next was the money. One way or another, she was leaving with somebody's money in her pockets. *That nigga has a safe around here somewhere and I'm gonna find it if it's the last thing I do.*

"He's on his way now, but I have a plan," Chanelle informed.

$$\$$$

Come in through the back door. It's unlocked. Got him right where we need him. **Sent: 9:25p.m.**

Ali slid his phone into his back pocket with a smile after reading Chanelle's text. He hated that he was late, but there had been an accident slowing down traffic on the highway. He would've felt much better about catching Trap when he came home, but he couldn't be choosy at this point.

It is what it is, he thought before entering the backyard cautiously.

He didn't completely trust Chanelle but figured that she had sense enough to know not to fuck with him. He didn't really have access to Desmond's body anymore, but knew that she didn't know that. It had allowed him to get exactly what he wanted.

Trap.

All these years Ali had waited for the golden opportunity to take over Trap's position, and now he would finally be able to cash in on it. He couldn't hide how giddy he felt knowing that things were finally about to start looking up for him. He would finally have the respect, the power, and the money that he'd longed for since he was young.

Stealthily, Ali opened the French doors that connected the backyard to the oversized family room. He then surveyed his surroundings before coming inside. Everything was dark and the only sound that could be heard was Chanelle's sweet moans bouncing off the wall. Ali headed in the direction of the seductive sounds and found himself standing outside the door of a second floor bedroom. The couple sounded so caught up in their lovemaking Ali knew that they would have no idea what hit them. He'd give them both two shots to the dome.

Just as Ali started to open the door, he felt a bullet pierce his right hand, knocking his Desert Eagle from his grasp. A second bullet connected with his left leg, dropping him to the floor instantly.

"Aghh, w-what... the... fuck?" he cursed before using his free hand to twist the doorknob.

When he saw Chanelle on the bed alone, he knew she'd set him up. Still, Ali pulled himself into the room slowly attempting to put some distance between him and his shooter.

"Snake ass, nigga," Trap said as he stepped out of the shadows of the hallway. "I know I was feedin' you well! So why the fuck would you do some shit like this?"

"I don't wanna hear shit that you got to say. It won't change anything," Ali hissed before staring Trap in the eyes with a piercing glare. If he was gonna go out, it would be like a man. He wasn't about to beg, especially not this nigga.

Trap nodded. Ali knew how the game went. No matter what was said, no matter his logic or reasoning, it wouldn't change the fact that he was going to die tonight. "You right. It won't."

"Nigga, fuck you!" Ali spat rebelliously, raising his middle finger on his good hand. "See you in hell!"

With those last words, Trap sent a bullet directly through Ali's skull. Ali dropped to the floor with a loud thud, as his body propped against the slightly ajar door. Even then, Trap didn't stop until the clip was completely out of bullets. He hadn't meant to waste them all, but Ali's act of defiance angered him more than he thought it would. Trap couldn't understand how ungrateful niggas could be. He allowed them the opportunity to make more money than they ever could on their own, but their greed wouldn't allow them to be content with that.

Now Trap had to deal with Chanelle. While he initially was going to let her leave, he'd changed his mind. If she could turn on her ex boyfriend and Ali, regardless of her logic, she could turn on him. It was obvious that this bitch had loyalty to no one but herself.

He looked into the bedroom, but she was nowhere to be found. "Chanelle?" he called out. *I know this bitch ain't get ghost that fast.*

The sound of a gun's hammer being pulled back caught his attention.

"Looking for me?" she asked with a smirk.

Shit, Trap thought. *This bitch got me again!*

$TWENTY-FIVE

"Don't turn around, drop the motherfucking gun, and put your hands up," Chanelle ordered with Ali's gun in her grasp.

She'd wasted no time disappearing into the connecting bathroom while Trap and Ali faced off. The bathroom also connected to the hallway, giving her the opportunity to help herself to Ali's fallen weapon. Chanelle had played the fool before, and she would be damned if she let it happen again. She'd heard the contempt in Trap's voice earlier, and couldn't believe the way that he'd put his hands on her. The guilt that she had once felt about setting him up had completely vanished.

"Hurry up! Does it sound like I'm joking?" she barked, noticing that Trap was taking his time following her instructions.

"You sure you really want to do this?" he asked in such a way to insinuate that she would regret it.

"Baby, I've never been so sure. Just show me to the safe and empty it."

Trap laughed bitterly. "You fuckin', bitch." He shook his head, realizing the irony. "You doin' me just like you did that nigga, JaQuez, huh?"

"Didn't I say shut the fuck up?" She kept the gun trained on him. "Lead the way."

Chanelle smiled to herself. She was finally in control. Things were going to pan out the way it should have originally. She was going to get her money, she was going to make a smooth getaway, and she wasn't gonna be stopped this time. Her whole life depended on this going well. If Trap even moved so much of a muscle out of turn, she would make him look no better than Ali did.

"I don't keep money here," Trap lied, while trying to think of a way to get himself out of his current predicament.

He only kept about two hundred thousand dollars in his home. His major figures were safely tucked away in offshore accounts. He didn't believe in stashing too much cash at home, for reasons such as this. If the money was taken, he didn't suffer much of a substantial loss, but if he needed to go off on the run, it was more than enough to take care of his needs.

Regardless of that fact, he would be damned if he gave Chanelle any of his money. That statement was reevaluated when Chanelle let off a shot that connected with the top of his chest. She was sure that his collar bone had been immediately shattered on impact.

"Fuck!" Trap yelled in agony as his uninjured hand flew to cover his wound.

Blood immediately began to stain his white shirt and seep onto his fingertips. Her precise aim had him wondering if she'd lied about killing JaQuez. This definitely wasn't her first time handling a gun.

My finger slipped that time, but believe me, next time I'm aiming for your heart," Chanelle stated. "We can do this shit either one or two ways! Either you can give me the money and keep your life or you can play hard and die!"

Chanelle's nerves were on edge, if Trap didn't have any money there, her entire plan would be thrown out of whack.

"A'ight!" he shouted out quickly, fearful that she might release another round. "Follow me." He led her out of the room and she maintained a safe, small distance between the two of them. She was close enough to hit him at point blank range, but distant enough that he couldn't just turn around and snatch the gun from her.

"You really gonna do this shit, shawty?" Trap couldn't say that he was surprised, but he hated that he was going out like this. *Like a muthafuckin' pussy,* he thought. *This bitch better hope she kills me.*

"I thought that much was understood," she replied smartly. "I need this money more than you know." Her voice trailed off before she went back into pitbull in a skirt mode. "So hurry the fuck up!"

Trap trudged down the stairs, leading her to the coat closet near the front door. "It's in there. Just turn on the light switch so you can see." Blood continued to gush from his chest.

"You do it!" Chanelle ordered. *What if this nigga got this shit booby-trapped?* The thought was silly, but she also knew that Trap didn't seem like the type to surrender so easily. She was sure that he had something up his sleeve. *If he does, I swear I won't think twice about murking his ass!*

"Shit," Trap hissed weakly as he removed his good hand from his injury and flipped the switch.

"Move," Chanelle demanded, nudging him roughly with the gun to make a point.

Trap did as he was told and stood off to the side while she peered inside. Chanelle darted her eyes back and forth quickly, from Trap to the contents of the closet. She was expecting some type of safe or secret compartment, but noticed nothing more than a couple of books stacked on one corner, a teddy bear, an umbrella, and about a dozen heavy coats.

"So, where is it? Is the safe behind the bear?" she asked with her face distorted in confusion. The bear was huge, nearly the size of a child, clutching a pink heart reading, 'I Love You'.

"Nah. Inside the teddy bear," he replied. "I got some in there and hidden in the books."

No wonder I could never find this shit. Here I was look-

ing for a damn safe, and the money was hidden in a fucking bear. "How much?" Chanelle wondered curiously.

"About two hundred thou," Trap informed.

He leaned his body against the wall, looking down at the floor. His face seemed to be paling and his once rich, caramel colored skin looked more like a pale yellow. He was losing a lot of blood and wasn't sure how much longer he could hold up, both literally and figuratively. He allowed his body to slide to the floor, too tired to stand up.

"Good enough." Chanelle's eyes brightened with greed. She'd been expecting more, especially after the huge payday she would've collected off JaQuez. Still, it was better than the eight thousand she had saved and definitely better than nothing!

Getting the bear and the books would be risky though. Chanelle remembered one of the other reasons she'd needed Desmond to help her rob JaQuez. Carrying the teddy bear would require the use of both of her hands and while Trap looked pretty defenseless, she'd seen plenty men do desperate things when their life was in danger. All it would take was her turning her eyes for one second and he would strike.

I'm just gonna have to kill this nigga. Ain't no sense in dragging the shit out. I need this money and I'll be damned if I fuck this shit up by tryna spare his life. If the tables were turned he wouldn't do that shit for me, Chanelle thought, quickly adjusting her attention back on Trap.

"Trap?" she called out in surprise.

Chanelle studied him briefly from where she stood, satisfied that he was beyond weak and barely conscious. With his head hung low, Trap's hand was no longer cradling his wound, but turned upwards. Wet blood covered his palm.

This couldn't have gotten any better.

Chanelle didn't feel an ounce of remorse, if anything she felt relieved that she didn't have to actually kill him. Smiling crookedly, she tugged on the teddy bear roughly, causing it to fall to the floor with a soft thud. She looked back at Trap who was still in his current position and breathing at a slower pace.

Satisfied, Chanelle placed her gun on the shelf and used her newly free hands to grab the small stack of books. Pulling back the cover on one of the hardbacks, she smiled after noticing the stacks of hundred dollar bills planted inside. The pages had been carved out in the middle and replaced with money, which reminded her of something out of a movie.

Quickly, Chanelle grabbed a gym bag that was on the floor and removed all the money from the books before placing the cash inside. After grabbing the gun, she placed the bag over her shoulder and proceeded to drag the teddy bear by its long arm. The bear seemed to weigh almost the same amount as a child. *Maybe it's more money in here than he let on.* Either way, she wasn't complaining. Chanelle was doing her best not to make a second trip. Her eyes watched Trap the entire time up until she disappeared into the kitchen.

Chanelle moved as fast as she could, heading towards the garage. She planned on making a getaway with his Benz since she still had the keys. She let go of the bear to grab her purse and the keys before continuing out of the door.

She pressed her hand against the garage door opener and unlocked the passenger door, tossing her valuables into the front seat. Tears lined her eyes as she thought of everything that would be possible with this money. She could get the hell out of Atlanta, open her boutique, and buy her a new whip. Life was finally looking up for her.

Chanelle had just gotten into the car and cranked the ignition when she saw the door leading to the garage crack open.

Her eyes widened with shock to see Trap standing there. His body rested against the door frame and a gun was in his hand. Waiting for Chanelle to exit the room had been excruciatingly painful, but necessary. There were guns stashed inside each pocket of the coats in the closet and Trap wasted no time helping himself to one. Hearing the kitchen door close had been his signal.

Trap knew he had to hurry if he wanted to get to her in time, but his injury slowed him down. *I'm gonna kill this bitch if it's the last thing I do,* he thought, taking aim at the car.

Suddenly, he sent a bullet flying through the windshield. The glass cracked and the bullet pushed through, luckily missing her and landing in the backseat similar to a pin in a pincushion.

"Argh!!" Chanelle screamed in panic as the gunshots continued to go off. Without waiting for the garage to open completely, Chanelle threw the car into reverse and slammed on the gas.

The sound of sirens filling the air should've been enough to deter Trap, but he continued to cry out obscenities and fire shots wildly in her direction. Chanelle ducked down, causing the car to swerve wildly down the long driveway. She could feel one side of the car drop and realized that he'd flattened one of her tires.

"Dammit!" she yelled before finally thinking to look at the rear vision cameras. She was too late to avoid the brick mailbox and crashed into it loudly before changing gears.

As Chanelle sat up, she noticed Trap coming toward her. He stood less than three feet away from her with his gun raised. Without thinking, she quickly pressed the gas but in her panic, she didn't realize the way the steering wheel had been turned. Before he could release the trigger, she plowed the car directly into him.

Fuck! Tears stained her cheeks as she quickly backed out of the driveway and skidded out of the yard just as the sirens got louder.

The car wobbled down the street, but it wasn't fast enough to evade the police. The red and blue lights illuminated her rearview mirror.

Oh my God, I'm going to jail.

$TWENTY-SIX

"Just listen to me," Chanelle pleaded as she found her-self shaking slightly. "I really need you."

Chanelle sat in the parking lot of a Subway on Buford Highway. She hadn't gotten very far from Trap's house, only about one mile, due to her blown out tire. Even when she was only going about twenty-five mph, she could feel the car wob-bling. Traffic raced around her and the last thing she wanted was to break down in the middle of the road. On top of that, it was incredibly hard to see through the cracked windshield. With the car partially riddled with bullet holes, she was drawing a lot of unwanted attention.

An ambulance whirled through traffic with its horn blar-ing and for a moment Chanelle wondered if Trap was the pas-senger that they were rushing to the hospital. She had gotten lucky when the police cars stopped in front of Trap's house, to-tally overlooking her ambling down the street. She could only count her blessings for that.

Still, the image of Trap laying on the ground with a pool of blood underneath him appeared before her each time she blinked her eyes. The sirens still played loudly in her ears even though she could no longer see anything. Chanelle wasn't sure if it was her imagination or if they were just this close.

"I really needed you, too," A'mya reminded her, finally breaking the silence between them.

"Listen, I'm really sorry that I didn't show up that day, but I promise, I'll tell you everything when you get here. This is really an emergency! I need you to take me to the airport, so I can rent a car ASAP!" Chanelle pleaded.

She didn't want to call A'mya for a favor, especially not after the way that she'd failed to be there for her friend, but her options were slim. Chanelle could've easily called a taxi to come pick her up, but didn't feel comfortable riding with that much money. She needed someone that she could trust.

A'mya sighed and rolled her eyes. "You are so self-absorbed, Chanelle. We've been on the phone for almost five minutes and you still haven't asked me if I was doing okay. If my baby was okay. The minute I pick up the phone it's been all about you, as usual," she said bitterly, obviously annoyed at her friend's lack of concern for her own predicament.

"Oh my God, A'mya. I'm so sorry," Chanelle apologized. "Is the baby okay? Did you ever get to the hospital?"

"Yeah. The doctor said that I had a urinary tract infection and that caused the bleeding. But I had to call Mike and I really didn't want to tell him about the baby," she said in a hushed whisper, hoping that he wasn't eavesdropping. "He says that I have to get an abortion though if I want to be with him. My appointment is tomorrow."

"What? Why are you with him if he thinks that way? Isn't it…" Chanelle came to a halt. She knew right now wasn't the time for a lecture. A'mya was already pissed and she desperately needed a ride. "Look, let's just talk when you get here, okay? I don't have a lot of time."

"Where are you?" A'mya asked curiously, seeming to momentarily shift her anger to the side.

"I'm in the parking lot of a Subway on Buford Highway. There's a Papa John's next to it."

"Okay. I know where you're at. I'm on my way."

Chanelle let out a sigh of relief as she disconnected the call. If there was one person that she could always count on to be there for her, it was A'mya. *And I've paid her back by being a really shitty friend,* Chanelle thought, hating that she hadn't been there for A'mya that day. Although it wasn't entirely her fault, she kept feeling that she could've done something differently. *Oh well. When I tell her what happened, she should understand. That was a damn life or death situation!*

Chanelle had to figure out what to do. With all the money, she couldn't get on a flight with alerting TSA, but with most of the rental car places at the airport open twenty-four hours, she could at least rent a car.

"It only takes about two hours to get to Birmingham, so I'll drive there and get a hotel. Then tomorrow morning, I can keep driving towards Houston."

Chanelle figured that Texas would be as good a place to start over as any. She would be over seven hundred miles away from Atlanta, and over a thousand miles from Raleigh. *Them muthafuckas won't find me there. And this time I'm not telling* anyone *where I'm going.*

Her mind went back to her recent conversations with both Loretta and Trap. Their stories weren't matching up. Was JaQuez really alive like Loretta claimed? Or was he dead and she was just working with Rob?

Chanelle kept thinking over and over again why she'd agreed for Loretta to come to Atlanta if she still had doubts about her mother's involvement. Loretta once again offered to give Chanelle money to get out of town, and after begging nonstop, Chanelle finally accepted her help, even though now, she didn't need it. What made things even more odd was the fact that Loretta insisted that she take a last minute flight to Atlanta and deliver the cash personally. At the moment it all sounded good so Chanelle agreed, but now she couldn't help but think it this was another ploy to get at her.

"And my dumb ass was about to walk right into it," Chanelle said.

Whether or not JaQuez was dead or alive, it didn't stop the bounty that was still on Chanelle's head and her money-grubbing mother would do anything for the almighty dollar. She'd witnessed it several times growing up. Money came before Chanelle in every scenario. Loretta was the epitome of greed.

"Speak of the devil," Chanelle muttered, seeing Loretta's name pop up on her screen as soon as the phone rang. "Hello?"

"Okay, I couldn't get a flight out tonight, but I got one for the first thing tomorrow morning at six. We should get to Atlanta around 7:20," Loretta updated. "I hope that's okay. I know I've changed the plans a little bit."

"Who's 'we'?"

"Me and the other passengers. Who else do you think?" Loretta snapped. "Are you still gonna meet me at the Hyatt Place by the airport?"

"I've been thinking. Why don't you just send the money? You really don't have to fly all the way out here."

Loretta sighed. "I know that but…you're never coming back to Raleigh, right?"

"You got that right," she stated proudly.

"Yeah, well." Loretta's voice lowered a few decibels. "I guess I just wanted to see my daughter one last time."

Chanelle laughed, unable to hold it in. Loretta had tried to sound sincere, but she wasn't falling for the okey doke. "One last time before you put Rob on me, right?"

"What the hell are you talking about? I thought we cleared that up."

"JaQuez is dead, Loretta," Chanelle said matter-of-factly.

"Where the hell did you get that from? Somebody's facts are fucked up."

"Nah. The only person with fucked up facts is you! The

police are looking for me, Loretta! They say I killed JaQuez!"

Loretta was quiet for a few seconds before finally speaking up. "Chanelle, you gotta believe me I…"

Click.

Chanelle hung up mid-sentence. She wasn't about to waste her battery arguing over an unlikely point. "I'll be damned if I get caught up in some dumb shit again." She shook her head thinking about how she could've possibly been murdered at the Hyatt Place.

"I wouldn't have even seen it coming either."

Chanelle glanced at the time on her phone as she continued to ponder. *This can't be life*, she thought before resting her head against the window.

Minutes later, Chanelle jumped, startled after hearing someone tap on the window. She turned her head and looked at A'mya with a smile before opening the door.

"Hey, girl! What the hell took you so long? For a second I thought you were gonna let me die out here," Chanelle joked in a weak attempt to mask her nervousness.

"What the hell happened to the car?" A'mya asked with awe as she examined the Benz. "Were you in an accident?" When she took a peek at the windshield her eyes grew bigger than golfballs. "Is somebody after you? What happened?"

"I'll tell you when we get on the road." Chanelle dragged the teddy bear from the front seat and crammed it into the back of A'mya's busted Honda. After grabbing the gym bag and her purse, she cleared everything out of Trap's car.

"You're just gonna leave it here? Is that a good idea?"

Chanelle shrugged her shoulders. "Probably not, but what other choice do I have?"

"Okay…" To A'mya it looked like Chanelle was in a lot of shit. She couldn't wait until her friend filled her in with the juicy details. A'mya couldn't pull out of the parking lot fast enough. "So what happened?" she asked eagerly.

"Girl, it's such a long story. But before we get into it, I

wanna know if you're really gonna get the abortion."

"Yeah," A'mya replied somberly.

"I can't believe that you're just gonna do what that nigga tells you." Talking about A'mya's problems were much easier than discussing her own. It was a welcomed distraction.

"It's not like you thought I should keep it anyway," A'mya retorted.

"That's true, but you should do things because you want to. Not because of a man that you've known for a short while."

"Well, he's the one taking care of me now. Hell, you would like him. He has money!"

Then why are you still driving this raggedy ass shit, and why did that nigga borrow your *car?* The questions were on the tip of Chanelle's tongue, but she repressed it.

"Let's be real, Chanelle, do you really think that Mike would want me and a baby that isn't his? I didn't even want him to know that I was pregnant! I wanted him to love me first and then he might be up to... you know, accepting the both of us," she added quietly.

Chanelle nodded. "I guess you're right. Do you, girl. If you like it, I love it." She tried to sound happy, but her voice still came out shaky.

When a police car whizzed past them, Chanelle ducked down in her seat, wishing that A'mya would drive faster. Against her will, her whole body started to tremble and to say that her nerves were on edge was an understatement. Still, the more distant they got from Trap's side of town, the more she could relax. But that wasn't by much.

"What the hell is wrong with you? And why is that car all messed up? Did you and Trap get into it?" A'mya fired off, looking over at her friend and noticing her strange demeanor.

"Trap is dead, I guess. I uh…" Chanelle struggled to find the words, not knowing whether or not she could trust A'mya with the information. She was the goody goody type. Bigger than that, she was super judgmental. "Some niggas robbed us and killed him, but I managed to get away."

A'mya looked at her skeptically. "Oh my God, are you serious? So, that's why you're so jumpy."

Chanelle only nodded.

"Are you okay?"

Chanelle nodded again. "I'll live."

"Do you wanna go to the police?"

"Hell no, then they might think I had something to do with it."

"I guess you're right. I can't believe this."

"Me either."

"So, what's up with the bear?" A'mya questioned.

"It was already in the car."

"I don't get it, Chanelle. I know there's something you're not telling me and I don't know why you always leave me in the dark about things. First that mess with you and JaQuez and now this! If it was a robbery, why do you wanna go to the airport? Are you in that much fear for your life?"

A'mya didn't even have to hear Chanelle's response to know that she was right. The evidence was all over her face. She'd noticed the faint red fingerprints around her neck and light blood staining her jeans.

"Trust me, A'mya, you wouldn't understand. I've been through so much shit." Chanelle leaned her head against the cloth seat.

"Maybe I could understand if you would talk to me." A'mya pursed her lips and glared in Chanelle's direction, but remained quiet with her hand resting on her forehead. "Fine but…"

Before A'mya could finish her sentence, the car groaned slightly, slowing down. She looked down, noticing that the car had gone into Neutral. "Dammit. I'm so tired of this car!" She banged her hands against the steering wheel.

"What's the problem?" Chanelle asked urgently.

"I think the clutch is going out. We gotta get to my

house so we can get Mike's car. There's no way Bessie will make it and I know you're not trying to end up on the side of the road."

"You're damn right."

"You'll like his car," A'mya brightened. "It's a Lexus."

"Oh yeah? I didn't know he had a car," Chanelle responded.

"Yup. He does," A'mya answered proudly. "He lets me borrow it sometimes. Luckily, we're not too far from the house."

The ride to A'mya's new place seemed to take forever, but Chanelle had never been so relieved when they turned on Edwards Drive in front of a small, semi-dilapidated house. It was dark so she couldn't see much, but could make out the older, brick house with blue-colored shutters. One of the windows was boarded up while the other was lit up from the lights in the house.

Damn, is this it? A'mya is still is doing bad. I think the apartment on Conley was better than this. I'll give her a couple stacks before I go. Maybe she can get a new car or find a new place.

A'mya could see the discontent on Chanelle's face and spoke up quickly. "Yes, yes, I know that this is beneath you and all that, but it's mine. The rent is cheap and it's nicer inside than outside. Mike really hooked the place up. Actually, come in really quick so you can meet him."

"Oh, no A'mya. I'm really in a rush. I just wanna get to the airport. I'll wait out here."

"Please," A'mya begged. "I don't want him thinking that I'm going off to see some other dude. He can be so jealous sometimes. I'm always talking about you anyway, so now he'll know what you look like."

Chanelle sighed. She didn't really want to but what would it hurt? She'd let A'mya down so many times before and it was the least that she could do after all she'd done for her.

"Okay, okay. Really quick."

"I think you'll like him," A'mya chattered on excitedly as she grabbed Chanelle's hand, mimicking a mother pulling her toddler along. She unlocked the door before stepping inside.

Chanelle frowned as she noticed a roach scurry across the almost bare room. It opened up to a dining room void of any furniture. The house had an open floorplan so she could see the kitchen, dining room, and the den all from where she stood in the small foyer. A hallway was to the left of her, but she couldn't see the end of it.

The back of the sofa faced Chanelle's direction so she wasn't able to steal a peek at Mike, but got more than a good look at the huge 50' TV. She wanted to panic when she saw that the Fox 5 News was on.

"Good evening, everybody, I'm Tom Haynes. Tonight a man was found murdered in the driveway of his home in Buckhead." The scene cut to a shot of Trap's driveway, now empty, but roped off. The familiar sounds of sirens filled her ears and several dozen police cars and an ambulance were parked out front. "Authorities say that he appeared to have been run over, as well as sustaining a bulletwound to the upper portion of his chest. The victim's name has not yet been released until the family is notified. They are also investigating…"

"Don't be rude. Say 'hello'," A'mya chastised Mike as she turned the TV off.

Chanelle was pissed that A'mya had turned off the TV. She was curious to hear about what else the authorities knew, and worried at the same time that they would some how find her responsible.

I need to get the fuck out of Atlanta. "Are you ready?" she asked A'mya.

Suddenly, Mike turned around to face Chanelle with a sinister grin. "What's up, Cha? Long time no see."

It was as if Chanelle had seen a ghost as her eyes increased three times from their normal size. She couldn't believe it. The loud thump of her chest echoed so loudly, she knew everybody in the room could hear it.

"Ja-JaQuez?" Chanelle stuttered.

"Who the fuck else?" he snarled. "I been dreamin' of the look on your face every fuckin' day since that shit wen't down."

Chanelle looked from A'mya to JaQuez and shook her head. *I must be dreaming. This shit can't be real.* She also wasn't gonna stand there and try to figure it out. Turning around sharply, Chanelle almost made it to the door to run outside, but it opened before she could touch the handle.

Rob appeared before her, blocking her exit. "Where the hell you think you're going? I told you I was gonna find you, bitch."

$TWENTY-SEVEN

I can't believe this is really happening, Chanelle thought as she closed her eyes together tightly. But when she opened her eyes, Rob was still standing there next to JaQuez. Menacing looks were on their faces and she instantly feared for her life. She knew that there was no way her life would be spared.

"What the fuck you closin' your eyes for?" JaQuez taunted with a laugh as he closed the space between them. "I assure you that this shit ain't a dream, bitch, but you'll be going to sleep soon enough." He drew his arm back and everything went black for her.

"Wake the fuck up, bitch!" JaQuez shouted several minutes later.

Chanelle's eye opened to see him only a couple centimeters away from her face. She immediately began to panic as she felt one of her eyes swollen shut.

"Faggh yugh!" she tried to speak, but it came out muffled due to a dirty sock that had been stuffed into her mouth.

She was lying sideways on the floor with her wrists bound tightly behind her. Another rope was tied around her waist and lower arms, ensuring that she wouldn't be unable to get herself out of this one. Her shoulders hunched over uncomfortably due to her position and her legs were also secured with rope.

Chanelle shook her head intensely. She couldn't believe the way things had panned out. *This nigga is really alive...* The realization that Loretta had been telling the truth all along hit her in the face like a ton of bricks. *So Loretta* wasn't *trying to set me up.*

"Y'all should've killed me, bitch," JaQuez spat venomously.

I fucked up big time.

JaQuez nodded his head as he could read her facial expression. "Yeah. You fucked up, but I ain't trippin'. I'm gonna enjoy watchin' you die." He removed the sock from her mouth. "And I'm gonna enjoy hearin' you scream, too."

Chanelle's voice broke as she became overwhelmed with tears. "I watched Desmond shoot you! You should've died!"

She could still see the incident as though it was happening again, right before her eyes. She'd had several dreams about it since the incident, so it came as no surprise.

"I probably would have if Rob hadn't stopped by the house," JaQuez reflected. "And lucky me, that pussy ass nigga you got to help you didn't hit anything vital."

The bullet just passed through the muscles surrounding his abdomen, and never entered the true abdominal cavity. If Desmond had been better about his aim, he could've hit a major organ like his liver or kidneys, killing him instantly.

JaQuez smiled at Chanelle's despair. "All they had to do was clean and sew a nigga up," he said, shrugging it off. "And now here I am. I almost feel like 50 Cent out this muthafucka," he joked. "Any more questions?" He was obviously getting a kick out of everything, meanwhile Rob stood to the side with a bored expression.

"But the police said I killed you!" Chanelle protested.

"Did that bitch, Triniti, tell you that?" Rob laughed widely. "Damn, I didn't think that shit was gonna work, but I guess it did. Your girl was the one who told me and JaQuez to go in the club actin' like the police. She put us up to that; made us fake cards and everything." He nodded his head in A'mya's direction.

"A'mya! You fucking, bitch!" Chanelle screamed. She'd been so caught up in the fact that JaQuez was alive, she'd overlooked the reason she was there in the first place. *And I trusted that scandalous, bitch.* "How the hell could you do this to me? I thought we were friends!"

"I'm sorry," A'mya uttered simply.

I can't believe her miserable ass sold me out to these niggas! How? Why? There were so many things that Chanelle wanted to know, but what difference would it make? Knowing wouldn't change anything. The end result would be the same…her death.

"A'mya, bring me the black bag in the bedroom," Rob commanded.

She nodded her head before rushing off like some type of lapdog.

"Now, where the fuck is my money?" JaQuez growled, getting to the point.

He was going to torture her until she begged for death, but needed to know about his money first. He'd gotten his bricks of cocaine on consignment and owed the Colombians a shitload of money. When Chanelle and Desmond had robbed him, they had taken literally all that he had to his name. It was imperative that JaQuez recovered all if not, most of his funds because his life was on the line too.

"It's gone," she squeaked.

"Bitch, you spent all my money?" JaQuez shook his head with anger. "I can't believe this shit." Reaching for her neck, he pulled Chanelle up from her position on the floor and raised her up into the air. "Don't play with me!"

His grasp tightened and he spoke, but Chanelle couldn't focus. She felt lightheaded and her vision had become blurry. She desperaty wanted to fight back, but it was impossible. Even if she could have, she was too weak.

Just as she felt herself about to pass out, JaQuez slammed her down to the floor. Chanelle couldn't catch her breath as she felt the wind being knocked out of her once again.

"This bitch is lying," Rob spoke confidently. "There ain't no damn way she ain't got it."

Chanelle wheezed for a bit before finally speaking up in a raspy voice. "Do you think I would've stayed with A'mya if I had money?" There was no way she was going to tell them about the money in the car. Sure, they'd probably discover it eventually, but it wasn't like her life would be spared if she shared the information. *Fuck these niggas. It's over.*

Rob looked at her skeptically. "Bitch, quit lyin' or it's only gonna drag this shit out more."

"As a matter of fact," JaQuez grinned devilishly. "I got some shit perfect for this." He walked to the back door, which was located in the corner of the small den. JaQuez stuck his body halfway out of the door and bent down, when he returned to his place in front of Chanelle, he was holding a thick, rusted, brown steel chain.

Chanelle's left eye grew wide. She'd endured a lot from being with JaQuez, and was no stranger to his punishment, but this didn't look good. "Please don't!" she begged in-between her sobs. "That nigga, Desmond, stole it all! I swear!"

JaQuez wasn't sure if she was lying or not, but he didn't care. That didn't excuse the penalty she had to endure for crossing him in the first place. He wrapped a piece around his fist and and swung the chain down on her roughly. Within moments, her screams bounced off the walls, but they only seemed to encourage him to hit her harder.

"Bitch… do you… realize… how much… shit you… got us in?" JaQuez asked each time he swung the chain down, not caring where it landed.

Chanelle's body felt like it was on fire each time he broke her skin. She couldn't do anything but scream helplessly. She couldn't believe that her life was going to end like this.

I don't deserve this shit, she thought.

"JaQuez, please!" Chanelle screamed.

"Shut the fuck up!" JaQuez's chest heaved in and out as he finally stopped and took a breath. He nodded his head towards Rob. "Your turn." He took a few steps back, handed the chain to his partner-in-crime, then grabbed his side. "This gunshot wound shit slowin' a nigga down."

"Shit, you ain't gotta tell me twice," Rob assured. He'd been waiting for this moment. For a second he thought that JaQuez was going to keep it all to himself.

Rob took the chain and wrapped a section around his hand, but then started to unbuckle his belt. "Hold up. I gotta do this first."

His smile sent chills up Chanelle's spine. She felt like he had it out for her more than JaQuez did. It was just the type of nigga he was. That kind of shit turned him on.

Oh my God... Is he about to rape me? She thought in panic. The look on his face didn't help to ease her fears. Chanelle looked over at JaQuez, but he peered on expectantly with a smile.

"Nah. It ain't what you think," Rob said to her finally, enjoying the cringing expression on her face. When he pulled his dick out of his boxers, releasing a stream of pee, both men laughed harshly.

"Ahhh!!" Chanelle shrieked as she struggled to wiggle. The hot urine stung like acid on her wounds. Some found its way to her lips, but she couldn't stop screaming. She just wanted to die.

POP!

Chanelle hadn't seen the gun, but she'd heard it even though the sound wasn't as loud as she was accustomed to. Undoubtedly due to the usage of a silencer. She waited to feel the sting of a bullet entering her skin, but didn't feel anything. At that moment, she opened her eyes to see JaQuez lying face down on the floor from a gunshot wound to the head.

Rob spun around to face the hallway. "A'mya, what the fuck are you…"

POP!

Before he could finish his sentence, she'd put a bullet into his chest.

POP!

A'mya let off another for good measure. She definitely didn't want anyone miraculously surviving. One to the heart would ensure that that didn't happen.

"A'mya!" Chanelle cried, wondering if she'd pegged her friend all wrong.

She used the term, friend loosely when speaking on A'mya, but at that moment, she was just happy that the beatings had stopped. She figured that she had a better chance of living if it was up to A'mya. Surely there was some sort of explanation for this. Things couldn't be as they seemed, right?

"Ssh, ssh. Calm down," A'mya soothed her as she walked closer. Her gun was still affixed firmly in her hand and stepped over Rob and JaQuez's bodies to kneel close to where Chanelle laid on the floor.

Tears ran down Chanelle's eyes. It was a mixture of re-lief and pain. "Why did you set me up? How could you let them do this to me?"

"I'm so sorry, but I had to. They blackmailed me," A'mya said softly.

"What? How?" Chanelle asked curiously, wondering how their encounter came about.

"I had no choice. Not when I found out about the money they were offering for you." Then her face contorted into a cruel expression, completely shedding her previous and usual demeanor.

She looked at Chanelle with a callous expression and let out a cackle. "When your cousin, Mimi, called me up telling me what happened in Raleigh, I knew some shit was up. I knew it was more to the story than you were telling me! We were supposed to be friends, but you couldn't even confide in me? Bitch, I gave you a place to live. I looked out for you when nobody else would! But how did you pay me back? You never helped out with the bills even though you were making more than I was. You always were a selfish bitch that put herself first!"

That damn Mimi, Chanelle thought. She knew that her cousin had probably just been fishing for more gossip and to find her whereabouts, but dreadfully needed to know when to keep her mouth shut.

"So, I got Rob's number, and told him where you were. If there was a bounty, I wanted to collect on it. What, do you think I wanna be broke forever?" A'mya shook her head before continuing. "Nah. You couldn't have thought that by the way you were always flaunting your fly shit in my face. You always thought you were better than me, Chanelle."

"No, I didn't," Chanelle spoke calmly in an attempt to change A'mya's mind. *She's my last chance.* "I wanted better for you. I was always…"

"Putting me down!" A'mya finished for her with tears in her eyes. She hated the way her friend always made her feel. It had truly fucked up her self-esteem and A'mya honestly believed that Chanelle was the cause of most of her problems. "You talked about my car, my weight, my job, everything! Bitch, who the fuck are you? Like your life was so put together? At least everything I had was mine! I paid for it on my own! It wasn't much, but it was mine!" A'mya yelled.

Chanelle could hear the pain in her voice.

"But I had to admit, when you came to Atlanta, I was reminded of all the shit that I didn't have. All the shit that I never even knew I wanted. Those damn expensive ass shoes, body like a model, or should I say a stripper?" A'mya smirked. "JaQuez was a good ass man, but you didn't know how to treat him! You always snagged the ballers while I snagged the losers!"

"A'mya, you don't know shit about JaQuez. He wasn't a

good dude! And if you feel that way, then why did you kill him?"

"The same reason I killed Rallo," she replied nonchalantly. "Nothing personal, but I didn't wanna share that money and now I don't have to."

Chanelle's eyes increased.

"I let Rallo in on the plan, but changed my mind after that nigga kept bragging about what he was gonna do with the money once we got it. He even had the nerve to call his fucking bookie, telling him he had the money to pay back his debt. I mean he was acting like it was his fucking idea," she spat. "Plus, I saw the way that nigga always looked at you. He always told me that I had to lose weight to be more like you. Do you know how humiliating that was?"

"There is no money," Chanelle told her flatly. "You know the story! Desmond stole it!"

"Bitch, tell me another lie!" A'mya shouted. "I'm far from stupid even though you never seemed to notice. It doesn't take a rocket scientist to figure out that there's something fishy about that shit you lugged with you. That gym bag and that big ass bear looked pretty damn suspect! Just to be sure I went outside and checked, and you know what? I was right!"

Chanelle shook her head. Her former friend had gone over the deep end. "A'mya, please don't do this. Take the money if you want, but please don't kill me. You got what you wanted, so just leave me alone."

"I can't do that. That was your mistake when you ended up with Rob and JaQuez on your ass. You turned on that nigga, Trap too, right?" A'mya narrowed her eyes at Chanelle. "I bet you murdered him, too. That was him on the news, wasn't it?"

Chanelle was quiet.

"Yeah, bitch. I know you had something to do with that shit."

"You always said that I should be more like you and now I am." A'mya smiled crookedly. "Well, I gotta be leaving now." She disappeared down the short hallway before coming back with a black bag over her shoulder and a gas can in her hand.

Chanelle's eyes widened as she heard crackling coming from the back and the unmistakable smell of fire.

"I've already done the back rooms, but…" A'mya circled around Chanelle, dousing the furniture with the contents of the can. "Don't worry. You'll die from smoke inhalation before the fire ever reaches you."

"A'mya! A'mya!" Chanelle screamed as she watched her final means of escape exit through the door without so much as a second glance. She could see the flames making their way to the den and while they weren't completely close yet, she could feel the heat as though she was standing next to an opened oven.

"The Lord is my Shepherd, I shall not want," Chanelle's voice cracked as she began the 23rd Psalm. She'd never been much of a spiritual person before, but now seemed like the appropriate time to send a prayer up to Him. She tried to finish, but the only thing that came out of her mouth were her coughs.

A'mya's words echoed in her mind '*You'll die from smoke inhalation before the fire ever reaches you*'.

She was right, Chanelle thought as she took her last breath.

$$$$$$$$$$$$$$$$$$$$$$$$

"And I'm on the money mission, nobody can stop me," A'mya sang along with the rapper, Cash Out as she cruised down 285 in JaQuez's rented Lexus.

She wasn't sure of where she wanted to go yet, but she knew that the possibilities were endless. She could finally live the life that she'd envisioned. Just her and well… She was alone. There was no baby; it was just something that she'd made up as an excuse for her weight gain and a desperate attempt to keep Rallo in her life.

Fuck him, she thought. A'mya didn't want to think about men for a long time. For now, she was seeing money, making love to the money, and engaged to money. "Got a condo 'round my neck, boy, I'm cashin' out!"

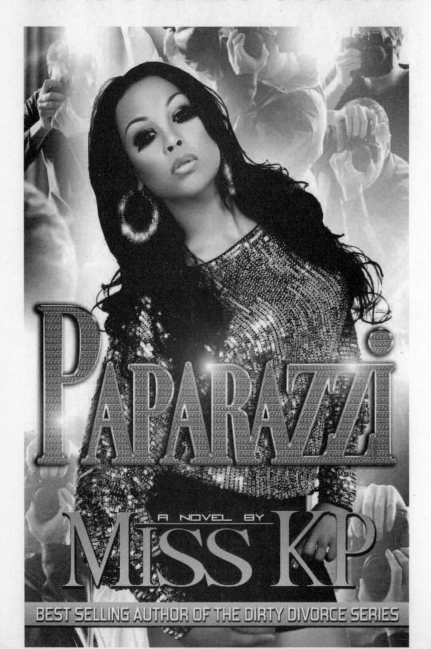

In Stores Now!!

PAPARAZZI

A NOVEL BY MISS KP

BEST SELLING AUTHOR OF THE DIRTY DIVORCE SERIES

LCB BOOK TITLES

See More Titles At
www.lifechangingbooks.net

ORDER FORM

MAIL TO:
PO Box 423
Brandywine, MD 20613
301-362-6508

FAX TO:
301-579-9913

Ship to:

Address:

Date: Phone:

Email:

City & State: Zip:

Make all money orders and cashiers checks payable to: **Life Changing Books**

Qty.	ISBN	Title	Release Date	Price
	0-9741394-2-4	Bruised by Azarel	Jul-05	$ 15.00
	0-9741394-7-5	Bruised 2: The Ultimate Revenge by Azarel	Oct-06	$ 15.00
	0-9741394-3-2	Secrets of a Housewife by J. Tremble	Feb-06	$ 15.00
	0-9741394-6-7	The Millionaire Mistress by Tiphani	Nov-06	$ 15.00
	1-934230-99-5	More Secrets More Lies by J. Tremble	Feb-07	$ 15.00
	1-934230-95-2	A Private Affair by Mike Warren	May-07	$ 15.00
	1-934230-96-0	Flexin & Sexin Volume 1	Jun-07	$ 15.00
	1-934230-89-8	Still a Mistress by Tiphani	Nov-07	$ 15.00
	1-934230-91-X	Daddy's House by Azarel	Nov-07	$ 15.00
	1-934230-88-X	Naughty Little Angel by J. Tremble	Feb-08	$ 15.00
	1-934230820	Rich Girls by Kendall Banks	Oct-08	$ 15.00
	1-934230839	Expensive Taste by Tiphani	Nov-08	$ 15.00
	1-934230782	Brooklyn Brothel by C. Stecko	Jan-09	$ 15.00
	1-934230669	Good Girl Gone bad by Danette Majette	Mar-09	$ 15.00
	1-934230804	From Hood to Hollywood by Sasha Raye	Mar-09	$ 15.00
	1-934230707	Sweet Swagger by Mike Warren	Jun-09	$ 15.00
	1-934230677	Carbon Copy by Azarel	Jul-09	$ 15.00
	1-934230723	Millionaire Mistress 3 by Tiphani	Nov-09	$ 15.00
	1-934230715	A Woman Scorned by Ericka Williams	Nov-09	$ 15.00
	1-934230685	My Man Her Son by J. Tremble	Feb-10	$ 15.00
	1-924230731	Love Heist by Jackie D.	Mar-10	$ 15.00
	1-934230812	Flexin & Sexin Volume 2	Apr-10	$ 15.00
	1-934230748	The Dirty Divorce by Miss KP	May-10	$ 15.00
	1-934230758	Chedda Boyz by CJ Hudson	Jul-10	$ 15.00
	1-934230766	Snitch by VegasClarke	Oct-10	$ 15.00
	1-934230693	Money Maker by Tonya Ridley	Oct-10	$ 15.00
	1-934230774	The Dirty Divorce Part 2 by Miss KP	Nov-10	$ 15.00
	1-934230170	The Available Wife by Carla Pennington	Jan-11	$ 15.00
	1-934230774	One Night Stand by Kendall Banks	Feb-11	$ 15.00
	1-934230278	Bitter by Danette Majette	Feb-11	$ 15.00
	1-934230299	Married to a Balla by Jackie D.	May-11	$ 15.00
	1-934230308	The Dirty Divorce Part 3 by Miss KP	Jun-11	$ 15.00
	1-934230316	Next Door Nympho By CJ Hudson	Jun-11	$ 15.00
	1-934230286	Bedroom Gangsta by J. Tremble	Sep-11	$ 15.00
	1-934230340	Another One Night Stand by Kendall Banks	Oct-11	$ 15.00
	1-934230359	The Available Wife Part 2 by Carla Pennington	Nov-11	$ 15.00
	1-934230332	Wealthy & Wicked by Chris Renee	Jan-12	$ 15.00
	1-934230375	Life After a Balla by Jackie D.	Mar-12	$ 15.00
	1-934230251	V.I.P. by Azarel	Apr-12	$ 15.00
	1-934230383	Welfare Grind by Kendall Banks	May-12	$ 15.00
			Total for Books	$

* Prison Orders- Please allow up to three (3) weeks for delivery.

Shipping Charges (add $4.95 for 1-4 books*) $

Total Enclosed (add lines) $

Please Note: We are not held responsible for returned prison orders. Make sure the facility will receive books before ordering.

*Shipping and Handling of 5-10 books is $6.95, please contact us if your order is more than 10 books. (301)362-6508